On the Other Side

On the Other Side

Vilis K. Michaels

The Pentland Press Limited
Edinburgh • Cambridge • Durham

© Vilis K. Michaels 1994

First published in 1994 by
The Pentland Press Ltd.
1 Hutton Close
South Church
Bishop Auckland
Durham

All rights reserved.
Unauthorised duplication
contravenes existing laws.

ISBN 1 85821 132 8

Typeset by CBS, Felixstowe, Suffolk
Printed and bound by Antony Rowe Ltd., Chippenham

To our daughter, Karen.

My thanks to the many
friends I have made in this
country without whose encouragement
and help this book probably would
not have been written.

Contents

Prelude	1
Part I	7
First Love	9
In Love with Flying	16
Flying School and a Wedding Party	24
Victims of War	32
Part II	43
Meeting Lena	45
Our Love Affair Grows	52
Defeated by the Class Barrier	61
Part III	73
Stationed at Riga - I meet Tamara	75
Under the Shadows of War Our Love Deepens	83
Heinz and Freda	92
The Growing Threat from Russia	99
Tamara and I Are Separated	109
Reunion and Marriage	115
Interlude at Hugo's Farm	125
Part IV	131
The Bombing of Dresden	133
Withdrawal to Martha's Family Home	141
Saved from Execution by the Arrival of the Americans	151
Part V	161
Life in an American P.O.W. Camp	163

A Boat for a Pair of Boots	168
The Price of a Dog	179
We Find Martha and Ellie	189
Re-united with Tamara's Family	205
We Begin a New Life	213

PRELUDE

It was a glorious morning. There was not a cloud in the sky as I left home for the daily walk around my lake, here in the beautiful Yorkshire countryside, much earlier in the day than usual. My faithful dog, who never fails to accompany me, appeared somewhat surprised at the early start. We had enjoyed a spell of lovely weather that week, and this was the last day of May. The conditions appeared to be just right for the many carp in my lake to spawn.

For several years now, ever since I was fortunate enough to find this place where I was able to build my home overlooking the river and the big lake, I have watched the exciting spectacle of the breeding habits of these large fish, taking me back to my early days. Then I spent many happy hours with my school friend, whose father owned a farm, a saw-mill and a large lake. As boys we used to lie in the long grass looking into the water to watch the spawning of the fish. That was many years ago in Germany and Latvia. But for me, in more ways than one, these places had become truly 'on the other side'.

*****

The Dream.
With my dog trotting behind me, I reached the nearest corner of the lake. The rays of the rising sun were striking the surface of the water, giving a slightly golden hue to the mist, which was broken by the long shadows of the overhanging trees at the edge of the water. There was still a fair distance to walk before I reached the usual spawning place at the far end of the lake, where the water was shallow and overgrown with water plants. A stretch of woodland grew almost to its shores,

providing protection from cooling winds. I never fail to marvel how the millions of animal species know exactly the right conditions in which to start the reproductive cycle, and for me this wonder has not diminished with the passing years. As I drew nearer, I could see the splashing water, indicating that the fish were performing the wedding act. Not wishing to disturb them, I made a quiet detour into the nearby trees, using the larger tree trunks to shield my presence until I reached the wooden bench I had placed there years ago so as to be able to rest and enjoy the magnificent view across the lake.

The sun had climbed higher into the sky, warming both the land and the water, and the breeding activity in the lake was in full swing. I was too far away, so I got down on my knees and crept forward through the long grass right to the water's edge. My small, well trained dog was bringing up the rear and although I could not see her, I knew that she shared my excitement at the spectacle before me. I crept close enough to be able to see a number of male carp rubbing their heads against the egg-filled bellies of the females. Then suddenly, tiny eggs were being released by the females, to be instantly fertilized by the males. The vigorous splashing of the water by the powerful tails of the males dispersed the eggs over a wide area of the water. They then started to fall slowly, and most of them would be attaching themselves to plants. The incubation process would be begun by the strength of the sun penetrating the water.

My terrier, now lying beside me, suddenly tried to jump up but anticipating this, I prevented it with my restraining hand on her collar. Seconds later I knew the reason for the excitement. A flock of mallards was flying towards the lake. The screech of the leading drake and the whistle of the flight feathers could be easily heard now. I looked up and saw them making an observation circuit of the lake. I could also see that a number of large cumulus clouds were slowly floating by and just watching the movement of them, my eyes detected the shape of a glider soaring under one of the clouds.

All my attention was now on the glider. I turned over on my back to follow its graceful movement. It was a beautiful machine up there under that cloud, and observing it, I saw how effortlessly it lifted itself in gentle circles nearer to the ever-increasing thermal. I watched with interest until the lift under the cloud must have been expended. I noticed the glider level out, the pilot searching for another lift. Slowly the glider became smaller and smaller and gradually disappeared from view.

I lay back, stretching myself out in the warm grass with the sun on my face. I closed my eyes and my thoughts drifted back many years to the time when I myself was a glider pilot sitting in the small open cockpit. I sensed once more the weightlessness and the complete freedom which engulfed me and I sank into oblivion ...

What caused me to wake up I don't know. Was it the barking of my dog or was it the terror of feeling myself spinning to earth in my glider? I sat up, exhausted and covered in perspiration. It had been a dream in which I had relived a terrible experience ... I had crashed.

Of course, it was partly my own fault, but then, gliding in those far-off days was very different to gliding to-day. The initial power for us to become airborne was supplied by a manual catapult action, requiring a team of men and tremendous physical strength to pull the rubber ropes sufficiently far back to catapult the glider into the air. It was always from the top of a hill, against the wind. From then on the glider pilot was alone and had to find a thermal if he was to stay airborne.

Normally he would find one, but on occasions conditions were such as to render him unsuccessful and give him no alternative but to land. As he would have lost height, he would have to land in a field well below his starting-point at the hill-top. Such landings were disappointing to the pilot's team members, and drew critical comments as they recovered the glider, pulling it manually to the foot of the hill, where an old two-stroke engine provided the power for a home-made winch, which would haul the glider back to the hill-top. Normally the criticism of the team was an accepted part of the disappointment associated with an aborted take-off.

On this particular occasion, I was very hurt to hear one of them say: 'I think he would be better flying a kite than a glider.' 'She' had not intended her remark to be overheard by me, nor in fact, did 'She' know that I had heard it, as I was some distance away from her at the time. I was stationed at the far end of the wing and my job was to hold the glider in a horizontal position. Hearing this aspersion on my flying skills quite naturally upset me, but especially coming from her, for 'She' was six years my senior. As the only woman in the team, 'She' was quite naturally admired by us all. On the occasions that 'She' was not with us, her absence was felt to a greater extent than that of other missing team members. This was not only because 'She' was female, but for the special qualities 'She' possessed, and which inspired us all. Eventually we hauled the glider back to the top of the hill. A discussion followed and, to my pleasant surprise, I was given another chance. The reason was that I was the only member of the club who had not yet qualified for the C test, the dream of all glider pilots of those days. The instructor took me to one side, but I already knew what he was about to say to me. I always answered him with an eager 'Yes'.

I did not find it easy to look directly at him because of his physical appearance, which was the result of horrific injuries which he had received as a fighter pilot in the First World War. He had been awarded the Blue Max, after being pulled clear of his aircraft just before it exploded. In spite of it all, flying remained his consuming passion and he had founded the gliding club. 'Are you ready then?' he said to me, and for a split second I looked at that face of his which was not a face. He was probably aware of the effect that his appearance was likely to have on those who mixed with him. Therefore he was probably not aware of the true reason for my red face. It was on account not of his grotesque appearance, but of the hurtful remark made by the lady member concerning my flying. It did not help that throughout the conversation I had with the instructor, 'She' was still joking with the other lads, presumably at my expense.

I fastened my crash helmet. The instructor lifted the wing tip. I climbed into the cockpit and went through the routine checking of the controls.

'Are you ready?', came the call. 'Ready!', came the response from the staring team. 'Pull!'

I could feel the jerk against the holding mechanism on the tail of the glider. 'Run!' and the ten-man team, five on each side of the catapult, were running down the hill, stretching the thick rubber rope to its limit. 'Let go!' The glider shot forward a few yards, and after a slight pull on the stick, was airborne. Rudder left, stick left to get the lift from the upsurging winds of the hilly landscape. So far so good, and as soon as I found a thermal from the cornfields below, I would be gliding. Alas, it was not to be! The glider did not pick up enough height, forcing me to ask myself whether I should abort the flight once again. If I did, I would be labelled a real kite-flyer by the object of my admiration. I could not do it! I tried a right turn towards the village, where we had found thermals before. 'Keep the nose up and try!' I did not notice that the fine whistle coming from the wind striking the diagonals of the wind stabilizers had stopped. My air speed was too low. 'Press, press, stick down!' It was too late! Everything seemed to turn and turn. It seemed to go on for a long time ...

PART I

CHAPTER ONE. FIRST LOVE

It is difficult to put things together. Is it Marianne? But what is she doing in the gliding club, and why is she dressed in white? Why not ask her when she looks at me again? She is rising from her chair and I try to see where she is going. What on earth has happened? What is on my head? I cannot move my arm. I will shout to her. 'Marianne!' I feel her hand on my face. Oh yes, I am right. It is Marianne. 'Can you understand me?' she asks.

'Yes, I understand. What has happened?'
'You crashed in the glider,' she said.
'Me crashed? Yes, I remember now. I was flying, then I was spinning. Marianne, stay with me!'
'Try to rest now,' she said as she gently stroked my forehead. I heard the door closing quietly and she had gone.

Although my injuries were quite serious, having Marianne to take care of me far outweighed the discomfort I felt as the result of the crash. From the first day I saw her, she was very special to me. She was one of the first people I had met when I moved with my grandparents to our new home in a small village a few miles from the hospital. That had been two years previously, when I was fourteen. Marianne was the daughter of the village builder. At the time my grandparents had been compelled to move for financial reasons.

I was raised by my maternal grandparents in Germany. My father was from the Baltic States but my mother was German. My father was an engineer, whose work took him to many different places. It had been decided from an early age that it would be in my best interests to make my home with my grandparents. This would enable me to receive an uninterrupted education, which my father's frequent travelling would otherwise have made impossible. I became so close to my grandparents that I came to look upon them as my parents and in the end they adopted me.

My grandfather was an orthopaedic shoemaker, who ran his own business in the town. For many years we lived in accommodation above the shop. However, with the changing times, many people were without work and unable to afford handmade shoes. For this reason my grandparents decided to leave the town and move into the country area, where living costs were considerably lower. They found what they were searching for in our present home. We occupied a flat, which was one of two created from one half of the most imposing house in the village. The house was owned by Marianne's father, who had built it for his own occupation and then found it be much too large for his present needs. He and his family occupied one half of the house and my grandparents lived in one of the two flats. A war widow, Frau Fisher and her daughter Martha, who was my age, lived in the other.

My heart belonged to Marianne. If I could get one glimpse of her, which I managed to do almost every day, I felt happy. Unfortunately, she was two years my senior and more unfortunate still, so far as I was concerned, was the fact that she attended a different school. She was a pupil at a private school in the town we had moved away from and, as her brother also studied in that town, he took her as a passenger on his 350cc motor cycle. For the next two years I watched her nearly every morning through the curtains of our sitting room helping him to push out the motor bike. Whilst her brother got the bike ready, she would be putting on her leather cap, her long golden hair flowing from beneath it almost to her shoulders. As the engine was ticking over, I would watch them mounting the machine and Marianne lifting the collar of her coat to tuck her blonde hair inside before closing the last two button holes. I would swallow the rest of my breakfast porridge still dreaming about her. 'Time to be off!' Grandma would call, 'Don't forget your cap.' 'You and your motor bikes,' she would add, 'one of these days you will get run over.' I was relieved that she believed my enthusiasm to be for the motor bike only.

As time went on, I became very friendly with Hugo, who was the son of a local farmer. Hugo and I were the same age, but our backgrounds were totally different. His family could be considered to be quite well off as they owned a farm and a saw-mill. We were also very different in physique. I was dark haired with a fair complexion and very tall for my age, whereas Hugo was much shorter and very strong and muscular. He had red curly hair and a freckled complexion. Our friendship was really based on our mutual love of nature. The opportunities to develop this were abundant because of the river which ran through his land and the beautiful lake. The purpose of both was really to power the saw-mill, but they also absorbed our interest and filled our leisure hours. Probably this was because of the limitations of the village school as compared to the school I had attended in the town. My waking hours progressively revolved around nature, with particular emphasis on the water life which, in later years, was to figure so prominently in my life.

For many years the lake was used in the summer months for swimming. Old and young alike, from the two villages which bordered it, bathed in it regularly. Many years previously the local farmers had transferred sand from a local pit to make a pleasant beach on its shore. It was here that we spent our long summer holidays from school. The weather was mostly good at this time of year, and there were plenty of children from both villages. One day Marianne appeared with two school friends who were spending a holiday at her home.

The village children were all playing together and enjoying a ball game. To my delight, Marianne and her two friends joined in. Someone then suggested a swim in the lake and Marianne and her friends disappeared into the bushes to change into their swimming costumes. As they emerged, I felt my full attention rivetted on Marianne's stunning figure in the swimsuit she was wearing. I thought that she was the most beautiful girl I had ever seen. My happiness was complete when she joined the ball game we were playing in the water and actually threw the ball at me. I watched her excitedly as she jumped up and down in the water and I remember wishing that time would stand still and the game would go on for ever. Very soon all three of them got out of the water and as they dried themselves on the beach, the game went on. Someone threw a very fast ball at me. Automatically I reached for it but could not catch it. Deflected, the ball flew directly onto Marianne's chest. She stood there wrapped in a bath towel, which she was holding underneath her chin as she stepped into her underwear. When the ball struck her, the shock must have loosened her grip on the towel, which fell down, and just for a second or so I saw her naked figure. I must have experienced the same kind of shock as she did. I threw myself into a dive and swam out into the lake. When I turned I saw the three girls leaving with Marianne wiping her tears away with her handkerchief. That night I could not sleep. Not only had I seen a woman in the nude for the first time, but it was a woman whom I secretly adored and in my fantasy of that night she became to me the most desirable thing on earth.

It was the start of my final school year, also Hugo's and Martha's and, as it happened, Marianne's as well. In a small village like ours opportunities for school-leavers were very limited and this worried me. There were so many people unemployed and the words of my grandfather were: 'You follow in my foot-steps!' My own wish was to become a seaman or an engineer or engage in some other occupation which would give me the opportunity I craved to see the world. I realised that my fate would be to become a shoemaker after the four-year apprenticeship and that I might as well forget about Marianne. She was to take up training as a state-registered nurse the following year, probably becoming a matron and marrying a doctor or someone rich and above my station. Then there was Hugo, who was also destined to follow in his father's footsteps. He was no scholar, but his father owned both a farm and a saw-mill. Hugo had a brother seven years his senior and already working in the saw-mill, which meant that Hugo was to work on the farm. Martha was to find a place as a mother's help on the next farm to Hugo's, where a baby was expected. Martha was already helping out there. In a small village such as ours everything was arranged with little regard to the wishes of the children involved. The overriding factor was that one should have a job, something to be thankful for when so many people were out of work.

One Saturday that autumn we obtained permission from Hugo's father to take the boat and fish in the lake for pike. As we sat there waiting for a bite, we began talking about the girls. Hugo knew that Marianne was my favourite, but he was rather surprised when I confessed to being very much in love with her. That confession must have given him the courage to tell me that he was very much in love with Martha, but that in spite of all the apples, pears and sweets he gave her, there was little response on her side. In any case, his family had farming friends in the next village and his mother continually commented on the fact that he would be a rich man when he eventually married their daughter. He could never marry Martha. His parents would never allow it. With all this serious discussion, we did not give our full attention to the fishing and missed a few bites. We did not catch a pike after all, but we shared our secrets and sadly accepted the fact that we had little chance of marrying the girls of our dreams.

So came our last winter at school. Spring followed and we once again celebrated the first day of May on the village green. The children were dancing around the Maypole. We sang and took part in sports and the winners received prizes. A brass band played and the grown-ups danced. Marianne was there. She danced every dance and always with the same man, the son of an engineering family from the next village, whom I knew. He had already finished his apprenticeship and worked in his father's business. He had just become the proud owner of a BMW motor cycle with a side car, and was the envy of us all. Marianne, now 18 years old, was more beautiful then ever and as we all walked home after the festivities, I could hear the motorbike in the distance coming towards us. Marianne was in the side car. She wore a blue silk scarf around her golden hair, and both were flying in the wind.

A couple of months later we started our last school summer holiday and Hugo and myself were in the lake almost every day. I was hoping that Marianne would turn up one day. Her two school friends were staying with her again and her brother also had a friend staying. Sure enough, one day the three girls were on the beach and it was not long before we were all enjoying a ball game again. I thought it was marvellous but I had to go home early that day. It was Grandma's birthday. The previous year I had got her some water lilies and now I wanted to do the same. I swam out into the corner of the lake, which was full of water lilies. The underwater plants were so thick in that area that it was almost impossible to penetrate. It was a real struggle for me to pull up half a dozen water lilies. When I came swimming out with them, Marianne was waving to me.

'Come here, let me look at those beautiful lilies,' she called.

'Marianne, I got these for my grandma. It is her birthday to-day, please have one of them.'

'No, no, you give them to your grandma.'

'No, no, no, please, have this one from me and come back tomorrow and I will get you some more.'

I pressed one lily into her hand and ran off. That night I did not sleep much and tried to figure out how I could get more of those lilies. It was very difficult. Of course, I could have asked Hugo to go by boat, but I knew that the boat was locked up and his father had the key. He would have objected because the fish were spawning amongst those thick water plants. The water was not really very deep at that point, about up to my chest, but the bottom of the lake was so muddy that one quickly sank into it. I knew that I would have to move quickly.

The following day I went to the lake early and had a good look so as to work out how best I could do it. Then I saw the three girls coming. I got into the water and swam to the corner of the lake. I do not know how long I was fighting mud and underwater growth, but by the time they arrived, I had so many water lilies that I could hardly swim back with them and I reached the beach in a state of exhaustion. I had not even noticed that Marianne's friend had arrived with his motorbike, as well as her brother and his friend. All were sitting in a circle, talking and laughing. For a moment I hesitated but then, 'a promise is a promise,' I thought, and marched boldly direct to Marianne. 'There are your water lilies, Marianne.' All was quiet, and then the boys broke out into loud laughter. 'You are too late, lad, she has been spoken for. Better finish your school first before you start courting.'

I ran off home feeling bitterly hurt and from that day I did not try to look for her. After all, in a matter of weeks she would be leaving home and would be some 30 miles away, living in a big hospital. Life would be different for all school leavers: different for Martha, different for Hugo, different for me.

The winter came. It was not too bad for me; I could at least sit in a warm room making and repairing shoes, but deep down I hated it. I was always waiting for 6 pm, when we stopped work. I would then quickly change my clothes and prepare for my paper round, which covered two villages.

That newspaper round was very good for me. It got me out of the house and, furthermore, I was allowed to keep the money I earned from it. My dream was to save up enough money to buy a motor cycle. Every penny I earned was put towards this dream, and on top of my earnings came a modest sum from grandma as well as an occasional tip when I delivered shoe repairs to customers. I did not get much sympathy regarding the motor bike ambition from my grandma. For her I was always a little boy and whenever I left the house I would be bombarded with instructions as to what I should and should not do and what time I should return. My grandparents were very religious people, as were all my relations. Once a week they travelled by bicycle to attend bible classes. Every six weeks the classes were held in our flat. I was often teased about this, especially when their singing could be heard in the street.

CHAPTER TWO. IN LOVE WITH FLYING

Spring came and one night, glancing through the newspaper before I set off on my rounds, I saw an advert for a glider exhibition the following weekend in the next town. I had never seen a glider. What could it be? A machine which flew without an engine! How did it look?

It was not very difficult to obtain permission to go and on the following Sunday off I went to see this mysterious machine. There it was, standing in the middle of the market place with ropes around it so that the public could not get too near. There were plenty of people about and amongst them were club members with collection boxes. The funds were exhausted and a new glider was being built. I tried to get as near as possible to the ropes so that I could hear what the club members were saying and their answers to the many questions. I was so fascinated by it all that I stood there for a couple of hours. One of the club members took notice of me. He looked at me for a while and came over. 'Now then, young man, you are obviously interested, aren't you?'

'Oh yes, very. I wish I could become a member of the club.'

'Well, why not?'

'My mum would not let me and I would not have the money to pay for it.'

'How old are you then?'

'Sixteen and a half,' I said.

'Well, you can fly a glider at that age, but you will need the permission of your parents. What is more, we only fly at week-ends and the hills are about 30 miles away. One night a week you would have to attend in our workshop where we build our gliders, and one night a month is theory night. As we intend to start a junior section in the club, you may get away with paying only half the fee.'

By this time I was nodding. 'Yes, yes, I can do all that.'

'Fine, come back to-night, we have a dance at the town hall. I will introduce you to our chairman and we will see what we can do.'

I jumped on my bike, wondering how I could get round Grandma and Grandad to allow me to go back that same night. It was a hard struggle, with tears on both sides, but in the end I was allowed to go.

The big room in the Town Hall was equipped with a large stage. The club members had transferred the glider from the market place on to the stage. I could not figure out how they had done it, but it just fitted in with one wing reaching out over the hall. As I came in, the chairman, who was also the instructor, gave his speech before the dancing began. He was talking about the history of flying – Icarus, Otto Lienthal, the Wright Brothers, and explaining what a great sport it was, how safe it was, the fact that the club was non-political, and much more besides. I was listening to every word so that I could repeat it in detail to my grandparents.

My meeting with the chairman was very short. 'If that is what you want, you get permission and we will have you provisionally for six months for half the fee. Be there at 8 pm next week in the workshop.'

I would have loved to stay longer that night, but I had promised to be home by 11 pm. So I jumped on my bike and rode off through the forest. It took about an hour to cycle home. Whilst pedalling along, I promised myself that, come what might, I would be a glider pilot. I was trying to work out how I could overcome the resistance at home and how I could convince my grandparents what a good sport it was; neither dangerous nor political. I would also have to learn how to build gliders. Oh, and the motor bike! I would have to have a motor bike, only a small one, and I would do that all from my own money.

Though both my grandparents put up a determined and prolonged resistance, I at last won my grandfather over by persuading him to accompany me on my next visit to the glider workshop. We were received with great courtesy and introduced to the club members, a dozen or so, all very busy making the parts for a new glider. Some members were working on the wings, others on the fuselage, while others were gluing together small diagonal sections in jig forms on a large table. There were rolls of cable, sheets of plywood, balsa wood and many other materials. The boys were whistling and talking. Grandad was absolutely fascinated. He was looking at the plans showing all the measurements. His face became pink with the excitement. Before we set off home, he had a quiet word with the leader of the group. On our way back he did not speak much, and when I asked him what he thought about it, he just said that he would have to have a word with Grandma. The following day I was granted permission to join the club.

It was another six months before I achieved my first flight. It was really only a hop. The glider was given just enough catapult power to lift it five to six metres high. I thought it was fantastic and I was more than ever determined to become a fully fledged glider pilot. I would attend every meeting, both in the workshop and at the flying meetings on the hills. Soon I was being given maximum starts and before long I had passed the A test. I was rewarded with a glider badge. The B test followed soon after and then came the training for the real thing – the C test, which was the glider pilot's dream. It meant being catapulted off the top edge of the hills into the wind, then gliding along the hill's edge until the thermal connection lifted the glider higher and higher.

Then followed the accident. Slowly I recovered. I had many visitors, mainly club members, and one evening the instructor came. He sat on one corner of my bed for over an hour, and we went through the whole story of what had gone wrong. I told him all about the remarks I had overheard, and how it had upset me. He said he understood but that it was no excuse and in a round-about way he told me off. The insurance company had paid for the repairs to the glider, which was nearly ready again. He persuaded me not to give up flying. He said that as soon as I was fit, he would give me a flight. It would be the best thing to do in these circumstances. He said that great things were in the pipeline, and he told me confidentially that a firm had given the necessary money for a brand new winch, a winch which would pull the glider right into a thermal. Another glider was going to be built and the club would then have two 'Grunau babies' and one 'Seagull'. The Seagull, the last word in gliders, was capable of making the silver C. The silver C meant five hours flying, and the Seagull was also passed for aerobatics.

Four weeks later I was back on the hills, after the anticipated resistance at home. The instructor kept his word and I got my flight. For a few seconds I was a bit nervous but as the landscape unfolded beneath me, I felt anew the wonderful feeling of freedom that only flying can give.

Things were changing rapidly; it was magic. The winch arrived, and with it came permission to use some 75 hectares of heathland near to the town for our flying activities. Six months later a hangar was built and this made things so much easier for club members; it was no longer necessary to travel 30 miles to the hills. But the most exciting factor was the flying itself. One was winched up by the pull of a lever and then one was off. Hanging on to a cumulus cloud, one could feel the lift. It did not take long for all the club members to become qualified C pilots. What a change this brought to my life! During the day I was repairing shoes, then quickly delivering newspapers, and twice a week going to the club. Every weekend, without exception, was spent on the airfield. Oh yes, I had a motor bike now which made things much easier. Little did I take note of, or care for, the changes taking place around me. A fever seemed to be gripping the people. Meetings and marches were taking place and demonstrations and arrests were common place.

One night, as I came home from the club, Grandma was sitting in the kitchen crying bitterly. A brick had been thrown through our sitting room window during the religious weekend. Next day Marianne's father came round to our flat and spoke for a long time with Grandad. The upshot was that unless the meetings stopped he would have to give us notice to leave. A time of political fever began. Everyone was pressed to join the Party, but my grandad kept a low profile and joined nothing. Because of this, his trade suffered, even though he was the only orthopaedic shoemaker in the district. We managed, however. Still Grandma continued to preach the gospel.

It was not long before it became apparent that the Third Reich had altered everybody's life. Most of my schoolmates were wearing uniforms of one kind or another. The girls were not affected so much. Most of them were engaged, and a number of weddings were already arranged. Rumour had it that Martha was pregnant. No one seemed to know who the father was.

Rumour also had it that something would happen to our club and sure enough, at the very next meeting, our instructor turned up in uniform. He looked most striking. None of us had seen anything like it before. It was not grey or khaki – it was blue! He had the rank of captain, a position he had held as a fighter pilot in the First World War. We were all given leaflets to take home. These had to be filled in at once and posted back to headquarters the next day. The leaflet took the form of a questionnaire and asked for the details of our life history. Signatures of parents were required on the forms of all persons under 21. The form was an authorisation for a medical examination to ensure that we were suitable for training as pilots.

Grandad and Grandma, badly shaken by the events of the previous months, pleaded with me not to go on. They considered it to be all evil. War was evil and destroyed people. I, on the other hand, was begging for their signature on the paper and explained that it meant nothing at that time as I might fail the test, in which case the entire disagreement would have been for nothing. Eventually they gave in and signed it. I could hardly bear to keep on repairing shoes. My mind was on that test and whether I would pass it and become a pilot. I did not care about the political aspect of it all; neither did I mind becoming a soldier. All I wanted was to fly, to escape from the little shoemaking shop and into the cockpit. To fly was all I could think about. I was dreaming of how I could fly over the village and see all my school friends run out of their houses to wave to me. Marianne would be among them. For once she would have to look up to me!

Sure enough, we were informed that the club would take delivery of its first real aeroplane in one month's time and that we would all have to work very hard to prepare the field. Every little bump had to be levelled out and every little hole filled in. From the members of our club a team was selected for training purposes at the aircraft factory, and this of course included our instructor.

One Saturday afternoon we waited eagerly on the airfield for our aeroplane to arrive. Eventually we spotted it and watched it grow larger and larger until we could hear the engine noise increase as it came nearer to us. It circled the field twice before coming in for a perfect landing and taxiing to the hangar. The afternoon sun glinted on this shining yellow, brand-new two-seater monoplane as it came very gracefully to a standstill. Then the engine was switched off and the wooden propeller whistled softly as it came to a complete stop. We all gathered around the plane to watch our instructor and the newly appointed engineer climb out of the cockpit. As the engineer looked the aircraft over, our instructor stood on the wing support, pulled off his goggles and his leather cap and we all eagerly awaited the speech which we knew would follow.

'Comrades of the flying club, it is with great pride and satisfaction that I present to you our first aeroplane, and I can tell you all that this is only the beginning. From now on we all have a very special role to play in the future of the Fatherland. From this day our club has been taken over by the Party. For all those members who wish to take part in this great event, there will be a meeting here to-morrow morning at 11 am. Those of you who cannot or do not wish to be part of our future development are herewith released and can take no further part in the activities of this club. Comrades, will you all please stand to attention. Long live the Fuehrer, Heil Hitler!' Then the salute to the Fuehrer was given.

The events of the day were very much in my thoughts as I swung myself on to my motor cycle and made my way home. What on earth could I say to my grandparents now? For what they had predicted was now a reality and I was deeply troubled in my mind. In the end I decided to say nothing and simply attend the meeting the following morning.

By now it was almost dark. I was close to home and as I passed through the village, I saw Martha going home to see her mother. She did not live at home now, she lived at the farm where she worked as a housemaid.

'Hello Martha, I don't see much of you these days.'

'No,' she said, 'you don't, and you know why?' As she spoke she indicated her swollen tummy.

'Oh yes, Martha, I understand. There are rumours in the village, is it true?' (the rumours were that Hugo was the child's father).

'Rumours are rumours, but the truth will never be told by me.'

'You don't mean it, Martha,' I said, 'you will need help when the time comes. I can have a word, you surely trust me? We have lived under one roof, we went to school together.'

'Thank you just the same.' A tear ran down her cheek as she turned and walked off into the darkness. I started up my bike and went home.

It was not until the very end of our meeting the following morning that we were told that all pilots would be given half an hour's flying instruction, starting the next week-end. Two more aircraft were to be sent to us, monoplanes with dual controls. Each of us would take our turn in these for instruction and would actually fly them, though not for take-offs and landings. I was so excited about all this that I was unable to sleep. I was going to be a pilot and my secret wish was that Marianne would be at home this coming week-end, so that she too would see me flying in the aeroplane.

All went according to plan and the following Sunday just after lunch we took off from the airfield and headed towards my village. As we climbed to 2,000 feet, the pilot told me to take the controls. I eagerly complied and quickly found the direction. I could see the stream leading to Hugo's house and the saw-mill. There was the winding road through the pine forest; the fields came into view, and a few minutes later I could make out the shape of the church steeple, the farm buildings and houses. We flew right over the village street from one end to the other. I pointed downwards to the pilot and he indicated that he wanted to take the controls. He went very low, down to a couple of hundred feet, and by the time we had made the first circle, nearly all the people of the village had come out of their houses. Many of them waved to us. I could see Grandma and Grandad. As we came round again, I saw all my school friends, Martha, Hugo and all the others, but not Marianne. What a shame!

Next day the postman brought a letter for me. I had to report in two days time for a medical examination in the capital. The medical would take four days. Another letter requested me to provide proof of my Arian descent. This worried me at first, because my father was not a German, and I was afraid that this fact might put an end to my hopes of being a pilot. As it happened, I had no cause to fear. Baltic nationals were classed by the present régime as Arians.

It was my first visit to the capital. The S.Bahn and the Underground were a new experience for me, but it was not difficult to find the large hospital where I had to report. The medical was much more thorough than I had expected. There must have been about 200 young men, all glider pilots. At the end we did not know whether we had passed or not.

In the meantime Martha's child was born, a little girl, whom she named Ellie. The baby was born at Martha's mother's home, and in little more than a week Martha was back at work but speaking to no one. Her mother cared for the baby. Martha just went from the farm to her mother's flat, never lifting her eyes from the ground.

CHAPTER THREE. FLYING SCHOOL AND A WEDDING PARTY

One morning the postman brought a registered letter. I held my breath as I opened it, and there it was – a post as a trainee pilot for four months in Halberstadt, to begin in two weeks time.

The day before I left I said goodbye to all my school friends, but when I came to Martha she did not look well. 'Goodbye Martha, get better soon,' I said, hoping for the best. Alas, it was not to be.

Three weeks had gone by at the flying school. We still saw aeroplanes only from a distance. It was all so different from what I had imagined. The newly erected barracks were about two miles from the airfield. Our civilian clothing had been handed in and we had all received a sort of training uniform. We got up at 6 am and had half an hour's physical training before we washed and dressed for breakfast at 8 am. Then there was military training, including the handling of weapons. All the people in charge of the morning activities were army and police officers. The afternoon instruction took the form of lessons in flying, navigation, aerodynamics, aircraft engines, instruments etc. All these lessons were given by civilian pilots and engineers. We were the second course on this particular airfield. The first course would be ending in a day or two, and then ours would start in earnest. After five hours on a dual control, I had my first solo flight. It was very exciting. To distinguish all the beginner solo flyers, we had little red bands fastened to the wing tips. These marks worked wonders; as we came in to land, everyone appeared to get out of the way. Suddenly everything seemed to be moving very fast. We had to concentrate on getting in our flying time, landings and take-offs, and soon we would be flying longer distances to other airfields.

One morning I was called to the office just before I was due to take off. I was taken into the Commandant's room. The Commandant, who was an officer in the police service and still wore that uniform, asked me to sit down.

'I am sorry, but I have some bad news for you. I have just received a letter from your Buergermeister at home, requesting leave for you to attend the funeral of a village girl called Martha.' He paused, recognizing that this news was a dreadful shock to me.

'Sir, she was a very close friend of myself and my family and she is only 19 years old.'

'Yes, I know, something went wrong and then she contracted pneumonia. The funeral is the day after to-morrow. You know that we are on a very tight schedule here at the school but, as your flying performance is satisfactory, I will give you two days leave.'

Everyone in the village attended the funeral. Afterwards we were asked to have a cup of coffee in the village recreation room. We stood around in small groups, talking about various things but mostly about Martha and the tragedy of it all. I looked for Hugo but he was not there. As I looked around, my eyes met someone else's and we looked at each other. It was Marianne. It was as if she had been waiting for me to look at her. She started to walk towards me. I had seen her in church as we carried the coffin. It had hardly registered then, but now that she was walking towards me she looked beautiful. She must have noticed that her presence affected me somewhat and she stretched out her hand before she actually reached me. As I recovered my composure I remarked that it had been some time since I had seen her, and we each expressed our sorrow at the occasion on which we had met again. Marianne said she had only heard about Martha last week when her mother had telephoned her, and she could only get three days off. She said she was very busy. I told her that I was also very busy and that it was no joke. She said she had heard that I was in training to be a pilot and asked me to confirm this. 'Yes, sort of,' I said.

'Go on, tell me all about it.'

'Big secret, Marianne,' I said. 'Big secret. First you must tell me about yourself.'

'Right,' she said. 'You know that I am engaged to be married to Heinz. You know, don't you?'

'Yes,' I nodded, 'I heard. The lucky man. Congratulations just the same.'

'I passed all my exams,' she continued, 'and was offered a job as a theatre sister in Hamburg.'

'Hamburg, of all places!' I said.

'Why?' she asked.

'Well, I have been there a couple of times in the last two weeks.'

'In Hamburg?' she asked. 'I thought you were somewhere in the Harz Mountains.'

'So I am, but that is not all that far in an aeroplane, is it?'

'And you fly alone all that way? Tell me how does it feel in the air?'

'It is just fantastic, Marianne. I think it is the second best thing a man can experience.'

'And what is the best thing?' she asked.

'Having a girl friend, I suppose,' I replied, 'but as I have not got one, flying is the best thing for me.'

She laughed, which made her look even more beautiful. 'It must be very exciting being up there amongst the clouds, nearer to God.'

'Well, yes, if you put it that way.'

'Good heavens, Marianne,' I exclaimed, 'is that the time! I have to be off. If I miss the van I shall not be able to catch my train and would not be back for take-off to-morrow morning. It was so nice to talk to you. Give my regards to your brother and Heinz, and if I come to Hamburg again, I would like to see you. But it is unlikely, because we land and are off again in such a short time. All the same, if it were ever possible, I would certainly come to see you.' As I said this, I stretched out my hand, she gave me hers and we looked at each other for a long time. I could have stayed in that spot looking at her and holding her hand for much longer, but it could not be. Reluctantly I released her hand and left her, waving goodbye to the other people in the hall.

All the way back to the camp I was reflecting on the events of the day and my own reactions to them: the sadness of Martha's funeral, but also the thrill of my meeting with Marianne. Marianne, the girl who had been in my heart from the moment I first saw her! She had come to me in that crowded hall and for a short time all the differences and difficulties between us had disappeared. We had been oblivious to everyone else in the room. She was two years older than I; she belonged to a higher social class; she was engaged to be married, but for a short time she had been almost mine. Then I thought of tomorrow and I knew that I had to forget the events of the last two days. There was no time for sentiment. In the cockpit I needed concentration. I could not afford to make the slightest error as this could jeopardise my whole flying career.

Rumours of war were circulating through the camp and were discussed in our living quarters and at meal times, but somehow we did not really take anything seriously. All we wanted to do was fly. Some said that it would never happen, some said it would happen very soon. Others said that it could never happen as our peace treaty in Versailles would not allow it. And then it did happen.

We were about three quarters of the way through the course when one morning we were all called into the lecture room and were told that if someone shouted 'Attention', we must all stand until we were given the order to sit. Next we heard 'Attention' and in walked three officers from the newly born Luftwaffe. From that moment we were no longer civilians. We were told that the school was now part of the Armed Forces and that in three days' time we would all be sworn in, unless we had good reasons not to be. We were to be issued with the newly designed Luftwaffe uniform. Immediately all flying was suspended and all leave stopped. So that was it. We were now in the armed forces.

The course finished as planned, and this was followed by an impressive passing-out parade. We were now among the first qualified pilots in the new German Airforce. We were then graded according to our academic qualifications. The higher grades were offered training as fighter pilots, the others, including myself, were to be bomber or transport pilots. At this time we were all given two stripes and two weeks leave. I proudly returned to my small village wearing my brand new uniform, something of a sensation as the first member of the armed forces, and even more proudly, I was the village's first pilot. I popped in to see Martha's mother and her little baby granddaughter. As I entered the flat, Martha's mother started crying. She said that it was so touching to remember the days when Martha and I had gone to school every morning. She pointed to the baby: 'Look how she has grown.'

'Can I pick her up?' I asked.

'Yes, of course you can.'

I picked her up, put her on my knee, got out my purse and put ten marks in her little hands. 'There darling,' I said. 'Tell your grandma to put it to good use.'

She started crying and said: 'I will, I will. Just think, Martha took her father's name (indicating the baby) to her grave with her. But everybody in the village is so good. I will tell you a secret. My sister in Bavaria has asked me to take the baby and live with them. They have a good business there and have no children of their own.'

'A secret is a secret,' I said. 'Give me the address and I will come to visit you.' Hastily I put the address in my pocket and said goodbye.

As I left, I ran into the Buergermeister's daughter Erna. She pulled me on one side and said: 'It is still a secret, but I am going to be married. It will be a big wedding.' She said she would like to invite me as well.

'Oh, great,' I said and explained to her the procedure she should adopt to invite someone serving in the Armed Forces to her wedding. I explained that the invitation would require a stamp from the Buergermeister and that since he was her father, it should not be difficult.

After my two weeks' leave, I had to report to Stendal, my new training centre. This was the real thing. New barracks, new hangars, new aeroplanes, big stuff – Junkers 52's. In the meantime, German troops were in Austria and we were still training, but not for long. On the passing-out parade we were presented with our wings and promoted to the rank of sergeant. New aeroplanes were arriving all the time, aircrews were being put together, and here we were with a brand new Junkers 52. My flying engineer, my radio operator and myself were dropping paratroopers as part of our training.

From the force and speed with which things were pushed along, one could sense that something much bigger was ahead, and as our Unit was ordered to fly to Breslau, it was not difficult to imagine what would follow. We settled down in Breslau and developed good relations with other aircrews. We all felt that our training had come to an end and we were now awaiting orders.

The invitation to Erna's wedding arrived, duly stamped by the Buergermeister. I went straight to the office but was given only two days' leave. I wanted to make a good impression, so I hired a car and borrowed an extra uniform. I secretly hoped that Marianne would be there; she was so often in my thoughts. I drove home to my 'little' village and when I arrived, Grandma excitedly briefed me with all the details concerning the wedding. There were 150 guests, music was to be provided by an orchestra, and the bride was to arrive at the church in a horse-drawn carriage. I asked Grandma if Marianne had been invited. 'Yes, Marianne and her fiancé. There are rumours that Marianne will be the next bride as all young men will be called into the army.'

The wedding started and everything went according to plan. I collected Elfrida, my lady for the day, in my hired car and she seemed happy enough to be chauffeur-driven. After the service all the guests were taken by horse and carriage to the reception hall except Elfrida and myself, who travelled by car. The orchestra was playing as we went in and were shown to our table. I was a little disturbed to find that our table was right opposite to Marianne and Heinz. I feared the dream would be destroyed, but then everyone started talking. I looked at Elfrida. She was a nice girl too, why not enjoy the occasion like everyone else? And so it was. After an enormous meal came the speeches and after the speeches the dancing was led by the bride and groom. After the first dance, they left the reception for their honeymoon. Following the old tradition, the bride threw her bouquet into the crowd and sure enough it was caught by Marianne. Obviously it had been pre-arranged. Everybody applauded and so it was accepted that Marianne would be the next bride. The dancing, talking and drinking went on and I noticed that Marianne and her fiancé did not miss a single dance together. I would have liked to dance with her, but did not wish to intrude, so I danced only with Elfrida. In a way I enjoyed it. Elfrida was a bonny little girl, a bit on the short side for me but an excellent dancer. When we were not dancing, we were sitting at our respective tables and Marianne joined in the conversation. I was able to have a real good look at her. To me she was beautiful. Perhaps I should have asked her for a dance, but what if she had refused? In any case, it would only have been polite to ask her fiancé first, and suppose he had refused? Marianne looked at me and it was as if she could read my thoughts.

'Hey, you two love birds over there, haven't you had enough of dancing together all the time? I would like to have a dance with a handsome pilot as well.'

'Look who is talking,' I said. 'What about you two? You don't give anybody a chance, but, if you don't mind?' I said as I looked at Heinz.

'Oh, help yourself,' he laughed. Just at that moment someone touched my shoulder and as I looked round, I saw two page boys making a wild gesture. One pulled down my shoulder to tell me that someone was interfering with my car. I was on my feet at once. I made a short apology and went outside to the car. I could see that one rear tyre was flat and I could hear the hissing noise of the air escaping from another. I could just see the valve cap lying on the ground and the valve itself half out of the holder. In no time I was surrounded by a number of boys all laughing and giggling and as I asked who was responsible they laughed even more. As I had to leave quite soon for my journey back to Breslau, I had to pump the tyres up again. So I secured the valve back in, got the hand pump out of the car boot and started pumping. I did not even notice that Otto was coming up behind me.

'That is for interfering with another boy's girlfriend. I was watching you all night, you bastard.' I could see that he was pretty drunk but, upset by what he had presumed, I said: 'If you were not so drunk, you pig, I would punch you on the chin right now.'

This was what Otto was waiting for. He grabbed me by my uniform jacket and threw me against the car. This attack was a complete surprise and caught me off balance but I struggled back to my feet. I still had the pump in my hand and I lifted it sharply and crashed it down on his head. In the meantime the word had spread and we were surrounded by a crowd of wedding guests. Otto was lying on the ground, bleeding heavily from the head. The bride's father, who was the Buergermeister, forced his way through to me shouting: 'What has happened?' Before I had time to explain, he shouted orders for the police and doctor and the ambulance to be called. A couple of men half dragged and half carried Otto into the hall. I sat on the mudguards of my car and wondered what on earth I had got myself into and what would happen if Otto should die. What will my grandparents say? What will happen to my flying career?

By the time the ambulance arrived, Otto had come round again. At first he insisted on going home, but was eventually persuaded to go to hospital. Shortly afterwards the police arrived and I was asked to make a statement. I declined, assuring the policeman that I was acting in self-defence but saying I would make a statement as soon as I got back to my unit. To my surprise, a couple of cycle riders, on their way back to the town, had witnessed the incident and they came forward and supported my story. In the meantime all the guests had disappeared. I was too upset to see anyone – not even Elfrida or Marianne. By the time I had rendered my car roadworthy again it was midnight. I got into the car and drove into the night, back to my unit.

I made my report and subsequently appeared before the commanding officer, a Squadron Leader and World War One fighter pilot. The result was that I was suspended from all flying duties until further notice. What a devastating shock that was! Two weeks later the matter was cleared up and once again I stood before my commanding officer, who had all the reports on his desk in front of him. 'Sergeant, as you acted in self defence there will be no charges against you. In fact, I congratulate you. A soldier, when attacked, should always choose the right weapon to liquidate his enemy and that is what you have done.'

'Yes, Sir,' I said.

'By the way, your attacker will be released from hospital in a day or so; he required twelve stitches on his forehead and cheek.'

'Thank you for telling me, Sir.' As I marched back to my quarters, I thought of Marianne and that one dance with her, which I would probably now never get.

CHAPTER FOUR. VICTIMS OF WAR

Another year had passed. It was 1939 and Czechoslovakia had been taken. None of us on the airfield were in any doubt as to what was to come. Our aircraft were ready, the paratroopers' training had been stepped up and all leave had been cancelled. Aircrews in waiting passed the time playing cards and writing letters. To some extent I took part in these activities too, but I liked to sit in the shade of the Junkers under the autumn sun, dreaming about the past and all that had happened. My grandfather had died, having suffered a stroke. He was buried quietly in the town from which we came. I was on a course at the time, and had been given only three days' leave. After the burial, Grandma told me about my real parents.

My mother was Grandma's daughter and my father, her husband, was a Latvian engineer who worked on a Hydro-Electric Plant in Latvia. They had always paid for my upbringing. I had known a little of my past as a small child, but I had never taken much notice. It was quite different now.

Six months later Grandma gave up her flat in the village and moved back to the town, where she took a room with a small kitchen. It seemed that all my connections with the little village had gone. There was only Hugo. I kept on writing to him and he always wrote back, so that I was kept informed as to what was going on. One day as I received one of his letters, I knew by the bulk of the envelope that the letter must contain some special news. I learned that Martha's mother and the child had left the village to live in Bavaria. The letter was also a confession. He was the father of Martha's daughter and, with hindsight, he said, everything should have been handled differently. But he and Martha had made a pact not to tell and both had honoured it. I was the only one he could trust and he was appealing to me for advice as to what he could possibly do now. I wrote back to him and told him that I would write a tactful letter to Martha's mother enquiring whether they were both happy in their new life. I did this and Martha's mother replied that everything was just fine. After some correspondence between us, it was decided that Hugo should make a Will in favour of his daughter. In his last letter he told me how quiet the village was now, as nearly all the young men had gone into the army. He had been excused Military Service as, now that his brother had died, he was the only one to look after the farm and saw-mill. Marianne had had a quiet wedding and her husband had been called into the army shortly afterwards. He was serving in a tank regiment.

What was that? The siren alarm! Was it a false alarm or was it real? It was real. Half an hour later we were flying over Poland. Anti-aircraft shells were bursting below us and beside us. They had the appearance of bubbles. We could feel the bursting of grenades as the force of them shook the cockpits. We got through to the dropping zone and the lads were jumping just as in training. We made a sharp turn and started for base. All aircraft returned safely and everyone was relieved. It was the first taste of war. Poland soon fell but England and France declared war and we all knew what lay ahead of us. We had settled on an airfield near Warsaw and, for a time, we were not involved in active service. We trained new aircrews and eventually the units were re-grouped. Most left for the Western front, but I stayed in Warsaw as part of a newly formed Transport Command. There was an opportunity to apply for leave so I thought I would like to go and visit Grandma for a few days. But just as I made my application I received a letter from the police at home saying that Grandma had been taken into custody for re-training. I did not realise at the time that that meant concentration camp. Poor old Grandma! Deep down I admired her for it. She refused to change her religious beliefs in the face of the political pressure in which we were all caught up.

It was 1941. Holland, Belgium and most of France were under German control. My Transport Command was still here in Warsaw, and from where we were it almost appeared a very easy war. Nevertheless, every so often we were given a grim reminder that it was in fact a very bloody war. Hugo still wrote to me regularly, and I never failed to reply. Three weeks previously he had written to say his father had died and that Marianne's husband had been killed in France in the final days of the fighting there. At first he had been reported missing and then he had been found, or what was left of him, in his exploded tank. Just yesterday I had received another letter saying that Marianne had come home. She had been pregnant but had miscarried – probably due to the shock of her husband's death. I did not know what to do. Should I write to her or not? Probably I would have written if the situation here in Warsaw had not been so tense. The attack on the Eastern front was in full swing. Our Headquarters were now in Kiev and we had to fly out men and machines alike, all that was humanly possible. We airlifted almost everything to the front and always brought back wounded soldiers. Low flying was our motto. The tiny Russian fighters appeared from nowhere, and we had no means of defending ourselves.

One day we flew back from Warsaw with a cargo of engine replacement parts, swinging nicely against the wind for landing. I felt a mighty shot in the aircraft. We had been hit by a Russian fighter almost over our own airfield and we had not even seen him coming. I felt a heavy drag on the elevator column, but between us, the engineer and myself, managed to get the aircraft down and we came to a halt with just yards to spare. The incident had been witnessed from aircraft control, and they managed to scramble two Messerschmitts. In no time they had engaged the enemy, and, we saw him crash-land with his engine on fire only yards in front of us. From the elevated position of my cockpit I could see the pilot leaving the aircraft and running away.

'Let's get him!' I shouted to my boys. Seconds later his plane exploded. We surrounded him shouting: 'Stop, stop!' A shot rang out and we all called to each other, checking to discover who had been shot. We all appeared to be all right, but did not know quite what had happened. Had he shot himself or was he preparing for a fight against the three of us? We doubted that. He would have had little chance of success. We pulled our pistols out and at a command jumped up. It was too late, he had shot himself. In the meantime our Unit had arrived. I borrowed a vehicle in order to take the maps we had found on him to our Commanding Officer as quickly as possible. The incident of the Russian pilot upset me and I was rather uneasy that night. By this time I was accustomed to the sight of blood, but we certainly would not have hurt him. However that is war and that is how things were!

My aeroplane had a couple of holes in the tail section but it lived up to its reputation to fly, even if only half of it was left. A couple of weeks later I was decorated for prompt action under enemy conditions and two weeks later I found myself promoted once more. How glamorous it all seemed!

The front moved east and south, and soon we were landing on an airfield near Stalingrad. Our flying distances became much longer and life was very exhausting. The mail was spasmodic. Marianne was often in my thoughts as I pondered on what the future offered her now. Sure enough, one day a letter from Hugo arrived telling me that his mother had followed his brother and father to the grave, and how many boys from our own and the surrounding villages had been killed or wounded. Bombs had been dropped on Cologne and Hamburg. He also mentioned that Marianne had returned to her nursing career and was now in a hospital in Berlin-Buch. In my reply to Hugo's letter I said how sorry I was about the passing of his mother and told him confidentially of how things were with me: that I had girl-friends on and off but still could not forget Marianne. I asked him, if he should ever see her in the village, to give her my regards and say how sincerely sorry I was for all that had happened.

Here near Stalingrad things worsened by the hour. Everything became increasingly difficult to obtain: food, spares and fuel. Wounded soldiers were piling up. We could not take them all and had to make heart-breaking decisions as to whom we took and whom we left behind. I felt the strain of this very badly and was unable to sleep at night from thinking of the badly injured men. There was just no room for them all on the aircraft.

One morning the airfield was attacked by long-range Russian artillery. We received orders to take as many passengers as we possibly could and get airborne. My instructions were to take wounded soldiers and make for Riga. There was panic all around us. The mobile aircraft control unit was badly hit and put out of action. The first plane to take off hit a grenade crater and exploded. The next plane changed direction and took off. As I followed him, a grenade exploded very close to the aircraft and a fragment hit my under-carriage. However, as I already had the necessary take-off speed, I managed to get airborne. As we prepared to land in Warsaw for re-fuelling, I radioed for advice. After a couple of low passes, it was confirmed that a wheel was damaged. With fuel running out I had no choice. I had to make an emergency landing. Ambulances and fire tenders were standing by as I held my aircraft to a very low speed on one wheel. For all my efforts, as she toppled over the wheel collapsed. She swung round, the wing broke away, and the propeller from that engine became embedded in the ground. We all got out safely, but the good old faithful was a write-off.

I had many reports to write and, after two weeks, my crew and I collected a new aeroplane from Berlin. Berlin of all places! Marianne's name came to my mind immediately, for Marianne, it will be remembered, was in Berlin. How I longed to see her!

I collected my papers together and hung around the office until I could obtain a lift for all three crew members to Berlin. I discovered that General Kesselring was to fly to Berlin in his special Heinkel. I smartened myself up and, as he arrived with his adjutant and another staff officer, I stepped forward, saluted smartly and asked him for a lift. All he said was: 'What do you want in Berlin?' I explained that I was to collect a Junkers 52 and he told me to hop in. The three of us, myself and my crew, got in and we were off. We were soon in Berlin and we landed at Gatow. All we had to do now was to get to Staaken, on the other side of Berlin, and this was not difficult. The only problem for me was how to make our stay in Berlin as long as possible. I thought it was my only chance of seeing Marianne.

It was easy to find the telephone number of the hospital in Buch, and I nervously pondered whether I should or should not ring. I decided that I would, but first I went to the canteen for something to eat. It was about 8 pm, a good time to ring. Eventually I got through to the nurses' quarters and there was a long pause. Then the voice came over the line: 'Ober-schwester Marianne.'

'Marianne Wittstock?' I enquired. By this time I was very excited.

'Yes,' came the reply.

'How are you Marianne?'

'Oh no, it is not you, is it?'
'Yes, yes, Marianne, it is.'
'What a surprise! Where are you ringing from?' she asked.
'Not very far from you. I am only here another day or so and I am wondering whether or not I can invite you for a meal? That would be nice, wouldn't it?'
'Oh yes, it would be, but it is not as easy as you may think,' she replied.
'I can imagine that, Marianne.'
'Let me just have a look. Yes, to-morrow I am on in the morning, and I finish at 2 pm. But don't forget that by 11 pm everybody has to be back home, there is no more transport.'
'Yes, I know. Can we meet at 4 pm on the Zoo underground station? I know a nice place just round the corner from there. It is called "The Grape". If I miss you for some reason, I will leave a message there, but I shall be at the station before 4 pm. I am really looking forward to seeing you to-morrow. 'Bye for now, see you to-morrow.'

That night at about 11 pm, the siren started. Everyone went into the air shelter provided. There had been siren alarms previously in Berlin, but no serious bombing. Further west, Hamburg and Cologne had been bombed in retaliation for our bombing of London. It was always the odd enemy aircraft which penetrated through to Berlin. The Berliners became accustomed to it. It was generally believed that the air defences in Berlin were so good that the enemy dare not risk an attack. That night hell broke loose. The anti-aircraft guns opened fire and the sky was filled with searchlights. Suddenly we saw a single enemy plane in the cross light. The guns opened up furiously, but the aircraft got away. He was assisted by the clouds. I went to bed but could not sleep. I was concerned that, if to-morrow night was like this, there was little chance of going out with Marianne. It could even turn out that leave would be cancelled.

The following morning we had to attend a briefing and, all being well, the afternoon would be free. The aircraft we took over, a Junkers 52, came from Spain as a contribution from Franco, but some modifications needed to be made. I knew that it would not be ready for the next day. The day after we would have a test flight and then in the afternoon we would fly off to Riga. But that seemed a long time away.

I arrived at the underground station and Marianne came at 4 pm. We stood with our arms around each other for a long, long time. Eventually she looked up at me and her eyes were full of tears. I got my handkerchief out of my pocket and wiped her tears away. She took my arm and without speaking we walked out of the station into the sunshine. I stopped walking and looked at her. 'Are you hungry, Marianne?' I asked.

'Oh no.'

'Good, because I have ordered dinner for 6 pm to 6.30 pm.'

'Fine,' she said. We walked round the corner past the Zoo and into the Tiergarten.

'Let me look at you.' I stepped back to look at her.

'Oh, don't, I am an old woman now, that is how I feel.'

'No, Marianne, you are not. You have lost a bit of weight since I saw you last and you look paler, but you are as beautiful as you were the first time I ever saw you. But of course, you would not remember that.'

'Of course, I do,' she said as she surveyed me. 'And you have been decorated and promoted.' She indicated the medals and the epaulettes. 'I always thought you were different from the other boys, but you were just a bit too young for me to give it more serious thought.'

'Now then Marianne, I don't want to embarrass you.'

'Yes, better not,' and we both turned round. She took my arm once again and we walked into the Tiergarten. It was a lovely afternoon. The Tiergarten was almost empty. We found a seat in a quiet corner and sat down. Time seemed to be standing still. In fact, we went back in time ten years or so. I was amazed at how much she remembered. 'The water lilies? Yes, I remember. I felt your humiliation at the comments made by the boys and I told them so.' We spoke of almost everything, and when Martha and her baby were mentioned, tears came into her eyes. 'Do you know that I lost my baby?' she said.

'Yes, Marianne, I know. Hugo told me in a letter. He still writes to me. I am so sorry.' And I took her in my arms. 'Do you know, Marianne, that my grandad died?'

'Yes.'

'Do you know that I am adopted?' I asked. She looked at me.

'Yes, I know.'

'Do you know that my grandma is in a concentration camp?'

'No, I did not. Poor Grandma! She believed so strongly and do you know, she may even be right. Just look at my hospital now, it is a lazarette, more like a slaughterhouse. Look at all these young men we are getting every day, and for many there is no hope. In a way – though perhaps I should not say this – at least Heinz was killed instantly. The grenade ripped his tank to bits,'

'Yes, Marianne, don't think I do not know. We pick the poor beggars up and fly them back to the lazarettes, and many do not even last the journey. Come on, its nearly 6 pm, our dinner will be ready. Let's make the best of it.'

'Yes, you are right,' she said.

It was a lovely dinner, and we even managed to have a glass of wine with it. Afterwards there was coffee and cake and a liqueur. We sat opposite each other and when we had finished the meal, she got up, put her arms around me, and gave me a kiss. It took me a while to recover and I said to her: 'If we were not in a restaurant, I would not let you go. You know that, don't you?'

'You made me very happy for a change to-day,' she said.

'Is it worth more than a kiss?' I asked.

'Perhaps,' she smiled.

'Come on Marianne, we have a couple of hours. Let's go back to the Tiergarten.'

So we did, and we made tender love. Walking back to the station, we promised to write to each other. The big question was, could we see each other again to-morrow.

She could manage it, but with me it all depended on the test flight the following morning, and whether I could persuade the test pilot to make one more day possible for me in Berlin. I would certainly do my best and arranged to ring her at 12 noon the following day. We had a long embrace and then she left. I stood there in a daze, not really sure whether it had all been a dream. Then I collected myself and went back to Staaken.

Next morning we performed the test flight on the Junkers. I insisted that number 1 and number 3 engines did not respond as they should, and my engineer agreed. We had won another day in Berlin. I rang Marianne. We met again at the station and ran into each other's arms. We went back to the Tiergarten, had another meal in 'The Grape', returned to the Tiergarten and were very happy. Then it was time to part. We had just passed the entrance to the Zoo when the sirens started. We didn't take much notice and kept on walking arm in arm. Suddenly anti-aircraft guns opened fire, the searchlights appeared, aircraft noise grew louder, and large flares dropped from the sky. The first bombs whistled down on Berlin. People started running, we started running. People were shouting: 'The air shelter, next corner!' I pulled Marianne along as fast as I could. We got to the shelter. Hundreds of people trying to get in were blocking the long concrete steps which led into it. Somebody pulled me on one side.

'This shelter is for women and children only. You have to run to the underground station.' I shouted: ''Bye Marianne, see you later.'

Next second all I could see was an almighty flash. I tried to breathe. I could not. I started vomiting. For a while I could see nothing, then all I could see was fire. Somebody shouted: 'Anybody here?' I tried to shout back but could not. I was half aware of being dragged along, and when I came round, I was lying on a stretcher on a lorry rattling along the road. I tried to move my arms and my legs. Why could I not move? I heard myself shouting: ''Bye Marianne, see you later, later, later.' The echo seemed to be coming from a long tunnel and became weaker and weaker.

When I came round again, I felt very sick and slowly I realised that I was lying on my tummy, heavily bandaged. Pain seemed to creep between my shoulder blades. The pain got worse and I felt that I had to shout for help. A couple of orderlies appeared, and shortly afterwards the doctor. He came twice a day, and slowly I realised that I was badly wounded. I was in constant pain, especially when the wound was treated. Eventually I got better and stronger again. All the memories prior to the bomb attack came back. I remembered Marianne going down the steps to the shelter. Surely she was all right? She would not know which lazarette I was in, that was why she had not contacted me. 'Shall I ask someone to ring the hospital,' I thought, 'to ask about her? No, I had better wait until I am well enough to phone her myself.'

Another three weeks passed before I slowly made my way to the telephone, and all the time I was telling myself that Marianne was all right. Had I not seen her going down to the shelter?

It did not take long to get through to the hospital. I asked for the department where Marianne was working.

'Hello, can I speak to Marianne Wittstock please?' I said.

'Who is speaking?' I gave my rank and name. 'Are you a relative of Marianne?'

'No, a friend,' I replied.

There was a long and dreadful pause. 'I am very sorry, Marianne is missing, presumably killed in the first bomb attack on Berlin.'

The lazarette doctor who had operated on me visited me daily. He suspected that something was wrong apart from the injuries I had received in that bombing. He sat on the corner of my bed and said: 'Come on, N.C.O., what is the matter?'

I shook my head. 'No, no!'

'Come on, boy, you have lost your will to live, what's the matter? You can tell me in confidence.' He sent the two orderlies away and I told him what had happened. Also that I had a terrible feeling of guilt, and that I did not want her parents or her in-laws to know how it had happened because of the short time since her husband was killed.

'But surely,' he said, 'she would have told someone at the hospital that she was meeting you?'

'Oh, no, she told me that nobody knew. She told her hospital colleagues that she was meeting a friend from her school days, a girl-friend. Sir, please give me leave for three or four hours to go back to Berlin to find out what has happened.'

'Right boy,' he said, placing his hand on my shoulder. 'If you improve in a week or so, I will. Then I shall send you for three weeks to a spa for convalescence. After that you can have two weeks' home leave, and after that we shall have to see what your doctor there is recommending for you. But I had better tell you, your flying days are over for a time.'

He left and I felt somewhat relieved. I could go back to Berlin and try to find out what had happened.

The surgeon kept his word and the following week I left the bunker hospital for Berlin. By the time I arrived at Bahnhof Zoo, I was totally confused. The place was unrecognisable. I wandered about until I found a policeman, who advised me to go to the nearest police station. After a long wait at the enquiry desk, it was my turn. 'Yes, the air-raid shelter near to the station?' The officer placed a map in front of me. 'It got two direct hits. One bomb fell on the centre of the shelter and dug a hole in the reinforced concrete about 50 cm deep and exploded. The other bomb fell right into the entrance of the shelter. There were 60 steps down to the shelter entrance. It is estimated that there would have been 200-250 women and children on these steps, and that all have perished.'

He must have noticed my distress and he offered me a chair. 'What was her name?'

'Her name was Marianne,' I said.

'Marianne, what?'

'Marianne Wittstock,' I replied.

'We have a list of all the people who could be identified, who were in the shelter. Just a minute, I will have a look.' He came back after a short time shaking his head. 'Sorry, she is not on our list.'

I can't remember how long I walked amongst the rubble until I found the spot where the bunker should have been. The flagged concrete top, with the impact mark of the first bomb, was clearly visible. I just stood there not knowing what to do. Marianne, Marianne! I could see us holding hands, running to the shelter. At least she had not suffered. I am sure she was happy that night, I am sure. On my way back to the station, I noticed a flower stand. 'Five marks a bunch of flowers, pick your own, Sir. Any cigarettes?'

'Oh, yes, cigarettes,' I said, 'here, 5 marks and 20 cigarettes.'

'Thank you, Sir, Heil Hitler!'

I went back to the shelter and pressed the flowers into the crevices amongst the rubble. There were many other flowers, mostly wilted, which had been placed there for the lost loved ones. 'Goodbye, Marianne, goodbye.'

PART II. LENA-MARIA

CHAPTER FIVE. MEETING LENA

The train was two hours late. The platforms were crowded with people, mostly soldiers. Some of these were fortunate enough to be starting a period of leave; others were going back to the front and perhaps a few, like me, were starting a period of convalescence. I was heading for the Thueringer Forest near Weimar, the town where Schiller and Goethe made their unforgettable contributions of wisdom and poetry to the world. So far this town had remained untouched by the War. Slowly I walked up and down the platform in an effort to exercise a little, as my limbs and joints were stiff from the long stay in hospital. My back was not actually hurting. Rather, it was numb and so were my toes. The doctor had told me that I would have to live with that. It did not worry me. I was glad to be out of the hospital. The surgeon had truly done his best for me. I think he had taken a liking to me. Before leaving, I went to his office to thank him. He shook my hand and told me that he had made a report to my commanding officer recommending that I be taken off flying duty, and possibly that I should be re-trained for something more suitable to my damaged back. This was something of a shock to me since flying had been my life, but then of course, it could have been much worse. On reflection I realised that I was lucky to have my life. I thought of all the boys I was leaving behind in the hospital who were far worse than I was.

Shortly after leaving the station, the door of my compartment opened and a young lady entered. She was wearing a Red Cross apron. 'Hello,' she said, 'Are you alone in here?'

'Yes, I am,' I said.

'Can I offer you some coffee and biscuits?' she asked. I accepted her offer gratefully, and I hastily placed myself in a more presentable position as she prepared the coffee in the corridor outside the compartment. I stood up. Something was wrong with my right arm. It felt sore and wet. I had suffered a shrapnel wound to this arm at the time of my serious back injury in Berlin, but little attention had been paid to it, for, compared with the back injury, it had seemed relatively insignificant.

'By the way, I have not introduced myself,' I said as I extended my hand to her. 'My name is Carl, Sergeant-Major Carl Decker. I am pleased to meet you. Do you live in Weimar?'

'No, not in the town, but not so far away, about 5 km,' she answered.

'And how do you get home to-night?' I asked her.

'On my bicycle,' she replied.

'What! On the bike, alone in the dark?'

'In the dark, yes, but alone, no. There are usually two or three of us going that way, and if it is very bad weather, my dad gets the horse out to get me home. We have a farm, although it is not our own,' she explained, and she went on to tell me that it was part of a very large estate.

When I arrived at the Sanatorium, I was given my new room number and was told that I would be sharing it with five others. Only in special cases could patients be given a single room, and I was not regarded as a special case. I could go at once into my new quarters and my luggage would be brought there. As I entered the room, I saw four men sitting around a table playing cards. A fifth man was sitting on his bed writing a letter. I walked straight over to the table. The boys looked up, and I could not believe my eyes when I saw a familiar face from my flying school days.

'It can't be Werner?' I exclaimed. 'Yes it is, Carl.' After a long and warm handshake I said: 'Just hang on a second until I shake hands with the other boys.' As I did so, Werner Kuehne was explaining to them how we had been together in the flying school in Halberstadt and in Stendal. He told them that I was always the villain amongst the trainees and that he, Werner, had always had to suffer for what I had done. He told them how in military exercises we always stood side by side, being the two tallest of the group.

'Stop it, Werner. I will tell you who was the bad one. It was he. He always kicked me in the ribs and I always retaliated by standing on his toes.'

'What a joke!' retorted Werner, 'Here you can stand on my toes as long as you like,' and he lifted his artificial leg.

'Oh no, Werner,' I said, 'I am so sorry.'

'Don't be sorry,' he replied. 'They did not bring you here for nothing,' and he pointed to my arm which was in a sling.

'It's not my arm,' I said, 'but I will tell you all about it. It is a pity that we can't have our beds side by side as we had them in the school.'

One of the lads looked up and said: 'My bed is next to Werner's, but you can swop if you like.'

'This is Franz from Vienna,' said Werner, 'he got shot up in a tank.'

'You really mean that Franz?' I asked.

'Yes, of course.' So we changed places and once again I was side by side with an old comrade. It was several days before we caught up on all we had to tell each other.

Shortly afterwards I received a telephone call from Elizabeth, the Red Cross nurse whom I had met on the train. She had managed to obtain tickets for the opera, she told me, and when I explained that I had met a friend, Werner, she found a way of getting an extra ticket for him.

When we met at the Opera House that evening, Elizabeth, looking very beautiful in evening dress, was accompanied by another girl, no less beautiful, whom she introduced as Lena-Maria. We took our seats and, as the opera struck up, I sat back and began to draw mental comparisons between the two girls. How very different they were! Elizabeth wore a long shiny pink-coloured dress. Her necklace seemed to be very dark. She had a roundish face with dark eyes and dark hair which appeared curly and just covered her ears. Lena was just the opposite. She wore a darkish blue velvet dress. Around her neck was a gold chain with a cross. I noticed that she wore a gold wrist watch. She was very blonde, her face was longish, and her hair was twisted into a knot at the back of her head in a modern style called the German Knot. This style was mostly favoured by women who were sympathetic to the policies of The Third Reich. In the middle of her chin she had a distinguishing groove and when she laughed, which she had been doing most of the time, one noticed the gap between her two front teeth. It was not excessively large but one could not miss it. Both girls were roughly the same height and this was somewhat disappointing for they were both rather small, only reaching to our shoulders. Both were rather young and I guessed Elizabeth to be the older of the two.

During the interval Lena came straight to me while Elizabeth talked mainly to Werner. Lena turned out to be a warm and lively conversationalist. When it was all over and we were taking leave of each other, I shook her hand. As I did so, I felt her pass a piece of paper into my hand, which I placed in my pocket. I was very eager to know what it was. I knew it would contain a message and I was burning with curiosity to know what this might be. However, wait I must. We did not say much on our way back to the Sanatorium as we did not want the driver to overhear anything of what had taken place during the evening. But as soon as we got out of the car, Werner started the conversation by asking me if we had arranged to meet again. 'I don't know yet, Werner. She passed a piece of paper into my hand. There could be a message on it but I don't know yet. But what about you, Werner?'

'Yes, Elizabeth would like to meet me again – at least that is what I understood. She did not speak very loud but she will contact me one way or the other. I took the piece of paper out of my pocket and unfolded it, making myself comfortable on the end of Werner's bed. Whilst Werner was undoing the straps of his artificial leg, I started reading. 'Hey, Werner, listen to this,' I said. 'Lena-Maria von Schulenburg, Trampe, Nr. Cologne', printed in the left hand corner.

'What!' said Werner, 'You pick the right ones, don't you, Carl! von what?'

The message read: 'Can we meet you at 3.30 pm on Tuesday outside the Sanatorium gate?' signed Lena and Elizabeth.

'Well, I never, I never!' laughed Werner bringing his hand down on the bed. 'What do you think Werner?' I said, 'Are we going?'

'Of course we are going,' Werner replied eagerly.

'We shall have to ask permission,' I said.

'Permission? We do not ask for permission,' answered Werner. 'Two NCO's wanting a couple of hours off? We will just tell them, that's all. Just leave it to me.'

'You know, Werner, I am not all that sure I want to go.'
'What's the matter with you now?' he asked.

'Look, Werner, I don't want to trouble you with my problems, you've had enough of your own, but it was only a couple of months ago that I lost the girl I had really loved since I was 14 years old, and had it not been for me, she could be alive to-day.' Then I told him all about Marianne. When I had finished he said: 'Listen, Carl, I knew from the first moment you walked in that something more than injury was troubling you. They would not have sent you here otherwise. But believe you me, you will not get better here or anywhere else if you don't change your attitude. It was not your fault and it was not my fault that I lost my crew that night.'

'No, I know it was not my fault, I did my best and so did you,' I replied.

'We are just lucky. Who knows? To-morrow it may be our turn. The War is not over yet. Let's face it, if you keep on flying in these conditions, it is only matter of time before it gets you. Come on, boy, we are going to see these girls! They want us. Look at you, sliding right into the nobleman's class! How lucky can you be? What do you think, how old are these girls?' Before he could say any more, we had to postpone the conversation as our room mates were coming back.

As we walked out of the gate at 3.30 pm on the following Tuesday, the girls were already waiting for us. They showed us their transport, a horse-drawn cart with a canvas top and as we examined it Elizabeth explained: 'This is now the family transport.' She went on to say that they had owned a motor car, but that it had been requisitioned by the military. We were invited to take a drive through the countryside. It was a lovely afternoon, and still warm enough to have a picnic. They had come well prepared for it. We watched in astonishment as they brought out all the foodstuffs which, they joked, had all come from their own coupons. We, of course, knew that this could not be so. We began to eat and during our meal the girls questioned us at some length, and also told more about themselves.

It turned out that Lena's uncle owned a very large estate nearby and that Elizabeth's father was one of his tenants. Lena had only been there for a couple of months. Elizabeth had met her as she came riding past their farm house, and in this way they had become friendly.

Lena had liked the idea of helping out at the Red Cross as much as Elizabeth and they saw each other quite often.

'And what did you do before you came here, Lena?' I asked.

'Not much,' she said, 'I only recently finished my education in a convent school near Cologne, and I would have taken a business study course but the bombing stopped all that. So my father sent me here.'

'Werner, you have not said anything for a long time.' I said.

'No, I am enjoying listening. It is all very interesting,' he said.

Elizabeth thought that it was time for us to be packing away our picnic things before starting the journey back, explaining that after dropping us at the Sanatorium they still had a journey to Weimar, and from there a further four kilometres to the estate. We all helped to clear up and were soon on our way back. As Elizabeth was driving the horse and cart down the hill, Lena asked whether we could meet again. Werner could not answer quickly enough. 'Yes, of course. Please.'

To this Lena said: 'I will tell you a secret, a very big secret.'

'Come on then,' I said, 'don't keep us waiting.'

'Right,' she said. 'The shooting season starts next weekend. My uncle has a lot of shooting ground in the mountains and he has a shooting lodge there. I know he has invited a number of generals and Party leaders to spend a week there. My aunt will be there as well, and so I have planned with Elizabeth to have a party of our own. There are only two servants at home and I will send them home early. If you can come to Weimar by bus, you can change there for another, which will take you to Elizabeth's farm house. We will collect you from there and take you to the estate. How is that?'

'It sounds like a fairy story,' exclaimed Werner looking at Elizabeth. On our way down the hill we had changed places, and Werner was now sitting on the front seat with Elizabeth. Lena and I were at the back and she had slipped her hand into mine.

Back at the Sanatorium we made for the canteen, as we both wished to talk over the events of the afternoon. The canteen would be a more private place for this purpose than our dormitory. We found a quiet corner and Werner could hardly wait to begin. He told me that he was certain that Elizabeth was fond of him. On the way back he had moved his knee against hers and she had not objected. Werner was obviously very thrilled at the experience, and he thought that Elizabeth was a lovely girl. He went on to say that Lena was also lovely and he considered me to be very lucky to have a girl like that. I tried to explain to him that although I might be lucky, I was not really happy about a new romantic situation at such a time. My heart was still heavy with recent events. Werner was a little concerned to hear me say such things. 'Hey, Carl,' he said, 'don't you change your mind or I will never forgive you.'

'Well,' I answered, 'the girl is nice, but just consider the situation. Elizabeth is a bit more mature, but Lena – she has just left school, a convent school. Do you realise, Werner, what that means? She has got away and now feels free, like a bird having flown from a cage.'

'Don't exaggerate,' said Werner, 'you don't have to go to bed with her if you do not want to. She may not even want that, but just consider the other side. How many of us ordinary chaps would even be able to take a nobleman's daughter in their arms? When the war is over, you would not have to worry about the future; you would be sitting on a mountain of money.'

'Don't talk such rubbish, Werner. There is another thing I don't like: her aunt and uncle going off to the mountains for a week's shooting of wild boar and deer, just for the fun of it, whilst our lads are being blown to bits. You and I are just out of a lazarette. You saw the cases in there. In my lazarette they brought them in by the dozen at night. The poor lads cried their hearts out and in the morning they wheeled them out dead.'

'You are right, Carl. Let's not talk about it any more to-night. Let's go to bed and just think that we had a very nice day.' We shook hands and went to our room.

CHAPTER SIX. OUR LOVE AFFAIR GROWS

The next day I was called to the office, and from there to the surgery. The doctor offered me a chair and said: 'Sergeant-Major, you are now half way through your time here at the Sanatorium. I think you have made excellent progress. Your Squadron Leader suggests that you take two weeks' leave after your release from here, but this will have to be cut short by three days, because you have been allocated a place at the Officers' School in Rudolfstadt. The three months' course begins on the 28th September. All the necessary papers have arrived here. Of course, I shall see you before you go, and good luck on your course.'

'Thank you, Sir. Heil Hitler!' I saluted and returned to my room. Werner was waiting, anxious to know what I had been told, and I repeated what the doctor had said.

A day or two later Elizabeth phoned to confirm the arrangements for our meeting with herself and Lena the following day. 'You are coming to-morrow, aren't you?' she began.

'All being well, we are coming,' I said. 'Elizabeth, can you talk for a minute?'

'Yes, go on.'

'What about Lena, is she just looking for a little flirt?'

'Look Carl, she fell for you from the first moment she saw you. She thinks you look like a real soldier. She always wanted a man from the Airforce and now she has got a real pilot. No Carl, she has really fallen for you. But now, tell me about Werner.'

'Well, Werner had a rough time as you can see. He was shot down and was the only one to survive out of the plane. On top of that, his fiancée let him down and he had a nervous breakdown. He likes you very much, Elizabeth, and his only worry is that you are already spoken for.'

'No, I am not. I have had a boy-friend who was really a school friend, a farmer's son from the village, but nothing serious.'

'Where is he now?' I asked.

'He is in the Army. We write to each other but that is all, honestly.'

'Shall I tell Werner that we had a little talk? And what about his injury?'

'You tell him, Carl, that I like him very much and his injury makes no difference. In fact I am very proud of him. You can tell him that if you wish.'

'Fine Elizabeth,' I said, 'I look forward to seeing you to-morrow.'

The house of Lena's uncle turned out to be an imposing mansion, the centre of a very large estate. We went up the steps into a vast hall. The walls were covered in antlers and horns, the teeth of wild boars, and other hunting trophies. Lena opened a pair of double doors saying: 'Please, come in and make yourselves comfortable.' We just stood for a moment and looked around. In front of us was a floor-to-ceiling glass door which opened on to a balcony. On the opposite side was a great open fireplace in which a welcoming fire was flickering. The other two sides of the room contained large oil paintings, mostly portraits. There was a grand piano in one corner and in the other a large chest of drawers with a radio set on top. A large chandelier hung from the high ceiling, and in the centre of the room stood a pedestal table on a large square carpet, which covered a parquet floor. I also noticed four heavy leather chairs and a matching sofa. That was about all I could observe of the contents of the room before Lena stopped stoking up the fire and asked us once more to sit down. Slowly we sank into the big leather seats. 'Yes, this is life!' exclaimed Werner. Suddenly the telephone rang and Lena went straight to it. 'Hello, Aunt,' she said, 'Yes, I am fine, thank you,' She went on to say that she had Elizabeth with her, but she did not mention our presence. 'Yes, I will tell the night watchman to check all the doors and gates. Don't worry, Aunt, we are fine here.'

'Sorry about that,' said Lena, 'Aunt always worries about me. Now you both entertain yourselves for a little whilst I make something to eat. I hope you are hungry. Elizabeth and I will be back soon.' With that she left the room.

'What about that?' said Werner. 'What do you think about that?'

'I don't think at this moment, Werner, I just let things happen,' I replied.

'I think we should have a very good time, if it's right about your telephone conversation with Elizabeth.'

'You can't wait, can you?' I asked.

The doors opened to reveal Lena with a large trolley packed with food. 'There,' she said, 'we had already been working hard before you arrived. I hope you have brought good appetites with you. I will make some coffee now and Elizabeth will soon be back.'

With these words she left us alone once again. It was not long before she returned, this time with Elizabeth. The blinds were drawn, the lights switched on, and the girls served sandwiches and cakes, all beautifully prepared. Werner was very happy and kept saying: 'Children, enjoy the war, peace may be worse.'

After the meal, the girls brought in glasses and a bottle of champagne. As the cork shot from the bottle and the glasses were filled, I felt that I should say a few words of appreciation. I stood up, raised my glass, looked at the girls and said: 'Ladies, Werner, I thank you very much for the wonderful meal you have made for us. May it be the start of a long friendship.' The touch of the long stemmed champagne glasses echoed through the room as we each drank the toast. The glasses were filled up again, and it was Werner's turn to speak.

'Silentium,' he said. 'May I propose a toast, and please excuse me if I don't stand up. I propose a toast to Carl, who is leaving us next week-end but not far away. He is only going to Rudolfstadt to the Officers' School. Soon he will be an officer. Good luck, Carl!'

'But first I have to pass,' I said, thanking him, and we touched our glasses once again. Lena looked with wide open eyes at me. She got up and pulled the big leather chair away from the others.

'Come here, Carl,' she said. 'Why didn't you tell me?'

'Sorry, Lena, I only got to know yesterday.'

'Can I come to see you in Rudolfstadt?' she asked.

'Of course, you can,' I said, and we had our first kiss. Lena made herself comfortable on the arm of the chair. I pulled her gently over into my good arm and we held each other close for quite a time. The other two must have done the same, and soon each couple became oblivious to anyone else in the room. We could hear the other pair happily whispering together, and there was an occasional giggle. Lena broke the silence.

'Sorry to interrupt you, but there is nice music on the radio now. Shall we have a bit of music?'

'Yes,' said Werner, 'as long as you don't ask me to dance.'

'We promise,' laughed Lena, and she switched on the radio. We all joined in the singing of Lily Marlene.

Suddenly the military music from the radio was interrupted and a voice said: 'Reichssender Berlin! Ladies and gentlemen, we are very sorry we have to break off the music for our troops' programme. It has been reported that large units of enemy aircraft have crossed over the west coast between Bremen and Hamburg flying east. For security reasons, this radio station is closing down. Please check that all lights are concealed. We shall resume this broadcast as soon as possible.'

My mind returned at once to Marianne. I closed my eyes and slumped back into my seat. Lena must have noticed the change in me. She knelt before me. 'What's wrong Carl?' she asked. 'Something has gone dreadfully wrong with you. Tell me, please tell me, what is it.'

'Yes, it reminded me,' I said.

'Please tell me, Carl,' she begged. 'I will do everything I can to help you.'

'I know you would, Lena,' I said, 'but please don't ask me any more; don't ever ask me. I will tell you myself when I am ready to tell you.'

'I understand, Carl, I am very sorry.' She sat down and put her head on my lap like a faithful dog. We were holding hands and the room was very still. Werner broke the silence.

'Does anyone know what time it is, and how are we getting home?' Lena jumped up and stood beside the wall light. 'It's nearly midnight,' she said. 'When have you to be home?'

'In our case, we can return when we please. We just have to inform the office where we are.'

'Well, then you can stay here until to-morrow, can't you? Please!' added Lena, looking at me. 'Werner can sleep on the sofa here, and we can made a bed from two big chairs and the pouffe for you. We have plenty of blankets. Look, we will go and make coffee while you get in touch with your office, Werner. It will be best if you can stay until lunchtime to-morrow. We have only the houseboy coming to-morrow and I will keep him away from this room. Elizabeth will go for the horse and we will drive you right home. Nobody will take any notice, and if anyone does see us, we have just given you a ride.'

'You are a good organiser, Lena,' I said.

'Well, if you don't get organised these days, you can get nowhere,' she giggled.

'Bravo,' said Werner. Elizabeth had disappeared. The radio came on again. Lena pointed to it and said: 'Thank goodness for that,' and she disappeared as well. I looked over to Werner. 'How are you doing over there?' I asked.

'You know, Carl,' he replied, 'I will always be in your debt for that girl. She is lovely! Come, give me a hand to get up, I will ring the office.' He soon got through. 'Sergeant-Major Kuehne here,' he said. 'I am ringing from Gruehntahl 267. We have been invited to stay overnight here at this number, and as we are all going to church to-morrow, we shall not be back to-morrow afternoon. Will you make a note, please, and will you also make a note for the physiotherapist for our session to-morrow morning. He will be pleased. Have you got it all? Yes? Heil Hitler.'

'You, bloody liar,' I said, 'and you don't even blush.'

'Look,' he said, 'I shall not be going to heaven anyway. Don't you think I have had it bad enough so far? I am just about to enjoy life a bit, and that goes for you as well, Carl. You know, Carl, this wooden leg of mine is killing me. I have to take it off. Come and give me a hand to take my trousers off.'

At this moment the girls returned. 'Are you going to bed already?' asked Elizabeth. 'You sit down, Carl. After all, we have been trained to help wounded soldiers. You just wait, Werner, I will soon have you comfortable,' and she helped him.

'Lena, let's have a blanket, then he can stretch himself out on the sofa. I will look after you, Werner,' she said and kissed him on the cheek.

Lena came back with the blankets.

Next morning we had breakfast served to us on our improvised beds. The girls joined us, wishing us bon appetite, and as we ate, they told us the programme they had planned for that day. First they insisted on looking at our injuries and attending to our comfort generally. Before our drive home, we were shown round the house. As Lena's aunt and uncle were due back at the house the following week-end, and also as I was due to leave at that time as well, we were invited to a farewell party for me on Wednesday night.

The visit was just as it had been the previous time, lovely food and excellent coffee, followed by champagne. When bedtime came, out came the blankets, but this time not as many, only enough for Werner and Elizabeth. Lena took me by the hand and led me to her bedroom.

The following morning Lena was to report for duty in Weimar at 8 am, so we travelled together. In a way it was lucky that it rained, and the canvas top covering the vehicle also covered our presence in it. In Weimar I said a special goodbye to Elizabeth. I also said that I would like to be best man at their wedding. We all laughed and on the way down, it was suggested that all three would come to the railway station to see me off. Lena, however, said she wanted to be alone with me. So the days in the Sanatorium in the beautiful Thueringer Forest came to an end.

Lena was already at the station waiting for me. There was still an hour to go before I boarded the train which would take me back to Berlin on the first stage of my journey. We sat down and I went for two cups of coffee. Lena gave me a parcel she had made up for me. 'They are nice things, all home-made,' she said. I took her in my arms and wiped her tears. 'You will come to see me?' I asked. She nodded. 'As soon as I can.' We started to talk of our families and I learned that Lena was the youngest of four children. The eldest, her sister, was married to a brigadier who was serving in the North African desert with Rommel. The eldest brother was a captain in the Pioneer Regiment, at the moment in France. The youngest brother was handicapped, but she did not say in what way. He was working in her father's office. Her father owned a factory which made components for the military. Her mother was at home in their villa about 20 miles outside Essen. Her mother was extremely nervous about her two sons being at the front, but she was a little happier that Lena was with her aunt in Weimar. Her aunt was very good to her. She and her uncle had only one daughter, married to a nobleman who owned a large estate in East Prussia.

'What about you?' she asked.

'Oh, Lena, there is not much to tell, not to-day.' I told her that I had been brought up by my grandparents; that my grandfather had died, and my parents were in The Baltic, where my father was working on a hydro-electric plant. 'That is, if they are still there. Since the Russians have occupied The Baltic States for a year, many of the people have been arrested and disappeared. My grandmother was living alone, but she has been taken away for re-training as she was very religious.' On hearing this, Lena gave me an enquiring look. I felt that she would have liked to pursue this point but I deliberately avoided reacting, so she said nothing. I went on to say that I was going to find out what had happened to my grandma's flat and then I was going to visit a friend of mine. She looked at me and closed one eye. 'A friend?' she asked. 'Yes,' I replied. 'A friend. We became friends when we were 14 years old. 'Look, Carl, she said, you don't need 10 days to see your friend. Stay here for four or five days I will find you a room in a hotel here where I know the proprietor. They will definitely put you up. Come on!' She picked up my luggage, took my hand and we walked out of the station.

I was surprised that Lena had been able to book a room for us at the hotel in Weimar and distinctly uneasy at her insistence that I should not pay a penny of the cost. 'It's a secret,' she explained, 'but that is how it has to be. My uncle with his shooting parties shoots a lot of deer and wild boar. We give some to the hotel and in return we get a room for guests whom we cannot or do not wish to accommodate. It's simple, is it not? I will see that they get something extra from last week's shooting.'

'Ah, that is how the rich people live. I will have to get used to it, but that may take me a long time.'

She looked at me and laughed, obviously not understanding what I meant.

Thanks to Lena, therefore, I could stay a few more days in Weimar, and I was very happy about it. I bought a programme, which I was reading when Lena arrived. She wanted to know how I had spent the day, but soon we went to bed and turned off the lights.

My last day in Weimar arrived. Lena came in the evening and she stayed with me all night. In the morning she accompanied me to the station. The train was on time and as it pulled out, I watched her standing there, waving a white handkerchief and wiping away her tears. Soon her slim figure and her blonde hair disappeared into the distance.

The train arrived in Berlin on time. I changed stations and promised myself not to think about the sadness of the past. By mid-afternoon I was back in my old town and my first call was to my grandma's flat, which had been locked up and sealed by the police. I knocked on the next door, which was opened by an elderly lady, Mrs Schulz. 'You must be Mr. Deckers?' she asked.

'Yes, I am,' I replied.

'Come in, you must be hungry. I will make you something to eat at once. Make yourself comfortable. I am so pleased that you came. Your grandma, yes, she was a nice lady, if she would only have stopped preaching they would not have taken her. I hope that she is all right. Just wait a minute, I have a letter for you.'

She opened a drawer and took out a large sealed envelope. 'Here,' she said. 'She gave me this two days before they came for her. She must have known. You have a look whilst I make you something to eat.' With that she disappeared into the kitchen. Somewhat apprehensively I opened the envelope. Inside it I found a photograph of my mother and father, a ring, a birth certificate, a bank book and a letter, which I started to read. In the middle of the page at the top of the letter she had written: 'Oh, Lord, forgive them, they do not know what they are doing.'

'Dear Son,

I hope you will get this letter, which I will give to Mrs. Schulz for safe keeping. You will find that all the money your parents sent for you is in the bank book. Your grandad and I saved it up for you for your later life. There is a photograph of your mother and father and written on the back is their last address. The ring was my mother's, which she left to me when she died. I think you had better have it and a copy of your birth certificate. May the Lord forgive you and bless you. Don't worry about me, Son, the Lord will always be with me. Love – Grandma.'

I just covered my head in my hands and cried.

That night I hardly slept. First there was the siren. Berlin was being bombed again. One or two bombers must have strayed off course without dropping anything but Mrs. Schulz was very frightened and I went down with her to the air raid shelter. When I got back to bed, I thought of Grandma.

The next morning I managed to get a seat on the post bus and went to see Hugo. He was very pleased to see me, and asked me to stay overnight. He did not work that day and we took a walk round the lake and riverside, so familiar to us over so many years. We talked of old times and we had so much to say to each other that our conversation went on well into the night over a bottle of Hugo's home-made wine. We renewed our promise to each other to keep in touch by letter, as we had always done. I did not feel that it was the right time to tell him about Lena, so I did not mention it. We opened a second bottle of wine, and we both agreed that the War might be lost. I was rather surprised to find that Hugo knew of the secret weapons which were being developed in Norway and Peenemunde and other parts of Germany. These weapons were said to be so powerful that the V weapons already in use against England were nothing by comparison. Of course these were only rumours, but until this evening I had not been aware that they were circulating amongst the civilian population. After we had made a start on a third bottle of Hugo's wine, he told me of the sadness which was now a part of life in the village. All the young men were either dead, badly wounded, or were prisoners of war. Then he spoke of the tragic disappearance of Marianne. It was believed in the village that she had gone into Berlin to meet an old school friend. She had not returned, and it was presumed that she had been killed in one of the first bombing raids on Berlin. I could not stand it any longer. 'Let's go to bed, Hugo,' I said. By this time I had had a lot to drink. Perhaps it was as well that I did not say anything to Hugo about what had really happened to Marianne. I thought it better not to comment.

CHAPTER SEVEN.
DEFEATED BY THE CLASS BARRIER

The next morning, with a very heavy heart, I said goodbye to Hugo. I got into the post bus and as it drove along the village street, I thought how different it all was. It was more like a ghost village than the place I knew as a boy.

The course in Rudolfstadt got off to a flying start. There were fifteen of us, all NCO's. All of us were airforce men, but only three were pilots. The course we took would normally have lasted three years, but because of circumstances, this was condensed to just three months. The study was, of course, intense. It had to be. Nevertheless, it was not easy to explain this to Lena when she visited me the following week. We arrived in the hotel room and Lena looked at me with pleading in her eyes. She looked lovely and I was touched. When she said: 'Don't you want me here?' I pulled her on to my knees, feeling very protective towards her.

'Of course, I want you here,' I said. 'All I am saying is that it will be a difficult time for me.'

'Look,' she said. 'I brought you some nice food so that you can have a bit extra every day. If you work hard you must eat well and when it is finished, I will bring you some more. Lena was really amazing. Here was a girl, a very young girl from a highly privileged background, protected and, perhaps, over-indulged. She had never known hardship and yet there were times, such as the present, when her mature outlook and shrewdness took me by surprise. 'Now we are going for a nice walk and to-night you will stay with me in the hotel.'

'Is that why you have got a double room?' I asked.

'Yes, of course, I did all that for you, Carl.'

'How did you do it?' I said.

'I asked for the proprietor and told him that I had come to see my husband. I gave him half a pound of coffee beans, and he gave us this nice room.

Lena informed me that Elizabeth and Werner were getting engaged and that we were both invited to the celebration.

'Please, Carl, you will get that one week-end off?' she pleaded. 'Won't you?'

'Yes, why not? I will just have to work a bit harder at night.'

Then she told me that she had told her aunt about me and shown her my photograph. 'Don't worry, Aunt is on my side. She understands and hopes to meet you soon. The only thing is, that she hopes you are a Catholic for my Dad's sake. Are you?'

'I am not a Catholic, Lena,' I said and quickly changed the subject back to Elizabeth and Werner's engagement.

A little later she said: 'While we are at the engagement party, we could slip over to the estate and meet my aunt and uncle if he is there,' she suggested. 'You don't mind, do you?'

'No, not really, as long as there are no generals about,' I chuckled.

'No, we do not get many of them at the house. It is usually at the shooting lodge.'

It was time to go down to the restaurant for a meal and there we met my room-mate and his fiancée. A very nice couple, we agreed later. The four of us had a meal together, and then spent the rest of the evening in conversation. Then the two false wives went to bed with their two false husbands.

Three weeks later, at the party, I could see that Lena was becoming somewhat nervous; she wanted us to go and see her aunt. We walked the short distance to the estate entrance, through the large ornamental gates and, this time, up to the imposing front entrance. Her aunt had obviously been waiting for us, as she opened the door herself. I made my military salute and as I entered, I removed my uniform cap, placed it under my arm and stepped inside. This time I was shown into a different room. Lena introduced us and a warm handshake put me at my ease. Her aunt was a good-looking woman. She had a warm round face and was very friendly. She started chatting straight away and it was obvious that she knew a lot about me. She knew that I was a pilot and said she had never flown in an aeroplane and would be terrified to do so. She said that she was even frightened to go up in a lift. At this point Lena chipped in. 'Aunt,' she said, 'shall I make coffee?'

'Yes, child, ask your uncle to come in just for a moment, please.'

'Do you know Mr ...' here she hesitated, obviously being unsure of my name, 'Decker...'

I immediately corrected the name saying: 'Yes, Deckers.'

'Lena is such a sensitive girl. I hope that your friendship is sincere.'

'Yes, I understand, Madam,' I replied.

'She is the youngest in her family. All that bombing over there is terrible; that is why she is here and I feel responsible for her. You understand?'

'Yes, of course I understand, Madam.'

At that moment the door opened and in came a tall figure in what was probably a shooting outfit. His grey hair was parted in military fashion over his left eye. He had a large moustache, and he wore a pince-nez. He wore riding breeches and long brown leather boots. He could easily have been a high-ranking officer. I stood up and saluted smartly as the lady said: 'This is the young man Lena told us about.'

'Oh, yes,' he said, and we shook hands. 'Where are you stationed, may I ask? And please sit down.'

I then began my story in a way that I had carefully prepared, realising before this meeting what they would wish to know about me. Lena appeared with coffee and cake. I apologised for being unable to eat anything, following the enormous meal at Elizabeth's house. Lena's uncle looked at the watch on the long golden chain at his waist. 'Just a few more minutes,' he said. 'I have one of my riding mares in foal and I must go round and have a look. Tell me, young man, after your course at the officers' school, what then?'

'I will go back to my old transport command, which at the moment is in Riga and there I will probably be put in charge of a technical unit for the time being. I know I would not be put back on flying duty. Perhaps later, when my health improves, I may be a pilot once again.'

'What about promotion?' he asked.

'First of all I have to pass at the school. Then in six months or so I should become a 2nd. Lieutenant. Because of my length of service in the Airforce, I should become a 1st. Lieutenant fairly quickly. For myself it does not make much difference. In fact, even as an N.C.O. I would be working there with an officer's responsibility and as far as my earnings are concerned, they are better now than they would be as an officer.'

'No, no, young man, an officer in the German forces is something to be very proud of. You pass your exams, it is very important. The Fatherland can do with boys like you,' and he pointed to my medals. 'Now I must leave you. Good luck, young man, for the future. You will make the grade, I am sure.'

'Thank you, Sir,' I said, and he left the room.

Lena stood up and said: 'Please excuse us Aunt, but we have been away from the party longer than we anticipated.'

'You are not leaving already?' she asked, looking at me, 'and I wanted to ask you so much about flying. You must come again and tell me more about it. All the best for your course, it is very important.' She emphasised this point by raising her index finger and pointing towards me.

I knew what she really wanted to say: 'You had better become an officer if you want to enter this family.' I thanked her, and as we shook hands, I rained as many compliments on her as I possibly could in the time until she showed us out. As we left, the long-haired gun dog which had been lying motionless under the table got up and followed us out. As soon as we had rounded the corner, out of sight of the house, Lena took my arm, stopped, and gave me a kiss. She was obviously very pleased with the meeting.

We were now more than halfway through the course and each day was more difficult, especially the homework. The sirens were the greatest obstacle. They sounded every third night on average and we all had to go to the air raid shelter. So far no bombs had been dropped in this area. The sirens sounded as a result of the tactical flying manoeuvres of the enemy aircraft, and as a result we lost many valuable hours.

I had not seen Lena for three weeks as she was standing in for Elizabeth. Now she was expected to visit me the following week-end and she had also told me on the phone that she would be visiting me two weeks after that. At the same time I had invited her to the passing-out parade at the end of my course.

Saturday came and I went to the station to meet her. She was waving from a distance and I noticed that she had changed her hair style. Instead of the usual knot, her blonde hair was hanging round her shoulders fastened with a broad blue band. 'Do you like my hair?' she asked even before the usual kiss of greeting.

'Yes, you look very pretty. Have you had a good journey?' I asked.

'Yes, no problem, but I have to tell you something, Carl.'

'Go on then,' I said.

'No, not here, it must wait until we arrive at the hotel.'

We kept on talking until we reached our room.

'Sit down,' she said, pointing to the bed. I sat down and she sat on my knees.

'What is the news then?' I wanted to know.

'Do you really want to know?' she asked. 'I am pregnant.'

'What! how do you know, Lena?'

'Look, Carl, don't be silly. How does any woman know she is pregnant?'

'Are you sure?' I asked.

'Pretty sure,' she replied.

'What now?' I asked, a bit shaken.

'What now? We are going to have a baby,' she laughed.

'Have you told anybody?' I asked.

'Not yet, but I will have to tell my aunt. I think she is the best one to tell, Carl.'

She then went on to say that it would be a good idea for us to become engaged as soon as possible. She felt that if we could say that we had been secretly engaged, it would all sound better.

'Don't you think so, Carl? Do you still love me, Carl?'

'Yes, of course. It is all so unexpected, just so near to the exams,' I said.

'Don't let it worry you, we just have to get married. So many soldiers are getting married and their wives having babies,' she replied.

'Well, Lena, is that what you want to do? Have you thought about it? The first thing to do is to become engaged without delay,' I said.

She went on to explain all that she had planned. How she would tell her aunt that we loved each other and that I had to go to the front. She also said that she would write to her parents explaining everything. She even said she would buy the rings, but at this I baulked. If we were to be engaged, I insisted that I would buy the rings. Then I remembered the ring my grandma had left me and I mentioned this to Lena, saying that I was sure my grandma would prefer the ring to be worn rather than lie in my purse. Lena tried it on. It was rather too large for her finger, but we agreed to have it altered to fit her. I would buy a cheaper ring for myself.

'And so, we are engaged now. Are you happy, Lena?'

'Yes, Carl, very happy,' she replied. 'Carl, you want the baby, don't you? You will love it, I know you will love it.'

'Lena, if it comes, I want it and I will love it. Getting married will be more of a problem. First you will have to get permission from your parents and I will have to get permission from the Commanding Officer.'

'I think my dad will not like it at first,' she said, 'but if you become a Catholic, eventually he will accept it.'

'We will have to see about that when the time comes,' I replied, 'but now, come, let's have something to eat.'

We had a meal and afterwards went for a walk. The siren sounded, and we went to the air raid shelter. The evening was over; it was time to go to bed.

Two weeks later, and just two weeks before the end of the course, we were all working hard for our finals when Lena came back as planned. She was very upset. She had told her aunt, who had thought it best to warn Lena's mother on the phone. Sadly, at that point it all went wrong. Her father had found out and had accused her aunt of neglecting his daughter. He had said he would never give permission for a non-Catholic to marry his daughter.

She sat on the bed in the hotel room and cried bitterly. On the previous day there had been heavy bombing of her home town and all the telephone lines were out of order. She knew that many people had been killed but she did not know and could not find out whether or not her family was safe. I tried to comfort her, saying that I felt sure that her father would have had a very good air raid shelter.

'Yes,' she said wiping her tears. 'My dad always said that our shelter was so strong that no bomb would destroy it.'

'Don't worry too much,' I said, putting my arm around her. 'They will be all right. The news of the baby would be a shock to them and they will need time to think about it.'

'Carl,' she said suddenly, 'why are you so much against Catholics?'

'I am not, Lena, truly, I am not,' I replied.

'But why don't you want to become a Catholic?' she pressed.

'Come, let's sit down and I will try and explain it to you.'

I then began to tell her about how I was brought up by my grandparents. I explained how very religious they were and told her that they called themselves Jehovah's Witnesses. The bible to them was the word of God; all Christians believed more or less the same thing, but the Jehovah's Witnesses believed that God had selected them to spread the gospel wherever they could. There were many children in this community, and all of them were influenced by their respective parents to believe the same thing.

'My grandma's belief was so strong,' I explained, 'that she is now behind bars for it. I respect her for that, Lena. Also I respect your father and your mother, provided their religion comes from their innermost conviction. What I do not believe is that any pressure should be put on anybody to achieve whatever it may be for religious gain.'

Lena was still standing and listening to every word I said. I took her hand and said: 'Come and sit down on my knee as you always do. What I really wanted to tell you finally is this. If we are getting married, for the time being it will have to be in the Registry Office. When the baby is born, I have no objections to it being christened even in a Catholic church.'

'Tell me, Carl, tell me honestly and truthfully,' and she looked at me again with those big eyes, 'Do you believe in God?'

'Yes, Lena, I believe in God. I can't believe that almost everything we look at is an accident, be it a flower, an animal, a tree, the moon, the sun, and the stars. Just look at a little baby, how in nine months it develops from an egg and a sperm into a complete human being. It cannot be an accident. Many millions of years of development some people regard as evolution. No, I think that behind everything there is a great planning, a great strategy, and that to me is God. What I do not understand is this, Lena: so many religions claiming that only theirs is the right one. That is very confusing to me. It is even more confusing now in war time, with people killing each other, even though they belong to the same religion. In the Ten Commandments it states quite clearly: "Thou shalt not kill". You see, Lena, I am a soldier and I know that I have to do what I am asked to do, but I need a lot more time to think about it all and that is why I am what I am. I am sorry I did not tell you all this in the beginning when we first got to know each other.'

'No, no, I would have loved you just the same,' and she cried in my arms.

In the morning she left. She wanted to be back at home to find out if there was any news about the bombing. I was somewhat relieved to see her go because I had so much work to do for the final exams. I took her to the station and kissed her goodbye. She promised to ring me the following week-end. As she got into the train she started crying again and this upset me. It was already pretty cold at this time of the year but she opened the window and stretched out her hand. I was holding it and as the train started to move, I was first walking and then running, still holding her hand. As the train picked up speed I had to let her go. I stopped running, took out my hanky and waved until she disappeared from view.

On the following Monday we started the final examinations in the class-room. This took four days and the remaining time was spent in preparing for the oral examinations the following week. The week-end came but Lena did not ring. I decided to wait until Sunday and if I still had not heard from her by then, I would get in touch with Elizabeth. Sunday came and there was still no telephone call from Lena so I rang Elizabeth. She told me that she had heard from one of the housemaids that Lena's father had turned up unexpectedly in a car and after an hour or so had left again with Lena by his side. At times they had spoken very loudly in the sitting room.

'That does not sound very good, Carl,' said Elizabeth.

'What do you think, Elizabeth,' I asked. 'Shall I try to get Frau von Goetz on the telephone? She may tell me what has happened.'

'Yes, do just that,' said Elizabeth. 'What can you lose?'

Elizabeth asked how my examinations were going and I told her that I was right in the middle of them. She offered to ring me if she heard anything further. I thanked her but told her not to bother as I needed every bit of concentration at present. I thanked her again and sent my regards to everybody. I told her that I would ring Frau von Goetz myself. We said goodbye and she rang off. I stood for a while, undecided as to what I should do. Then I decided to ring. Surely she could not eat me over the phone! I found her number, put the money in the phone box and asked the exchange to connect me. One of the servants answered.

When Frau von Goetz came to the phone, I told her who I was and she said: 'You are ringing about Lena.'

'Yes, Madam,' I said.

'Well, I am sorry to tell you that Lena left with her father on Friday. Her father had arranged a place of further education for her, and she went with him. I am sending a letter to you in the next few days. Good-bye, Mr...Deckers...'

So that was it, then. Her father had interfered.

The last week at the school had been for me the worst of the whole course. The saving grace was that I had passed. I did not think too much of that letter Frau von Goetz had promised me on the telephone. We spent most of the last day pressing our uniforms in preparation for the passing-out dinner that evening. Everyone was allowed to invite one guest and nearly everyone had someone coming, but not me. I knew how much Lena had been looking forward to that night and so had I.

The following Tuesday we all queued up for our travel documents and the next day we were off to new posts and new responsibilities. My destination was Air Command I. Its headquarters were in Riga. As we all left, I am sure we all had mixed feelings about the future. I most certainly had. The promised letter from Frau von Goetz had not arrived. Lena was unexpectedly removed from my life. I knew for sure that it was not of her own choosing. I was heading north for a new post. Winter was just around the corner and furthermore, my new post was bringing me nearer to the place where I had spent the first years of my life. My father had worked here at the Hydro-Electric Power Station before the country was taken over in 1940 by the Russians. Perhaps I would now be able to find out what had happened to them. I knew that they were not in the area as we had had no further news of them since that time.

The unit I was assigned to was an experimental unit. This was because the previous winter in the Eastern section had been very severe and the considerable snowfalls had caused problems for air transport. Therefore I knew that the unit I was now joining would be disbanded before the oncoming winter and that rail and road transport would be used instead. The whole unit was commanded by Captain Heinz Klinker and my position would be to take charge of maintenance.

When I reported to him on arrival, we recognised each other. We had been in the flying school at Stendal at the same time. I was a lance corporal on flight training and he was a sergeant in charge of the ground staff. He had previously served in the police. This meeting with Captain Klinker was an unexpected bonus for me, as taking up a new post always entails a certain amount of uncertainty. He greeted me with a warm handshake and later reassured me that I would have a completely free hand in my department, provided, of course, that I kept things rolling. Things were looking none too rosy at the front and at the time this greeting gave me some degree of comfort. Captain Klinker told me that two sergeants, a number of lance corporals and a large number of men, all with some engineering training, would form my staff. Also I could recruit civilians from the town if necessary.

At the end of my first two weeks in this new post, I was quite satisfied with the way things were going. Most of the replacement engines and spare parts were supplied by a large depot in Daugavpils, which was about 200 km. south-east of Riga. I had been accompanying my sergeant, who was in charge of the spare parts department, and noticed that a quarter of the way to Daugavpils we were passing close to the Hydro-Electric Power Station. I knew that the first two years of my life had been spent there. My father had worked there before he had returned to Germany. As I had my own transport, it was not difficult for me to make a stop in this area and make some enquiries about my parents.

One morning I received three letters. One was from Martha's mother, telling me that Ellie had now started school. It was a sharp reminder of how quickly time was passing by. It seemed such a short time since she had been a tiny baby, lying next to her mother in the cot. There was a letter too from Hugo, telling me of two more boys from our village who had been killed on the Russian front. I knew that the third letter was the most important. It had the crest of the von

Goetz family and I was almost afraid to open it. It seemed to be a pretty thick letter. I felt it first and there was something hard inside the envelope. I pressed again. It could not be! Yes, it was – a ring, my ring. It was, of course, the ring I had given to Lena in Rudolfstadt. What had she to say, I wondered? Not much, as I looked at the written part. It was written by Lena's aunt, Frau von Goetz, and what it said was:-

'Dear Mr Deckers,

Here is my letter as discussed on the telephone. Lena asked me, when she left home, to return the ring to you as she would not be able to contact you herself. I hope you will understand the situation and I am personally very sorry for both of you. Unfortunately, I cannot help you any further.

Frau von Goetz.'

I put the ring into my purse and tore the letter into a thousand pieces, saying to myself as I did so: 'Give me the grace to accept the things I cannot change.'

PART III. TAMARA

CHAPTER EIGHT.
STATIONED AT RIGA – I MEET TAMARA

The next day I was on my way to Daugavpils. I drove right into the Hydro-Electric Power Station and asked if anyone knew Mr Deckers. No, no one did, but I was advised to call at the nearby public house, where the landlord had lived for many years. I called and, yes, he remembered. Like so many other people, the two Deckers (my parents) had been taken away by the Russians one night. But some 50 km further down the road on my way to Daugavpils, near a village called Skriveri, lived a relative of my father. He had a farm there. After further enquiries I made my way to the farm, which turned out to be only 2 km out of the village. When I was half way down the farm road, a Great Dane sprang towards my car. It followed the car to the farm, making a lot of noise, which brought a young man out of the house. He was blond, broad-shouldered, and possibly slightly taller than myself. He proved to be Eriks Deckers and we greeted one another cordially. Even the dog was aware of the warmth of my welcome, as his long tail wagged from right to left. In no time Eriks had a bottle of degvins on the table. This was corn brandy, a national drink and very difficult to obtain at that time. After we had drunk each other's health, I explained that he lived in a part of my district and that there would be other opportunities to celebrate, but that to-day I must leave for Daugavpils.

Eriks had been a law student at the university of Riga, but had returned to the farm to take possession of what was left of it. He was managing fairly well. Everything he produced was controlled, both under Russian and German occupation. He had his own little distillery, where he made his own schnapps. He also made his own beer. He laughed as he told me that it was not allowed but that everyone else was doing it. He told me that the 'black market' was well organised to subsidise the rations, and that they had to learn to live with it. I asked him if he was married. He was not, but he was engaged and intended to marry when things improved. His fiancée, Olga, was working as an interpreter in Riga. He asked about me and I told him briefly. I was surprised to learn that he knew more about me than I knew about him. It was comforting and exciting to find that I still had roots which I had thought were lost. It was late and I was eager to be on my way, so we made a compromise, to have a re-union dinner at Eriks's farm the following week. I planned to do this by making my usual journey to Daugavpils on the Friday, then phoning my unit from there to say that I was delayed for some reason. That way I could spend the week-end at the farm. 'Great,' said Eriks. He also said that he would invite his cousin, who lived on a farm nearby. He was a couple of years younger than we two, and his girl-friend would be invited too. A girl was living in Riga at the time whose father had a farm quite near to Eriks's cousin. He would try to arrange for her to be invited as well. Olga interrupted at this point and asked who the girl was, as she might, in fact, know her. 'Yes, of course you know her,' said Eriks. 'She very often comes to the station with a racehorse and a little trotting cart to pick up her mother or her little brother.'

'The tall blonde girl? Ah, she is good looking,' said Olga.

'You will like her,' Eriks said to me, 'she is a real sporting character and always laughing. But, whether she will like you is a different matter.'

'Oh boy, you don't waste any time finding me a girl-friend,' I laughed.

'No, no, it is not that,' he said. 'Look, we have our girls and you would just be sitting there looking at us. She is a nice girl and I think you will like her.'

I asked how old she was and also her name. He replied that she was a few years younger than ourselves, about 20, and that her name was Tamara. I thanked them and said that I really had to go, but that I was looking forward to the party on the following Saturday and hoped that I could make it.

So far, I could understand Eriks's philosophy; he had my interest at heart. He rightly thought that three couples would be better than two and a half. I began to look forward to Saturday and as I prepared for bed, I tried to imagine what this nice girl would really be like. They had told me that she was good looking, that I would like her, and that her name was Tamara. It sounded Russian to me.

Thursday came and after some difficulties I managed to get through to Eriks. Everything was in order and the party was on. I arrived at the farm just in time to drive with Eriks to the station to collect Olga and the other girl, called Valeria, the girl friend of Juris, Eriks's cousin. As we arrived back at the farm, Juris had just arrived on horseback. After the introductions, Eriks and I set off once more to collect Tamara from her farm. On the journey over there I tried to find out more about her. I asked Eriks why he thought that she was the right girl for me. He said it was because he liked her himself. She was very different from Olga; she was a sporting type and she was still at the university. During the Russian occupation she had been selected to take part in the Stalin Parade in the Red Square in Moscow. This was a gymnastic display in the square, and only the fittest young people had been selected for it. They were all training in a very remote place near the Russian border. Then right in the middle of the training programme, the Germans had declared war on the Russians. As the Germans marched into the Baltic States, Tamara and one of her girl friends ran away from the camp. They slept rough in hay stacks and farm houses, well away from the main roads. It had taken them nearly a month to get home, walking all the way.

When they arrived home without shoes and with blistered feet, the Germans had taken Riga. Everyone was very happy to be freed from the Russians. Tamara's father had been very badly wounded whilst fighting in the First World War for Latvian independence. When the Russians overran Latvia in 1940, he escaped being deported by them because he was hiding in the woods when they came for him. He told me that Tamara's father had a newsagent's shop in Riga and that they had a large flat there too. Here on the farm, in addition to farming, he bred and trained racehorses. He seemed to be mad on horses. The farm was run by a manager, who occupied half of the farm-house. The other half was kept for his own use. Eriks told me that they were due at the farm to-morrow afternoon and would be bringing some racehorses from Riga, because the racing season was finished. Tamara, he said, was already there. She had agreed to come to the party but he felt sure that her father did not like the idea. 'You know how fathers are,' he smiled. I told him that I knew very well; I had not got over the last one.

By this time we had arrived at the farm, the track to which branched off the main road up a fairly steep hill. The black labrador had spotted our car and came running towards us making a lot of noise. The front door opened and a young lady appeared, calling the dog back. Eriks was delighted.

'Here she is! Isn't she lovely?'

I just nodded back. My impressions were decidedly favourable. She was tall, blonde and her shoulder-length hair had a natural wave that seemed to hold it in place. She wore a dark green velvet dress and an amber necklace. By the time I had stopped the car, Eriks had jumped out and was walking towards her. She was holding back her dog with one hand and waving with the other. 'Hi!' she said. Her whole face was laughing and there were dimples in her cheeks.

'Hello Tamara,' said Eriks and they shook hands.

I had got out of the car, and after Eriks introduced me to her she invited us into the house. Eriks thought, however, that we should go straight back as the other guests were already there and waiting for us.

'Right,' she said, 'I will just get my coat whilst you are turning the car round and we can be off.' As she said this she was looking at me and laughing.

A few minutes later we were rolling down towards the main road on our way back to Eriks's farm. Eriks and Tamara sat together in the back seat. They discussed what each was doing and Eriks explained to her how I came to be there. She seemed to be very interested. I could see her in my driving mirror and whenever driving conditions allowed, I had a quick look at her without making it obvious. I had to admit that Eriks was right. She was extremely attractive, with a milk-and-honey complexion. She seemed to be smiling all the time and laughed when others would have smiled. For all that, one could detect a degree of shyness in her when she was talking to Eriks.

I enjoyed her company on the journey and I was sorry when it came to an end. I had also enjoyed looking at her in the mirror. Whenever she laughed, the two dimples appeared, which I thought made her look heart-stoppingly pretty. When we arrived at the farm the other two girls were busy preparing the meal and Tamara joined them.

We were soon seated round the table and for the first time I had a chance to take a real look at my companion for the evening. She must have noticed for she turned towards me and we looked at one another for a second. Oh yes, I thought, nice – very nice, and what blue eyes! By the time we had finished the elaborate meal it was almost midnight. The girls cleared the table and set it again for coffee and cake later on. We men moved the furniture around to make room for dancing. Eriks brought in a hand-operated gramophone but admitted that he had only two records left. One was a long-playing one of Strauss's melodies and the other had a tango on either side. We had to be satisfied with this, and it was not long before we invited our ladies for the first waltz. We danced for the whole of the long playing side, which switched from waltz to polka, and finished with the Radetzky March. Tamara was a delightful dancer and after a time we felt more comfortable with each other.

'How did you come to know Eriks?' I enquired.

'There is really not much to tell,' she replied. 'Every so often he turns up in our shop in Riga and if I am about we have a natter. I have met him once or twice at University dances and at winter skating in the park. Do you skate?' she asked.

'As it happens, I do,' I replied.

'We have a beautiful skating rink in Riga. It is right in the city in a park,' she said, and she went on to describe the beauty of its setting and the facilities that were available there. She said that it would be opening again when there was some good frost and that I ought to go and see it. I told her that I would but, still wanting to know a bit more about Eriks, I asked:

'Coming back to Eriks, did he tell you that I would be your partner this evening?' She laughed aloud.

'Oh no,' she said. 'As a matter of fact, I did not even know that he was engaged. I thought that I would be his partner tonight, and I am quite sure that my mum and dad are of the same opinion.'

'Oh! Well then, Tamara, are you disappointed?' She looked at me, laughed again and said:

'No, not disappointed, just surprised.'

'Fair enough,' I commented. 'Let me tell you that I am surprised as well, pleasantly surprised. You are a good sport, a very good dancer, and if I may say so, a very good-looking girl.'

I moved away from her a little to get a better view and she just looked at me for a second. I saw that she was blushing all over her pretty, round face.

The music had stopped and Eriks put the other record on. Then he came straight to Tamara to ask for a dance.

'I have to separate you for a minute, do you mind Carl?' he said.

'Heavens no, Eriks, it gives me a chance for a courtesy dance with Olga.'

Olga started talking after the first few steps of the tango: 'It is a real treat to see you two dancing,' she said.

'Ah, big sister is watching, is that it?' I replied.

'No, Carl, I suppose it reminds me a little of the days when we started courting.'

'But Olga, we have only known each other for a couple of hours. You can hardly call that courting!'

'Perhaps not,' she said, 'but that is what I would like it to be. You both seem so well suited to each other.'

After a time, Olga lit the candles, switched off the electric light and said:

'Carl has not fulfilled his commitments yet. Officially he is still Mister to us, and we are still Misses. Come on, Carl, do your duty now.'

I was on my feet in a flash. I knew that Olga was referring to the fact that we had not drunk brotherhood yet. That meant that we could not be on Christian-name terms until the ceremony had been performed.

'Nothing will give me greater pleasure,' I said, and I started with Olga. We interlocked our right arms, each holding a glass in the right hand. Then we looked at each other, said something naughty, and then kissed. All the others applauded. Olga and I had now drunk brotherhood, and henceforward would forever be on Christian-name terms. Now it was Vali's turn. She also was a good sport and after filling my glass again, we repeated the ceremony with a smacking kiss. I got out my handkerchief, wiped my mouth and mockingly said:

'Olga, I will always be grateful to you for suggesting this. It will now be Tamara and Carl.'

Tamara stretched out her glass to me, we looked at each other, drank and kissed. I had my other arm round her shoulders, and for a few seconds I held her tight. The others gave us rousing applause. I looked at Tamara and she was blushing and laughing at the same time. As she sat down, I bent over her and said:

'Sorry, Tamara, but I thought it was my only chance to-night.' She promptly reassured me.

'You may well be right, Carl,' she said. By now we were all in a happy frame of mind and Eriks started to sing the famous student song, 'Gaudeamus Igitur'. In the traditional way we stood on chairs, linked our arms together, and sang the song through. The evening continued as we sang, drank, danced and laughed. Everyone enjoyed themselves and I could never remember being happier than I was that night. Not only had I traced a member of my family, but I also felt that the girl at my side (if only for that night) was something special. What it was, I don't know. Was it her good looks, was it her personality, her blue eyes? I only knew that I did not want to let her go.

From the kitchen came the smell of eggs and bacon. I looked at my watch and it was 7 am. Where had the night gone, I wondered? I looked across at Eriks.

'I saw you looking at your watch,' he said, 'that is why Olga is making breakfast. We know that you have to be in Daugavpils by 10 am. Will you be able to take Juris and Vali home? Tamara's farm is almost on your way, but don't get lost with Tamara! I have been watching you two,' he laughed.

It was now daylight, and I drove Juris and Vali to Juris's farm. Then, for the first time, I was alone with Tamara. I was already preparing myself for any questions I thought she was likely to ask, questions such as whether I was married, whether I had a girl-friend – that sort of thing. To my surprise, however, she did not ask anything. We spoke of what we were each doing and she told me that she was at University reading economics and languages. In fact, she said, she was actually in the course of taking examinations at that time. As to her future, it was as yet uncertain. There were so few students left. Most of the young men had either volunteered for the war effort or had been directed elsewhere. She went on to say that if, as she feared, the University should close, she could help out for the time being in her father's shop in Riga. I told her that I would be back in Riga the following day and suggested that perhaps I could call.

'What time would that be?' she asked, as she had to return to Riga herself and would have to leave very early to get a train ticket, unless I could give her a lift. She looked at me and blushed a bit.

'Is it worth a kiss?' I asked laughing. 'As long as it is not a definite "no", I shall be quite happy,' I added.

I went on to explain to her that it was forbidden for people in my position to give lifts to anyone unless they were employed in the Airforce. That meant that even for this present journey, she was 'employed' by me. Fortunately, I was able to sign my own traveller's permit and I always carried these documents. In order to cover today's journey, I would make out a document showing her as working in my stores section.

As I said goodbye, I was holding her hand and now pulled her towards me. I felt her arm around my shoulder as we kissed. Only the singing cockerel on the fence reminded me that it was early morning on the farm and it was time to leave.

CHAPTER NINE.
UNDER THE SHADOWS OF WAR OUR LOVE DEEPENS

I had a 1½ hours drive before me. Strangely enough, I did not feel tired at all, despite the fact that I had not slept a wink in the last 24 hours. On the contrary, as I thought about the party and the strong sense of belonging I had found, I was very much awake. I felt I had a family again. Then there was Tamara, this lovely girl. At this stage I did not dare to hope that the relationship could be permanent, and yet ... that kiss had been something really special! I wondered whether she had felt the same way. Dare I hope that she did? I was to see her again to-morrow and perhaps I might be able to persuade her to see me again in Riga. I wondered whether her parents would object, but then I comforted myself by the thought that she was old enough to make up her own mind. Olga had liked her and I knew that she viewed with favour the prospect of Tamara and I being friends. If all else failed, I could always ask Eriks to have another party and invite Tamara again.

I tried to concentrate on my driving but it was not easy. Normally, after a Saturday night party such as the one I had just so thoroughly enjoyed, I would have had the benefit of Sunday in which to relax and think it over, but in this instance it was not possible. We were at war and every day was the same. When I reached the distribution centre in Daugavpils, I found myself at the end of a long queue. It took some time to convince other ranks that my orders had top priority. I knew that if I failed to convince them, I would have to stay another day and this would mean missing my date with Tamara.

Somehow I managed to arrange matters so that the following morning I was first in the queue and by 10 am I had completed my business and was on my way to Tamara. She must have seen me driving up the farm road, because I could see her waving to me as she walked from the door of the house. She was dressed in a blue and white polo neck sweater with a blue skirt and looked prettier than ever.

Before I could say anything of consequence, she introduced me to her mother and her younger brother. It was all completely unexpected and I did not really know what to say.

'Please sit down,' she said, reaching for my hat and as I removed my belt, she pointed to the pistol.

'Is it loaded?' she asked.

'Of course it is,' I replied.

She looked at her brother, who appeared engrossed in our conversation. She told me that he liked uniforms, pistols and daggers.

'I think all boys are interested in these things,' she said.

'Yes, unfortunately,' I said.

'Why unfortunately?' she asked.

'To look at them may be fine,' I answered, 'but to use them in earnest is a very different matter. But if your brother is so interested, I had better make it useless.'

I stood up, got out the pistol and removed the magazine.

'Come here, Alfred,' I said. 'If you like uniforms, you should see yourself in one. Look in the mirror.' I took off my uniform jacket and held it out for him. He was eager to put it on and I took the belt from the hook and fastened it round him. Then I put my hat on his head and pushed him to the mirror.

'How old are you, Alfred?' I asked.

'I am nearly 13,' Alfred replied.

'Well, I understand. Most young people have a dream and, I think, boys more than girls. I had a dream when I was your age, or perhaps a bit older. My dream was to become a pilot and as you can see, my dream has come true, but I had to pay a terrible price for it.' At that moment the thought of Marianne crossed my mind in a flash. I paused and looked at him in the mirror. 'Perhaps one day I can tell you the story,' I said – 'perhaps.'

At that point Tamara's mother came in carrying a plate with a large piece of pork on it.

'Look, Mum,' exclaimed Alfred. 'How do I look?'

'Oh dear, he is mad about uniforms. Can you not take him with you?' she laughed.

'Yes, I will take him,' I chuckled, 'and your daughter as well.'

The joke was well received and the ice had been broken. We sat down to a meal of pork, sauerkraut and potatoes, a traditional meal at this time of the year. It came out in the course of conversation that Tamara's father had been at the farm for the week-end as well, but had gone back to Riga because of the business. Tamara's mother did not say very much but I was greatly struck by her compassion. She was concerned as to whether I had enough to eat and enough warm clothing for the coming winter. She said that she had heard of the terrible sufferings of soldiers at the front and it had obviously distressed her. I had to admit that some of her fears were in fact well-founded, and I explained that it was due to the activities of the partisans, which were increasing. The transport difficulties on the long supply routes constituted an added problem. It was precisely to try to resolve some of these difficulties that I had come here at this time.

As I was walking to the car I felt very good. There was a lot of warmth in the words of Tamara's mother and I had thoroughly taken to her. Tamara came out of the house carrying a large suitcase. I told her how pleasantly surprised I had been at meeting her mother and brother.

'I think your mother is a very nice lady,' I said. 'She made me feel at home the minute I entered your house.'

'I am glad you like her,' Tamara replied, 'perhaps it is mutual.'

'I sincerely hope so. I think you have inherited quite a bit from her,' I said. I considered that she had inherited her mother's looks and explained what similarities I saw, particularly the round face and the dimples in the cheeks. She paused and looked down for a second. Then she looked directly at me and thanked me for being so complimentary to them both.

'Let me tell you a little bit about my mother. Eriks told me that your mother was German. Well, my mother was born Russian. She was caught up in the turmoil of the Russian Revolution and was travelling from the Black Sea to Leningrad. She got to know my dad, who was fighting in the Russian Army in the First World War, and he brought her here to Latvia.'

'Has she been back to Russia?' I asked.

'Yes, once when I was little. She took me with her but her father had died in the meantime and her mother had married again and had more children from that marriage. Since that visit we received no more news from her. Russia is a very big country and it is all too easy to lose contact with people.'

By this time we were approaching the Hydro-Electric Plant.

'Look, Tamara,' I said, 'we are nearly in Ogre where my father used to work. I spent quite some time here when I was very young.'

'Can you remember it?' she asked.

'No, not really, but I can remember when we went on holiday to the coast. My father rented a villa there and I can remember playing on the beautiful beach and the dunes. We used to walk along the coast and look for amber.'

'Carl,' she interrupted excitedly. 'that is just what we used to do every summer when we spent our holiday there with friends. My father rented a villa too and we all spent the whole summer there. My father used to go back to his business in Riga three or four days a week, and we children used to go to the station to meet him in the evening. He always used to bring us sweets and presents. Oh, that lovely white sand, the dunes and the pine trees!'

'Yes, I have flown over that beach many times, and I always hoped that one day I would be able to go back there. If I do, I hope that you will be there as well.' As I looked at her, she blushed.

'You sound really romantic now, Carl,' she rejoined.

'Yes, I am. Surely we must see each other again – please!' I exclaimed.

'Perhaps,' she replied after a pause, 'it is not as easy as you might think. First, I am right in the middle of my examinations; second, there is my father. He is not like my mother, you know.'

'Thank you, Tamara, at least you did not say an outright "no".'

'Look,' she said as she put her hand on mine on the steering wheel, 'I have only known you for three days, Carl. I like you. Otherwise I would not have come with you. All the same, let us get to know each other a little better.'

'Thank you again, Tamara. Is it only three days? I feel as if I had known you all my life. Can I see you again this week, please?'

I removed my hand from underneath hers on the steering wheel and took hold of hers in earnest, holding it for a moment. She paused for a few seconds before saying:

'If I give you the phone number of our shop, will you ring me there on Thursday afternoon after 3 pm? I will be there with just one other girl. If I do not answer, ask for me. I will try to arrange things so that my father will not suspect that I am with you. I usually go out with my friends, three fellow students. Mother is all right, and I am sure that she likes you. I will see what I can do. Are you satisfied now?'

She slipped over to me and gave me a peck on my cheek. In the meantime we had reached Riga and I asked her to give me directions as to where I should take her. When we arrived at her place, she said that she would have to get out of the car and open the gates. Then she would have to check that all was in order in the flat before we went in, because one room of the flat was sublet. This was a legal requirement and it was occupied by a woman who had a men's hairdressing saloon in the town. She herself was all right but sometimes she had visitors, and it would be far better for no one to see us unloading the case.

Everything worked out to our advantage. Tamara got into the house and after a couple of minutes she came out again, followed by a middle-aged man.

'Carl, can I introduce you to my father,' she said, opening the door of the vehicle.

I had, of course, expected her father to be in the shop rather than at home, and I was taken by surprise.

'Pleased to meet you, Mr Berg,' I said.

'Pleased to meet you too,' he answered, 'I understand that you have a rather large present for us.' He smiled.

'Yes, that's right. I will get it for you,' and I jumped into the back and got the suitcase. My word, that case was heavy!

I jumped out and carried it into the house.

'Let's have a quick drink,' he said, once we had entered the house.

'I am sorry,' I said, 'I have to report to my big chief and even though I know him pretty well, I would not like to smell of alcohol. Thank you just the same.'

'No, no,' he said, 'it is for me to thank you. You must come again when you have a bit more time. I always like to hear about life in the forces these days.'

With that I took my leave. Tamara and her father both came out with me and as I was backing out Tamara blew me a kiss. I felt sure that she had not known that her father was at home. I had another half an hour's drive to the airfield. Darkness was falling and it was beginning to rain. In spite of all the traffic in the town, I could not stop thinking about Tamara and could hardly wait to phone her the following Thursday. When it came, I had to endure a long and frustrating delay before I could get a line. My heart was beating faster as I heard her voice at the other end. She told me that she had been surprised to find her father at home when we arrived.

'Yes, and so was I. Did he have anything to say about me?'

'Oh, no,' she said, 'and why should he?'

'No, he should not,' I said. 'After all, you are in good hands with me.'

I heard her laughing and eagerly asked if we could meet the coming week-end. She agreed, but told me that it must be kept from her father. Then she asked me where I wanted to go.

'Anywhere,' I said, 'as long as you are with me. To the pictures, if you like. I have already found out what they are showing in one cinema nearest to the station.' She asked me what it was. 'It is a film called "The Crash Pilot". It is about flying,' I replied. 'I would like you to see it.'

'And if I do not come?' she teased.

'Then I will just come to your house and get you. And if your father is in, I will ask him if I can marry his daughter.'

We agreed to meet at the cinema and she told me that she would be bringing a friend of hers.

The next week-end, therefore, dressed as smartly as I could and clutching a box of chocolates which I had managed to get from the canteen, I arrived fifteen minutes early and walked up and down the street near the cinema. The girls had obviously spotted me parading up and down and they sneaked up on me from behind. When I turned round, there they were right in front of me, both laughing heartily. Tamara introduced me to her friend who had so kindly acted as a decoy for the benefit of Tamara's father. She was anxious to be off to see her boy-friend. Tamara would soon be alone with me in the cinema, and this was what I had been so much looking forward to.

The film was a comedy, all about flying, and Tamara was enjoying it.

'Is that what you do in the Air Force?' she exclaimed.

'I wish I could do that right now,' I replied, and went on to tell her briefly what had happened to me and that I had been taken off flying duty for the time being.

'Oh, I have said the wrong thing then,' and I could feel that her hand was searching for mine. I pulled her tight over to me and we had a long kiss. As we walked home arm in arm through the dimly lit streets, the first snow flakes were falling. To me they looked like falling stars. I was in love in good earnest. Was Tamara? I was not to know that yet, but at least I felt that she liked me.

For the next four weeks we met every week-end, visiting the cinema, the circus and the opera, for luckily Tamara had managed to get two tickets for this through one of her friends whose father was conducting the orchestra.

Over a period of four weeks, I had been in Daugavpils a couple of times, and on each occasion I had called at Eriks's farm and at that of Tamara's father. Each time I had carried food parcels to both Olga and Tamara. On my last visit I hinted to Eriks that it would be a good idea to have another party just before Christmas. I had been able to save chocolates and drinks from my allocation. Eriks was delighted and so was Olga when I mentioned the idea to her. Now I had only to see Tamara and since I had a parcel to deliver to her, I would soon know what she thought.

When I called at her house, all the family was at home. Her mother insisted on giving me a cup of coffee. Her father was on the telephone and her brother never left my side. I wanted to tell Tamara about the party, so I removed the ammunition from my revolver belt, gave it to him, and sent him off to find a mirror. By this time Tamara was laughing.

'What's on your mind?' she asked.

'Yes, you guessed right. We have decided to have another party at Eriks's place. What about it?'

'Oh, Carl, that is not so easy.'

'Tamara, please,' I begged.

'Well then, you had better ask my father, but don't be surprised if he turns you down.'

'If that is the only solution, I will.'

'Then, of course, there is the problem of transport,' Tamara continued, 'the trains are often overbooked and they simply refuse to take you.'

'Well, first let me sort out the more urgent matter,' I replied, 'namely speaking to your father.'

When he had finished his telephone call, he came into the room and Tamara went out. Resolving not to postpone the matter, I began:

'Mr Bergs, I have what you may feel is an unusual request to make.'

He looked at me but I continued.

'Could I ask your permission to invite your daughter to a party?'

There was a brief pause before he replied.

'Sit down, Carl,' he said quietly.

'Don't get me wrong,' he continued, 'you have been very good to us, but I would not like anybody to buy my daughter with a few favours. I have been a young man myself and, for what it is worth, I have been a soldier as well. You may have noticed the scar on my face.' Here he pointed to a large scar on his left cheek. 'That same piece of shrapnel also took my left eye. What I mean to say is, not only have I been a soldier, I have been in the war as well. In these times soldiers are here one day and gone the next. Of course, they like to have a good time whenever possible, even though they may have a wife and children at home. Personally I like you, but I would not like my daughter to be subjected to a bit of an affair. She is still very young and still at the university. I really would not like her to become involved in anything passing.'

Now it was my turn, and I was well aware how much my reply could affect my relationship with Tamara.

'Thank you Mr Bergs for being so open,' I rejoined, 'and I appreciate everything you have said; but the points you have made are just not applicable to me. In the first place, I am really no stranger. You have probably heard that Eriks is my cousin. I do not claim that I have been an angel in the past, but I have no such commitments as you have mentioned. I admit that I could be married; I am old enough, in one month's time I shall be 27 years old. Nevertheless, I am not married and never have been. You see, Mr Bergs, there are circumstances which occur in everybody's life which cannot be explained in a few words. You mentioned your injuries. I had my problems as well, though nowhere near as serious as yours. I have the greatest respect for what you must have been through. But as far as your daughter is concerned, now that I have got to know her, I am truly and deeply fond of her. I hope that she likes me too. I can assure you that, as far as I am concerned, it is far from being a passing affair. It is true friendship and I hope it will lead to an everlasting relationship.'

We looked at one another.

'Well, if you can say that and mean it,' he replied, 'as from one man to another, then I have nothing more to say.' With this he stretched out his hand. We put our arms around each other and then he went to the door and called:

'Mother, come here a minute.'

She came in from the kitchen wiping her hands on her apron. 'Mother, he continued, 'I want you to meet Tamara's boy-friend.' She stretched out both hands to me and we hugged and kissed one another.

'Welcome to our house, Carl,' she said.

'But where is Tamara?' I asked.

'She has retreated into Freda's room. I will call her.'

Seconds later she returned, arm-in-arm with Tamara and we kissed all round. Even Alfred joined in. Then her father brought out a bottle of vodka and we had a celebration drink. Then Freda joined us and I was introduced. In the ensuing conversation Freda told me that she had a men's hairdressing saloon in Riga which she ran with the help of three assistants. She proved a real live wire and very jovial. She told us how happy she was for both of us. Unfortunately I could not stay long as I had to report to Capt. Klinker. As I took my leave, Tamara came out with me. We were holding hands and I asked her if she was happy. She squeezed my hand and said:

'Yes I am. And you?'

'Yes, of course, I am the happiest man in the world.'

She went on to tell me that her mother had helped enormously in a quiet way, as she had liked me from the first meeting at the farm. I arranged to ring Tamara the following day so as to arrange our next meeting.

CHAPTER TEN. HEINZ AND FREDA

When I reported back to Capt. Klinker in his private quarters, he got out a couple of bottles of beer and we had a drink. Meanwhile I was making my progress report to him from Daugavpils. After our business was over, we continued to talk for a while and I thought it was time to tell him about Tamara. As we had known each other intimately for a long time, off duty we were on Christian name terms. Now I asked him whether he wanted to hear a love story.

'Go on then,' he said, and so I told him as much about Tamara as I dared, being careful not to jeopardise my duty trips to Daugavpils.

His reaction was that he envied my good fortune and wished that he could find a pretty girl himself. At this point I had a brainwave. 'Wait a minute,' I exclaimed, 'I met a woman to-day at Tamara's home. She has a room in their flat and keeps a men's hairdressing saloon. She is married but is separated from her husband who is an alcoholic and in the care of the authorities. She is good-looking, very lively, and she is about your age. I am ringing Tamara to-morrow. Shall I mention it and see what she says?'

Capt. Klinker was all for it but I asked him what was in it for me.

'I thought there was a catch in it,' he retorted. 'Go on, what is on your mind?'

I told him that in two weeks' time we were planning to have a party at my cousin's farm, which was situated about 100 km. from the camp. I told him that two ladies who were invited to the party lived in Riga and I asked him if he could help me with transport. I mentioned that if he and Freda became friends, they would be invited also. He scratched his head and said that he would think about it. In the meantime I must try to find out the position regarding Freda and let him know the following night. By this time it was almost midnight and we parted, wishing one another sweet dreams.

The next day I rang Tamara and told her of the new arrangement. 'You, devil,' she laughed. 'You would do anything.'

'Anything for you, Tamara,' I replied.

She warned me to keep our plans for Capt. Klinker from her father, for she knew that he would not approve of them. She suggested that Capt. Klinker and I should both go to Freda's saloon and have a haircut. That would be the best way to introduce them. She asked me when we could go. I suggested the following day, and Tamara said that she would give Freda a little hint later that evening. I said that we would be going in Capt. Klinker's car and that I would hope to call and see her afterwards, if that were possible.

The following day we drove into Riga together in style in Capt. Klinker's chauffeur-driven service car. On the way we made calls at various places to buy certain equipment, and then went to Freda's saloon. Freda had obviously been briefed by Tamara as she looked extremely smart. I introduced them as Heinz and Freda adding that Tamara had recommended Freda's saloon as being the best in town. Freda attended to Heinz herself and spent so long a time on it that I assumed that all was going well. I excused myself and went off to see Tamara. I was nearly there when I met Tamara's mother carrying a big shopping bag. I gave her a hug and a big kiss, which made her blush. I took her shopping bag and we walked to the house together. I was anxious to tell Tamara how things were going, so I gave my jacket, hat and pistol to Alfred to get him out of the way. After the longed-for kiss and cuddle, we sat down. I was holding her hand in mine and told her that my plans were to take the things I had been saving for the party to Eriks's farm the following day on my way to Daugavpils. If Heinz and Freda should decide to become friends, I knew that Heinz would organise the transport for all of us. I told her that I felt under an obligation to invite them both to the party and asked what she thought about it.

'Well,' she said, 'Freda is a very good sport and she can be great fun if she is handled properly.'

'Tamara,' I said, 'I just want to be serious for a minute. Come on, give me a kiss and listen very carefully.' I kissed her tenderly and continued: 'Now that we have your parents permission, I thought we might announce our engagement at the party.' She started to interrupt me. 'Shush, let me finish,' I said, gently covering her mouth with my hand. 'You see, Tamara, we have your parents blessing and we love each other. But we have to recognize that I could be posted somewhere else. If that happens, it may be very difficult to get what is left of my little family together again. In view of that, I would like to marry you as soon as possible.'

I explained to her that as well as making me very happy, she would have definite advantages as the wife of a member of the Armed Forces. I went on to tell her of the plans I had formulated in my mind for which I just needed her approval – getting everything ready for the party, for instance, and trying to get rings on the black market.

The door opened and her mother came in.

'You have been alone long enough,' she said. 'It's time to have a little bite.'

'We have been having a serious talk, Mum,' said Tamara, pointing to me. 'You tell her now, Carl.'

So, I went over to her, put my arm around her and said: 'Mum, can I tell you a secret?'

'Not another one! Is it about the party next Saturday?'

'Look, Mum,' I said, 'I love Tamara and she loves me. I am thinking about an engagement.' I was still holding her as she looked up at me and said:

'Carl, you are both old enough and if you want to be engaged, so it shall be.'

'That's nice, Mum,' I said, giving her a kiss, 'but what about Dad?'

'Well, you know Dad by now, but I will try to prepare him a bit,' she smiled.

Tamara said nothing, but quietly put her arm around her mother and for a second we both held her.

When I got back to the barracks, I went straight to Heinz. He was obviously attracted to Freda. I went on to tell him about the party and that I had intended to invite him and Freda as well. He thanked me and said that they would like to go. He also told me that he had made plans for transport for the party in any case, and this had been done before he knew that he would be invited.

We had recently received two new ambulances, which were already in service. The two old ones would be going to the home front in a couple of weeks' time. Heinz had intended to offer one of them to transport the girls to the party. He went on to say that in the event of a check being made, I should put on a siren and the revolving light. Then no Military Police would have the authority to stop it. Since he was now invited, he would ride in the front and if there should be any difficulties to leave all the talking to him. I was delighted and tried to thank him, but he assured me that thanks were not necessary and that it was he who should be thanking me. He thought that Freda was the best thing that had happened to him since he had arrived in his present posting.

Everything went as planned. I picked Eriks up on my way back and we called first at Tamara's house. Her mother answered the door and as we entered, we heard a piano being played in the sitting room. It was Tamara. Her mother invited us into the kitchen and explained that Tamara had finished her exams that lunch time and now that it was all off her mind, was relaxing by playing the piano. We listened as she played 'The Blue Danube' by Johann Strauss. Her mother told us how she enjoyed listening to music, particularly if a violin was played as well. I said that it was a pity that I had not got a violin because I could play it. Eriks said that his violin was at Olga's house and offered to lend it to me. I put my arm around Tamara's mother and told her that the following evening she would be able to listen to 'The Blue Danube' played on piano and violin. Tamara must have heard us and came into the kitchen. After the greetings, I told her all the news and asked her what Freda thought of Heinz. She told me that Freda liked Heinz and considered him a gentleman. 'Fine,' I said, 'will you then invite her to our party?'

I then asked for Eriks and myself to be excused as we had very important things to do. As Olga was not yet home from work, we went first to the jeweller and after some bargaining, we bought two rings which now had to be engraved. We then went on to Olga's and we told her everything, including the invitation we had given to Heinz and Freda to come to the party. Olga was delighted. The violin was brought out. It was still in good order and the bow and strings were in good condition. Olga made supper and we talked happily together for an hour or two, Olga repeatedly saying how happy she was at my engagement to Tamara. I told her that I was grateful to her for the part she had played in making it all possible.

When I got back to the barracks, I had two reports for Heinz – one official and one private. He was most anxious to hear what Freda thought of him. By the end of our conversation it was clear that the party was on.

The following morning I made my way into town with the violin under my arm. Tamara's mother and Alfred watched me as I unpacked the instrument. I explained to them that because of the cold weather, the violin must be left to stand in the room for quite a time before it could be tuned.

However, it was not long before we started practising, and when Dad arrived home we were half way through 'The Blue Danube', which just happened to be one of my own favourite tunes. I could see that Dad was pleased and as we both finished more or less at the same time, they all applauded.

The next evening I made my way to Olga's home, and from there to collect the rings. It had started to snow. I was lucky to get a passing taxi. At the jeweller's I asked the driver to wait, and I was soon back at Olga's house with little money left but with two lovely 22ct gold rings, both engraved with initials and dates. Olga and I discussed transport arrangements for the day of the party, and we decided that it would be best to collect all the girls from her home. It had a concealed entrance, and we thought that this would attract least attention. I left Olga and went to see Tamara. I could not wait to show her the rings.

As I left that night, much snow had fallen. Tamara and Alfred came with me to the taxi stand, but outside we had a snowball fight before I left. By now I felt deeply that I had found a new home. Tamara's mother was especially nice to me. I watched her as we played our music, listening as she knitted socks and gloves for me.

As time passed, it was becoming obvious that the situation on the Northern Sector of the front was not good. We could not supply what was needed and when we were able to take supplies by road or train, the supply vehicles were often attacked by partisans. Half of our transport planes were diverted to the Western Front. However, my old crew was still situated in Pleskau, flying supplies right up to the Leningrad front and bringing wounded men back. I kept in contact with them by telephone and I was aware that their spirits were very low. Every other evening I went to see Tamara and if Heinz happened to be going to see Freda, I would travel with him.

On our way to the eagerly awaited party at Eriks's farm, we had safely passed the point where we were most likely to be stopped by the Military Police. This particular road, which we regularly used to reach Eriks's farm, was not classed as one of the main roads out of Riga, and we considered that this was to our advantage. While the girls in the back of the ambulance were happily chatting and singing, I took the opportunity to tell Heinz about what Tamara had said about the sleeping arrangements; that the two men had to sleep separately from the girls. Heinz started laughing and as we talked it became clear to me that he and Freda were already on intimate terms and hoped to continue to be. To-night's arrangements, therefore, would be quite acceptable to them.

'Well, I am speechless, Heinz,' I said. 'You do not waste any time.'

'No, Carl, there is a war on and we cannot afford to waste time.'

When we arrived at the farm, Eriks and Juris were waiting for us. After introducing Heinz and Freda, we all sat down for coffee. Heinz had brought drinks as well as myself, so we could afford to be generous with the brandy. Thus we made a good start to the party. This time we had a wider selection of music, as Olga had brought some records to choose from. As to-morrow was the second Sunday of advent, Eriks had given the room a festive look. The girls prepared the dinner, the pièce de résistance being the biggest goose that Eriks could find. During lulls in the cooking, the girls would come in for a dance. It was nearly 10.30 pm before we sat down for the meal, and on the stroke of midnight we announced our engagement.

After that Eriks put a record on and we spent the rest of the night dancing, not breaking off until the first streaks of dawn began to appear. Then, after an early breakfast, we decided we ought to get some sleep. Heinz, Freda, Tamara and I drove to Tamara's farm as planned and, as the good boys we had been told to be, we slept in one room and the girls in another. In the afternoon, we collected the rest of the party guests and drove back to Riga. Heinz suggested that he drop Tamara and me at her home whilst he spent some time with Freda. He then generously said that he would collect me the following afternoon, and so Tamara and I were free to celebrate our engagement with her family at greater leisure than we had first hoped. Some of her father's relatives had arrived to join in the celebrations, which went on until the early hours of Monday morning. Tamara's brother Alfred had gone to stay overnight with a friend and when we eventually got to bed, I slept in his room. Heinz arrived in the afternoon and after introducing him to the family, we all had a meal together before we left to return to the camp. When we got back to camp, I invited Heinz and two lieutenants, colleagues of mine, and my two sergeants, to the Mess, where we had a celebration of our own. They expressed a wish to meet Tamara, so I promised that I would invite her to the Mess one day soon.

It was now nearly Christmas but the expected snow storms did not materialise and neither was it as cold as it had been the previous year, when temperatures fell to 25°C below freezing. On the Northern Front near Leningrad, temperatures had fallen to 40°C below. This winter, by contrast, was rather mild. The snow came but it turned to slush, making transport by road extremely difficult. Supplies which would normally have gone by road without much difficulty became stuck in the appallingly slushy conditions, and were not helped by the state of the roads, which had suffered from lack of maintenance. A further setback was the fact that supplies could only be sent in daylight because of night attacks on convoys by partisans. The week before Christmas, however, conditions improved. Temperatures fell low enough to freeze the roads, making it easier for supplies to get through. The drop in temperature resulted in a bonus for Tamara and myself, because a large area of land had flooded and frozen over, making a natural ice rink which was open for public use. News of this soon spread around, and we were able to enjoy a spell of skating with Olga and Vali. Tamara told me that before the war some parks in Riga were converted into ice rinks, which were lit up by night while live bands played music for the skating. There were also numerous stalls selling plenty of refreshments, including hot food and punch.

The greater part of Christmas was spent very happily with Tamara's family.

CHAPTER ELEVEN.
THE GROWING THREAT FROM RUSSIA

The following week I was confined to camp as Camp Duty Officer, which meant that I could not see Tamara and had to be content with talking to her on the telephone. It also meant that I could not take part in the camp's New Year celebrations for all officers and men, which traditionally took place in a hangar.

On the morning of the 1st January 1944 an urgent message came through. It was a request for immediate help. One of the three remaining Junkers transport planes stationed in Pleskau had been shot down on a flight to Leningrad by partisans. It had crashed on to the railway line north of Luga and the wreckage was blocking the line. The message took the form of an order from Headquarters to free the railway line and at the same time to establish the number of casualties and find out what weapon had been used to shoot it down. It was my job to organise the recovery of the wreckage and within two hours we were on our way with the heavy recovery equipment which we had in readiness for such incidents.

In the meantime the crash investigator had arrived at the camp and an aircraft was placed at our disposal so that we could fly out at once and organise an advanced rescue team. I was very upset and for that reason I did not ring Tamara; instead I asked Heinz to do it for me. The reason for my apprehension will be evident. I feared that those involved in the crash could be my old crew, as it was one of the three operating on that section.

We landed in Pleskau and once we had been briefed on arrival, my worst fears were confirmed. It was indeed my old crew. The aircraft had left Pleskau for a flight to an airfield just south of Leningrad, taking medical supplies to the front. It had a crew of three, plus one

Red Cross Orderly, as it had been intended to return with wounded men from the front. Visibility in the area had been quite bad for the previous four or five days, and for this reason the pilot had obviously used the railway line as a navigation aid. He should have known that when flying over partisan territory, the same course should not have been used twice. To the north of Luga, about half way to his destination, the partisans had been waiting for them and the aircraft had crashed into the railway line, blocking it completely.

The whole district was one vast forest and this of course made it difficult to reach some sections of the single-line track. The line was regularly mined by partisans and trains were shot at. Trains using this line were always heavily guarded and always pushed two empty wagons in front of the engine to act as mine detectors. It was only due to the keen observation of the engine driver that another tragedy had been averted, as he had managed to stop the train just in time to avoid colliding with the wreckage. The military unit on the train had sent a coded signal back to Luga and the Commandant at Luga had sent armed track vehicles through the forest to the site of the accident to guard the wrecked aircraft. They reached the spot just before us and as I was organising my own armed command, news reached me that it was believed there were no survivors. I sent instructions that nothing must be touched before we arrived. The train with the armed unit on board was to be towed back to Luga but the motorised unit was ordered to remain until we reached the spot. It was feared that partisans would plunder the wreckage. Conditions would have been very favourable for them as the ground was frozen, making transport much easier. As there was no snow, it would be difficult to track them. In the meantime I had my Command ready, but darkness was falling and I considered that it was much too dangerous to move out. Also I had been informed that my two recovery vehicles were well on the way, and as there was no partisan activity up to Pleskau, they should be back at camp by 10 pm. So I planned to go very early the following morning. I telephoned Heinz with an up-to-date report. He told me that he had spoken to Tamara, who sent her love and asked me to be careful. He was intending to drive into Riga that evening to see Freda, and he said that he would first call to see Tamara and tell her all he could about the situation. Heinz could remember my two crew mates from Stendal and was, of course, upset as well.

The motorised unit had received orders to make camp and guard the wreckage overnight. One of the track vehicles was to make its way back through the forest early in the morning and take my convoy to the spot. As the ground was frozen, we did not expect much difficulty in getting through and we reached our destination at midday. By nightfall we had recovered all four bodies from the aircraft. It was a terrible task. I went through the motions automatically but when it came to recovering the personal identity discs from the necks of the victims, I had to sit down for a while. My whole body was shaking. These identity discs were in two parts, and my next task was to remove one section for sending off to Control Registration in Berlin. I trembled as I printed down their familiar names: Lance-Corporal Fritz Colmer, Pilot Sergeant-Major Helmut Maler, Flying Engineer Sergeant-Major Hans Weidemann, and Radio Operator Sergeant-Major Siegfried Baumann. Siegfried had been my pal and room-mate for such a long time. He was so full of life and humour. What a waste this bloody war is, I thought, as I performed my grim duty.

We camped overnight on the railway and I lay down in one of the vehicles. More men had joined us in the afternoon from a Pioneer Unit whose job it was to repair the damaged railway line, so essential for supplies to the front. We set up a strong night guard to protect ourselves from unexpected attack. I could not sleep a second that night and I was relieved to see the dawn. We soon had the wreckage cleared from the line and by midday we were on our way back.

I was leading the column of vehicles and when we reached Luga we found that the road was blocked. I got out of my car to try and find out what had caused the stoppage. I saw a number of Military Police trying to clear the road, which was blocked by both military and civilian personnel. I asked a sergeant from this group what was going on, and he told me that they had just witnessed a public hanging, which had taken place as a reprisal for the shot-down aircraft. He went on to tell me that the Commandant was desperately trying to put a stop to the partisan activities in the area, so he had given the order to round up the men here in Luga and for three Russians to be hanged for each man killed in the aircraft. 'Look over there,' he said, 'and you can see them.' I looked and saw a large beam fastened between two big trees. Twelve men were hanging from the beam, their hands tied behind their backs and their feet roped together. Their heads were leaning over to one side and the bodies were swaying in the wind. I felt sick. I could not continue the conversation with the sergeant and walked back to my car. So that, then, was the real war, I thought as I walked. Four men killed by partisans, the bodies of whom we were actually taking with us towards their final resting places. For that, twelve men had been hung in this way, without trial, without justice or mercy, just taken and hung. I got into my car and told the driver to drive on whenever he could. I buried my face in my hands. I was ashamed of myself and ashamed of the uniform I was wearing. I thought about my grandma's words in her last letter to me when she had said: 'Oh, Lord, forgive them for they don't know what they are doing'.

We arrived back at Pleskau and stayed there overnight. The next morning I supervised the departure of the transport taking the crashed aircraft back to Riga. The crash investigator, who had the rank of Inspector, made his preliminary report and I made mine. Then the Inspector, the pilot of our aircraft and myself attended the funerals of the crew at the cemetery for fallen soldiers in Pleskau before flying back to Riga.

When I reported back to Heinz I felt pretty bad, and my condition did not go unnoticed by him. He insisted that I saw a doctor. The doctor diagnosed a feverish cold and ordered me to bed for three days, giving me plenty of aspirins. I knew that this was not a correct diagnosis but decided to follow his instructions. First, however, I would ring Tamara. I was lucky to find her at home and she was happy to hear from me. I told her that I had a temperature and had been ordered to bed. I would see her as soon as I felt better again. So back I went, took twice the stated dose of aspirins, and was soon asleep. When I woke up I was very confused. The door of my room was wide open and the lieutenant, my opposite number from the Armoury, who occupied the room next to mine, was standing at the foot of my bed. As I looked at him, he told me that I must have had a terrible nightmare as I had been shouting for help so loud that he could hear me next door. I felt uncomfortable and my bed clothes appeared to be wet through. He had noticed it and said he would ring for an Orderly. 'Oh,' I said, 'that dream was terrible!' It was as though I had been caught in a big square cage, like a parrot cage. Vicious looking men wearing masks were standing on the top of it and were trying to push ropes through the bars. The ropes had nooses which they were trying to get round my neck. I tried to dodge them by jumping from side to side, but eventually one rope fell over my head. The other men then dropped theirs, and all pulled together on the one around my neck. I tried to hold myself for a time by clinging to the bars of the cage. Then I could hold on no longer and with a big jerk I was pulled up to the top bars. Then I must have woken up.

In the meantime my batman had turned up and was at once dispatched to the medical station to summon assistance. A doctor and two orderlies were quickly at my bedside. They made me comfortable and then I was examined. The diagnosis was severe stress and the doctor ordered me to spend a further two days in bed. I told them that I had been unable to sleep on account of what I had been through, but I said that I really did not want to talk about the ordeal any more. I just felt I wanted to be left in peace to get over it. I asked Heinz if he would kindly ring Tamara, but he said that he would go into town and tell her himself. After they had all left my room, I fell into a deep sleep and did not hear my door being opened. I woke up to a kiss on the cheek. It was Tamara. Heinz had brought her into the camp. 'Oh, Tamara,' I said as I took her in my arms and held her for a long time. She had brought some flowers, and her mother had sent some cake and plenty of food. I just wanted to keep hold of Tamara and caress her all the time but she said: 'No, no, Carl, not now. You are having visitors. Heinz has brought Freda as well and they will be here any time.' By the time they arrived, Tamara had washed my face and adjusted my pillows ready to receive them. Freda had brought her hairdressing equipment and I was treated to a trim and a shave in bed. Heinz then appeared to become serious and I wondered what he was going to say. 'Sergeant-Major Deckers,' he began, 'you will be transferred.' I caught my breath until his next words, which brought me immense relief: 'to Tamara's care for one week so that she can look after you.'

'Hey, what does that mean?' I asked.

'It means what I said. I am giving you a week's leave. I shall look after your department and Tamara has agreed to look after you. When are you fit to go?'

'Oh, Heinz,' I said, 'I am fit right now. Thank you very much. Can we go?' and I looked at Tamara.

Three days later I was fit to go. Heinz had prepared my papers and then armed with a box of pills from the doctor, Heinz took me to Freda's saloon instead of to Tamara's house.

'What is going on?' I asked.

Heinz was grinning. 'Just wait and see.'

'You are all plotting something against me,' I said but Heinz only repeated: 'Just wait and see.'

We went through the saloon into a small kitchen which was used mainly for making coffee for customers and there was Tamara. Heinz said 'Hello and good-bye' and then left us alone. After our greeting and some longed-for precious minutes alone, Tamara explained why she had wanted me to come here first. It was to discuss my one week's leave. Tamara had already asked her parents if we could go to the farm, as it would be much quieter and more restful there. She would be able to look after me. Her mother did not mind at all but her father had some reservations, mainly because of what relatives and neighbours would say. After all, we had only been engaged for a short time. Tamara had suggested to her parents that if we took Alfred it would silence the gossip. Alfred, who was still on school holidays, was very keen to go. The farm foreman had a son of the same age and they often played together. Tamara had also suggested to her father that if we went by train, we could bring back a case of meat quite safely as no one would check on my luggage. Her father had then agreed on condition that Tamara slept in one room and Alfred and myself in the other. Tamara wanted to know what I thought about it.

'You are an angel, Tamara, let's go.'

We had to leave quite soon for the station and as we walked out into the street it started to snow. By the time we reached the station it was snowing heavily. As the train pulled out, everything was already covered in a layer of fresh white snow. Steaming through the countryside, we passed through some breathtaking scenery of fir forests. When we arrived at our destination we were greeted by the farm foreman, who had received instructions by telephone to collect us. As a special treat, he had travelled in by horse-drawn sleigh. Both horses were decorated with bells, and after being wrapped warmly in blankets and fur skins, we set off on the eight-kilometre journey to the farm. It was as romantic as it was beautiful. The horses trotted through the snow with the bells chiming in rhythm with their hooves. Tamara wore a big scarf round her head, which she rested on my shoulder. I loved it and wished that the journey could have lasted for ever.

We arrived at the farm to find a roaring fire burning in the open fireplace. The room was warm and welcoming. Alfred had gone off to talk to his friend and for a time we were alone. We sat down in front of the fire and hugged and kissed before going to meet the foreman's family, who had invited us for dinner that night. They were all very friendly to me. There was the foreman's wife, their eldest son, who also worked on the farm, a daughter, who worked in a nearby dairy, and the youngest son, about Alfred's age. It was too early for dinner and the three boys gathered round me and would not leave me. I sat down with them and of course the talk was about flying. Whilst I was with the boys, Tamara went to her own part of the house to do some work in the kitchen and to look at the horses. Even after the dinner, the boys were still eager to talk flying, but Tamara said that that was enough. I had come here for a rest. Shortly afterwards we returned to our part of the house, leaving Alfred for a while to play with the other boys. Tamara and I made ourselves comfortable lying down in front of the fire wrapped in rugs. We switched off the light. The warmth of the fire and the flicker of the flames was the perfect setting for two young people in love, and I was able to forget, for a moment, the horror of the past few days. It was about 10 pm when Alfred came round from the neighbour's house and went to bed. When we heard him snoring, we closed his door quietly and went into Tamara's bedroom.

In the course of that week we spent many hours lying in front of the big log fire telling our life story, and we both agreed that the past was the past and should not cloud our happiness. Even so, I did not tell Tamara the full story about Marianne. I did however, tell her all about Lena.

Our stay at the farm passed all too quickly, and before we left we made another visit by horse-drawn sleigh to Eriks, and from there to his cousin Juris. This time we returned earlier than on our previous visit, and spent some time playing cards, darts and dominoes with Alfred.

After he had gone to bed, Tamara and I lay once more in front of the fire, continuing our talks. Tamara told me of the instances she knew of families just disappearing when the Russians arrived, and how jubilant everyone had been at first when the Germans came. But the jubilations had been short-lived. It had soon become apparent that the Germans were doing the same sort of thing. People were being subjected to forced labour. For instance, if the Germans needed some people for work in a particular factory, they simply stopped people in the street and, unless they had a very good reason for being exempted, they were sent to work in the factory concerned. Apart from that, Jewish people, particularly those in Riga, were required to wear the 'Star of David' and were not allowed to walk on the footpath.

I told her that I had indeed noticed it, and I explained to her that such conditions were not confined to Riga. My own grandma had been sent to a concentration camp simply because of her religious beliefs. I told her how upset I was by this, but also how helpless I was to do anything about it. I told her of my long-standing dream of being a pilot, how very proud I had been when I was presented with my wings, and how proud I was to wear that uniform. I went on to say: 'I *was*. I have had to revise that feeling. I am no longer proud of it anymore. In fact, I am ashamed; I did not want to tell you, Tamara, but it was not for nothing that I was so ill when I got back from Pleskau. It was terrible to have to bury your own comrades, comrades you had relied on every minute you were in the air, and with whom you had been together constantly since we had first flown into Poland in 1939. But that was not the whole story.' I then went on to tell her of the public hangings which I had almost witnessed, and of the terrible effect the sight of the hanging bodies had had on me. I told her that they were just twelve ordinary individuals, innocent people who were most certainly not the partisans who had shot down our plane or who were putting mines on the railway lines or attacking convoys. Therefore these attacks were likely to continue and the Commandant had murdered twelve innocent men. These men, no doubt, would have had wives, children and parents. Imagine the grief to so many people as a result of this, the most degrading thing a man could do! I looked at Tamara. Tears were running down her cheeks.

'I am sorry, Tamara,' I said.

'No, no,' she said, 'I am glad you told me but do not tell Mum. She was brought up in Russia and she would be very upset to hear that.'

I reassured her that I would not tell her mother. I also said that I felt so much better for unburdening my sad story to her. I felt that it had brought us so much closer together.

The week had flown by and to-morrow was our last day at the farm. We lay contentedly together in front of the fire until it died down to the last embers. Then I said:

'You know, Tamara, only one good thing has come out of this bloody war.'

'And what is that?' she smiled.

'That I found you. Come, let's go to bed!' I laughed.

We arrived back in Riga in daylight and as my luggage was heavy, we took a taxi. Everybody was happy to see us back but the news was not at all good. Tamara's application to work in her father's shop had been turned down, and she was commanded to work for the forces. Her mother was very upset about it and I tried to console her. I told her that if Tamara did not like the work, I would do something about it. Her mother replied that I was not a general.

'Oh, no,' I said, 'but I can marry her.'

'Marry her?' She looked at me.

'Yes, Mum, if I marry Tamara, she will then become German, just as you became Latvian when you married Dad. She may still have to work, but I would have some say in what that work would be.'

The next morning we had an officers' meeting at which we were briefed about the general situation in the Northern Sector. It was pretty grim. The Russians had launched two tank attacks, one in the north near Leningrad and the other further south near Novgorod. The attack on Novgorod was so fierce that it was expected to fall back into Russian hands at any time. We would then lose one of the major supply points, which in turn would put pressure on Pleskau, and Pleskau was our responsibility. We left the meeting with instructions to organise an effective programme under Capt. Klinker. We were instructed that three officers, myself being one of them, must take an active part in these operations. This meant that we would be supervising the convoys and travelling with them. After the emotion of the meeting, I sat quietly for a while and pondered on the changed situation. Tamara had to report for work and I knew that this could result in her living away from home. I myself would be mostly on the move and I was dismayed at the prospect of us seeing much less of one another.

It was planned that my first convoy would leave Riga for Pleskau in three days' time. Heinz gave me a lift into Riga the following evening and as I greeted Tamara she was smiling. I took this to mean she had received some good news and indeed she had. She had reported for work and because of her knowledge of languages, she had been given a position as interpreter at the Headquarters for the distribution of wounded soldiers. This meant that she could continue to live at home.

'That is good news, Tamara, but I have not been so lucky,' I said.

CHAPTER TWELVE.
TAMARA AND I ARE SEPARATED

I told Tamara of the changes which would be affecting me from now on. I assured her that I would be back whenever I could to see her. Her mother, who overheard our conversation, handed me two parcels as I was leaving. One contained warm clothing and one some extra food.

On the 19th of January 1944 the Russians had finally taken Novgorod, and from then onwards conditions went from bad to worse. We did what we could from our base to stem the ever-increasing Russian attacks. We were transporting back our injured soldiers and material which had to be recovered, and also taking supplies to the front. In spite of it all, I still managed to see Tamara and whenever possible I stayed overnight.

This went on for about six weeks or so. In the meantime the situation had worsened to such an extent that plans were formulated for the evacuation of our Headquarters from Riga. Again we had a meeting and advance secret information was given to us: unless the Russian advance could be stopped, our Headquarters would be moved out of Riga and be split up.

Capt Klinker's section would go back to the district of Memel and I was to be sent with a number of corporals and men to prepare suitable sites for the move. From what I knew of the situation at the front, I was convinced that nothing could stop the Russians now. On occasions when I returned to camp and had lunch in the Officers' Mess, I was saddened to hear men still pinning their hopes on the imminent use of secret weapons. I did not become involved in such talk and as I watched them discussing this from the comfort of their well-upholstered chairs, I knew that one trip to the front, the first for many of them, would give them a very different view. In fact, they had no idea of the actual situation. This, combined with the news we were receiving from Germany, left me in no doubt that the secret weapon was little more than a dream.

By now Berlin was reduced to rubble, as were Hamburg and Cologne, along with many other towns and cities. U.S. bombers had reached as far as Regensburg and Schweinfurt in broad daylight, and had dropped heavy loads of bombs on to these towns. The fact that these places were so far from the front provided further confirmation of the gravity of the whole situation. I thought it was time to have a talk to Tamara before things became even worse. I asked if she had considered what she would do in the event of the Russians taking Riga and her Unit giving her the choice of evacuating with the troops or staying there. She said that she would not stay under any circumstances under the Russians, and neither would her family.

'Will you marry me then?' I asked.

'Yes', she replied. 'I accepted it for better or for worse when we became engaged.'

'I was hoping you would say that, Tamara, but to marry you I have to get permission from Headquarters and that will take time. You know, everything is now in uproar and when we start evacuating, it will get worse.' I went on to say that in normal circumstances my promotion would have come through by this time, but my feelings now were that I would prefer it not to come yet. Perhaps, even, it would be better if it never came at all. I told her of the plan to move our Headquarters to Germany and that when this plan was actually put into operation, it meant that I would be the first to go to prepare for the changeover.

'I hope it does not happen, Tamara, but if it does, we will marry as soon as permission is given. Then if things get worse for you, try to get a travel permit and go to Hugo. I will write to him and you can be sure that he will make you welcome and your family as well.'

When Tamara's parents returned home that evening, I asked their permission to marry Tamara.

Four weeks later the orders I had been dreading came. I was instructed to leave Riga and I thought it would be forever. The uncertainty for Tamara made me very edgy and unhappy. It was very hard to say good-bye to her and the family. I made the farewell as short as possible to try to hide my feelings but as I drove back to the barracks, I was unable to restrain my tears.

I was now in charge of a Company, a mixed crowd made up of men from several units. There were radio technicians, armoury-trained men, engineers, mechanics, drivers, office staff as well as some sergeants and lance-corporals. It was my job to find sufficient operational space to accommodate the full Headquarters in the Memel area. This involved power supplies, food supplies, spare parts and supplies in general. For the first two weeks all went well and I was able to keep in contact with Capt. Klinker. Messages to and from Tamara were delivered satisfactorily and on a couple of occasions Heinz even brought her and Freda to his quarters, where we were able to talk on our service line. This, of course, was contrary to all regulations, but we managed to get away with it. The situation at the front appeared to improve temporarily as the weather improved and no one was happier about this than myself. I was hopeful that the whole advanced operation here in my present post would prove to be unnecessary and that we would all return to Riga.

However, one day in June the Russians began a massive attack in the region of Minsk. At the same time we heard, at first unofficially then officially, that British and American troops had landed successfully in Normandy and were not only holding on to it, but had seriously breached our defence line. The Russians, obviously encouraged by this progress on the western front, made further attacks on the weakened Minsk section and this resulted in heavy losses for our troops. To prevent a total collapse, the commanding general had to re-group his fighting units and build a new defence line. To do this he needed more men and in less difficult times these would have been drawn from the West. But by now the West was in no position to spare any men at all. The British and American Forces had made such progress that Cherbourg was now in danger, so the reinforcements had to come from the Northern sector.

The situation was now so desperate that men from the Air Force were to be used for ground fighting. I had just sat down for lunch one day when a dispatch rider brought the order to stop all the preparations immediately and have the whole unit in battle dress ready for the following day. Four troop carriers and my own commando wagon were to be made ready as well. Only ten men were to remain behind to safeguard our camp.

I rang Heinz that night. He was fully in the picture and assured me that he could do nothing to prevent it. He said that it would be temporary as we were urgently needed for our own operations. We were not the only Air Force Unit ordered to hold the defence line near Minsk. Minsk was to be defended at any cost as it was a very important supply point. If it could not be held, the whole Northern Sector could be cut off and this would include our own headquarters in Riga. I asked Heinz to tell Tamara what had happened but not to upset her unduly. If anything went wrong unexpectedly and she had to leave Riga, she should try to reach Hugo or at least contact him. I begged Heinz to try to push through my marriage application. He assured me that he would do everything he could. I thanked him and wished him luck.

We reached Minsk by evening, where I reported to Major Gruene as instructed. I was given a lengthy and very detailed briefing. The place my Company had to defend at the front line was a stretch of river. The Russians had advanced to the river and our job was to prevent them crossing it. All bridges had been destroyed and the Russians had to bring in Pioneer Units to build a pontoon bridge. Such an operation by the Russians was not, however, expected to be attempted on my section, nor yet on the sections adjoining on either side. The whole area was marshland and therefore not suitable for heavy equipment. The idea was to get his trained fighting men out of these unlikely areas and into the strategic sections of the front. The difficulty was that the area assigned to me was well within enemy view, which meant that we had to be vigilant. It was impossible to dig deeper trenches because of the high water table. Furthermore, everything would have to be done under cover of darkness and even then we were not safe from snipers.

When I inspected the Command Post, I noticed that it was fairly well concealed by reeds and bushes. We were to relieve the outgoing unit by nightfall and in order to reach the spot we would have to travel on a major supply road. This road was under long-range artillery fire from the enemy. We would travel as far as we could on it and make the remainder of the journey on foot. It was expected that the changeover would be completed by dawn except that the heavy machine-gun crews would remain until such time as my men could handle these weapons.

As the last bit of daylight disappeared, we set off. It was not long before we heard the first grenade exploding nearby. Shortly afterwards, I saw one of the dispatch riders disappear just in front of my vehicle. He was our first casualty. As we were moving without lights, he had not seen the hole that the exploding grenade had made in the road. As we got him out, we found that he had suffered a broken leg and that the bike had a broken fork. I stopped a supply vehicle which was travelling towards Minsk to take him back, and we drove on. It was not long before we reached the point where we had to leave our vehicles and proceed on foot.

As daylight came over the marshy landscape, the changeover was completed. The next three days and nights were not too bad, but the Russians opened up with their machine guns and ack ack at the slightest movement on our side. We always returned their fire. Movement was confined to the night time whenever possible, and even then it was dangerous, as every so often the Russians sent up flares which illuminated a large part of our section. When this happened, everyone went down immediately on his stomach. If someone could not get down quickly enough, bullets started to fly about. It was in this way that we suffered our second casualty on the third night there. It was one of our soup carriers, for soup was the only warm food that we got each day. The soup was carried by four men in canisters on their backs and as the flare lit up, one of them could not get down quickly enough. A bullet went through his arm and then through the canister, spilling the hot soup all over him. We got him back to the road where he was picked up for hospital. He was lucky.

The next day, just as it began to get dark, I was telling one of my sergeants that I would try to get to sleep for an hour or so when an exhausted messenger arrived with a message which read:

'Enemy broken through and has taken the road to Vilna. All units to withdraw immediately south of Minsk.'

Through radio communications, we knew that Minsk had fallen on 3rd July 1944. The radio operator also established a link with my

Battalion Headquarters, which had been set up between Minsk and Brest.

The ensuing withdrawal was a nightmare. Under heavy fire and already suffering several casualties, we made our way back across a canal, eventually reaching the new defensive line south of Minsk. Here I was able to report to my immediate superior, Major Gruene, who was delighted to see that I and the men under me had survived. To my surprise, he told me that he now had enough replacement troops to hold this section. My Commander, Major-General Jacoby, had ordered our release. This meant that we would be rejoining our old unit, which was on the way to Memel. Transport would be provided for us at the earliest opportunity.

While waiting for our transport, we spent the time in smartening ourselves up, cleaning our weapons and repairing our torn uniforms. The moment I found any time to relax, my thoughts flew to Tamara. Since I knew that our Headquarters were no longer in Riga, this could only mean that Riga was being evacuated, and I wondered whether Tamara would be able to get out. All I could do was wait until we got back to Memel. Heinz would surely know where she was.

CHAPTER THIRTEEN. REUNION AND MARRIAGE

We had now been at the camp site for a week and I began to worry that our transport had still not arrived. I decided to wait another day and if the transport had not come by then, I would accompany the daily foot patrols back to Headquarters to see Major Gruene. However, the next morning the troop carriers did arrive, though one of them had broken down and had had to be towed. A motor cycle belonging to one of the dispatch riders had also broken down and he stayed behind until it was repaired. Now our morale improved; we were mobile again. I decided that since I had a number of trained engineers in my unit, we could repair the truck ourselves. One of our men remembered seeing an overturned truck of the same make somewhere along the road. Transferring the whole gearbox from this to our own truck presented no problem to my men. The blue skies we had seen for most of the week were gone now, and there were quite a lot of cumulus clouds. There were occasional sounds of aircraft, which we identified as Russian observation planes. We nicknamed them 'Coffee Mills' because of the grinding noise they made. The occasional break in the clouds enabled the pilots of these small observation planes to look below and take photographs. As we were well camouflaged, we did not worry too much about them but next morning we were rather shocked when we were attacked by a Russian fighter bomber. We could hear him approaching, flying above the clouds. He throttled back, broke through the clouds and disappeared again. He missed us by a long way, but we were quite sure that the fresh truck-marks leading to the wood had been spotted by the observation planes, resulting in this attack. I decided to pull out the next day.

Shortly after the attack the dispatch rider arrived on his repaired motor cycle. He brought new orders for me, my travelling orders back to Memel, and also a personal letter from Heinz. The rider started to speak to me but as I recognised Heinz's handwriting on the letter, I asked him to wait. I went to my tent and nervously opened the letter. It was brief. He told me that Tamara had left Riga on a Red Cross ship to Danzig, where she was working as part of a medical team. Also my marriage licence had come through and I would be given further information when we reached Memel. I did not like the thought of Tamara being on a ship. Even a Red Cross ship was not always respected by the Russians, but at least she had got out of Riga. At this stage, however, I did not know whether or not the Russians had taken the city.

I called the company together and told them that we would be leaving the following morning for Memel. Then I tumbled into bed and fell asleep at once. In my relaxed state it took me a long time to realize that someone was calling for me in a very loud voice. I looked at my watch; it was 1 am. Outside my tent I found a dispatch rider looking for me. He handed a sealed message to me stamped 'Top Secret'. The message was signed by a Major-General of the First Air Command, and said that I must immediately get my unit into full battle dress and move them towards Brest. There was a location map showing where I had to report and the name of a Colonel, who would give me further orders on arrival. I signed to acknowledge the receipt of the message and the dispatch rider continued on his way.

On arrival at the airfield outside Brest, I went in to report to the Colonel. Even though it was only 7 am, there was plenty of activity in the camp. I reported to the Adjutant and was soon face to face with the Colonel, reporting my numbers of the Air Force Fighting Unit Jacoby as ordered. The Colonel asked the Adjutant and myself to sit down and reminded me that what he was about to say was secret. He went on to say that yesterday an attempt had been made to kill the Fuehrer. The Fuehrer had been injured but was in full control of the situation. There was definite proof that a number of Army generals were behind the coup, and that an armed attack on the Fuehrer's Headquarters was a possibility, mainly by Army Airborne Units. As the Air Force had the full confidence of the Fuehrer, all Air Force Fighting Units were called in to defend the Fuehrer's Headquarters together with the adjacent territory, including the airfield. He paused and rolled out a map of the Fuehrer's Headquarters and detailed to me all the positions which I would have to defend if such an attack should take place. I was then asked whether I fully understood the position. I replied that I did but also explained that I had lost both men and weapons in my last engagement. The Colonel ordered his Adjutant immediately to make good all my losses, to provide rations for three days and to give me a second dispatch rider. I was also to receive a commando vehicle for my own use. As the expected attack was thought to be imminent, timing was vital. I was to find the section I had been ordered to defend, take my men and organise the digging of trenches to be ready as quickly as possible for the attack. I saluted, and withdrew.

I returned to my unit, briefed my men, and within three hours we were on our way to our new location. We arrived in the vicinity of Hitler's Headquarters and Air Force Police at the road block inspected my papers. We were given directions as to how we could reach our section and were soon in position, having dug ourselves in.

For the time being our presence here was kept secret. Food was brought to us but no mail was allowed in or out. Our duties consisted solely in watching our section of the airfield by day and night. The weather was sunny and warm and I passed many hours writing letters, even though for the time being I could not send them anywhere.

By now it was August 1st and we had been stationed in our position for ten days. Compared to our last assignment, this felt like a tropical island. All I had to do was watch for the occasional aircraft flying in and look out for the green flare which was a pre-arranged signal to us that everything was in order.

I was wondering how long this would go on. Every day I was thinking about Tamara. By now she would be travelling on a ship. Once we were relieved of our present duty, she would be my first priority. After all, Heinz had written that permission for my marriage had been given. I wondered why I had had no further news from him. Just as I was thinking about this, I noticed a car travelling towards us. I immediately recognised it as Heinz's. I heard my men shouting: 'Capt. Klinker, Capt. Klinker!' I ran towards him, dressed only in my trousers. I saluted and we shook hands. He laughed, and then asked his driver to leave us alone. 'Heinz, since I saw you last, I have been through hell. Nine men dead and eight injured, some of them badly. If we had not had a bit of luck, we would probably be in Siberia by now. But now, Heinz, please tell me, how is Tamara?'

'I wish I knew,' he answered. 'The Red Cross Headquarters she worked for was controlling seven hospitals and as they started to evacuate, all wounded soldiers had to be moved to Germany. This, by the way, is still going on. Road and rail transport is strained to the limit. Most of the wounded are being transported by ship from Riga to Danzig. Medical staff on board is desperately short and Tamara and four other girls were ordered to assist. Look, Carl, I could do nothing to prevent it. So that is where she is, between Riga and Danzig. As for Mum, Dad and Freda, I was lucky enough to get them registered on to our own Red Cross Unit but they will have to travel by train, first of all to Posen. At the moment the front is holding on the Estonian border and hopefully there is enough time to get everybody out.'

'What about Tamara's brother, Alfred?' I asked.

'He will get out with them.'

He went on to tell me that Memel was only a temporary place for his unit and that we would have to move on to Posen and possibly even further back, as the Oder-Neisse line was already being prepared. He said that that was the line where the Russian advance would be stopped and they would be prevented from advancing any further. Hitler's Headquarters, where we were at the present time, would most likely be transferred to Berlin. Therefore our duty on the airfield would cease forthwith and all the Air Force fighting units which had been called in to defend the Headquarters would be returned to their original units. That was what he had really come to tell me and we began at once to break up our camp before returning the men to their own units.

Our stay in Memel was short-lived and we soon received orders to move on to Posen. This time everything had to be loaded on to trains as all possible fuel had to be conserved for use in tanks. The only functioning Panzer Division fighting here on the North front had been diverted to the West and all the fuel reserves had gone with it. Heavy fighting was going on in the West. Allied troops were close to Brussels and were nearly through Holland. Rail transport was also difficult to obtain, as everything was on the move.

We needed four trains to carry all our equipment, which had been moved by road from Riga to Memel while we had been fighting at the front near Minsk. A group of men were already on their way to Posen to find a suitable site for it. The first empty train was pushed into a small goods yard at Memel and we were packing again.

Heinz had tried for two days to get a telephone message through to his wife, who was living with her mother on the Island of Ruegen. The civil lines were either overloaded with calls or were out of order, so that he could not get through. On that particular day he was lucky, but the news he received was unfortunately not very good. His wife needed an operation and he applied for one week's leave to see her. The leave was granted and he left, leaving me in charge.

This meant an increased work-load for me and much more responsibility, but I also had more freedom. Moreover, I was able, without permission from anyone, to use the service long-distance telephone line. I wanted to find out which ship Tamara was on and when it would be in Danzig Harbour. I had to make a lot of calls and seemed to be getting nowhere, but I persevered and eventually I got through to the distribution depot for wounded soldiers at Danzig. I asked whether there was a Red Cross ship from Riga in harbour. They asked me which one, because one of the ships had been attacked by a Russian submarine and had many casualties. However, it had reached harbour where it had been unloaded and was now lying empty. The other one, named the Robert Moering, had just left for Riga and was due back in three days time.

This was distressing news to me as I did not know which ship Tamara was on. Nevertheless, I had to find out. I tried to ring the Red Cross Station in Riga. All through the night I did not leave the telephone. At last, in the early hours of the following morning, I managed to make contact with the Red Cross officials and asked the man on the other end of the line if Tamara Bergs was on the Robert Moering. He asked me to hold the line whilst he made enquiries. I could hear my heart thumping as I waited. Then a sergeant answered. I identified myself, and he told me that he knew Tamara. 'No one could miss a girl with her looks,' he added jokingly. 'Are you her fiancé?'

'That's right', I replied. 'I am so glad I can speak to you, is she on board?'

'Yes,' he said, 'she was when the ship left here.' He added that he could see no reason why she should not be on board the ship still. He went on to say that I was lucky because the next trip would be the last one from Riga; after that, all trips for the Robert Moering would be made from Libau. Riga was getting too hot, he remarked. I asked him to give Tamara a message that I would contact her in Danzig as soon as I could, and to have ready her birth certificate and passport as I had a reason for needing them, a reason she would understand. I thanked him again and again and it was with great relief that I replaced the receiver.

I calculated that the Robert Moering should be back in Danzig Harbour that same day, but after numerous unsuccessful attempts to contact the harbour depot by telephone, I eventually got through, only to be told that engine trouble had developed on the outward journey and that the ship would therefore be delayed for the necessary repairs. It was expected that this would take three days. I found this news deeply disturbing. At this stage, I well knew, those three days could be crucial in deciding whether the ship was able to leave Riga. The Russians might well take the city in that time.

Mercifully I was kept so busy that my mind did not dwell continually on the matter. There was the urgent business of loading our equipment on to the transport in readiness for transferring it to its new destination. One trainload had already left and I had received orders that the remaining equipment must be loaded within the next two days. There was a sense of urgency all around me. We were working day and night to meet our deadline. As I worked, my thoughts were occupied mainly with the Robert Moering and I was trying desperately to find some solution to my problem. There was really nothing I could do until Heinz had resumed command. I sent a telegram to him saying that he should go straight to the new quarters rather than return to our present site.

The last train was loaded and we steamed towards our new destination south of Posen and behind the newly erected defence lines which were intended to stop the Russian Army for good.

Two days later, to my great relief, Heinz joined us at the new camp and resumed command. Not only was I now free of the additional responsibility, but he was my only hope of saving Tamara. Heinz was pretty depressed. His wife needed a gall bladder operation but because of staff shortages at the hospital, the operation had been cancelled time after time and she was in pain. In addition, there was the grave situation faced by all the Islanders, that the Russians could arrive at any time and take over the Island. Most of the defending troops had already left, leaving the people defenceless and without escape. I opened a bottle of schnapps and we had a drink. I told him about my problem and how desperate I was to get Tamara off that ship. I told him that the sister ship had already been attacked and I wondered how long it would be before the Robert Moering was at the bottom of the sea. My plans were to get married. The necessary documents were here. Once married to an Airforce officer, no one could keep her on the ship. The question was, could Heinz provide a vehicle so that we could fake a journey to Danzig or alternatively, could he give me four or five days leave?

Heinz studied the situation over another drink and then said: 'The best thing, Carl, is for me to give you a week's leave to get married. Then it is official and we are all covered.' That was the best news I had had for a long time. Now I had to find out when the ship would be arriving at Danzig and to find a train to take me there. We also discussed Tamara's parents and Freda, but all we could do was to hope that they would get out of Riga in time.

That same evening I sat by the telephone for hours trying desperately to get through to the Red Cross station at Danzig Harbour. Eventually I got through and learned that the ship was now operating from Libau, which shortened the sea journey by half. This meant that she would be in dock more frequently than before. Next morning I told Heinz what I had managed to find out and he instructed the office staff to get my papers ready. I left the following morning and by a stroke of luck I was at Danzig Harbour by midday.

To locate the Robert Moering in that vast and complex docking area was a considerable problem but eventually I found her and managed to interview the Red Cross officer in charge. I told him my reason for being there, whereupon he confirmed that Tamara was in fact on board the ship and said that she was due to sail that evening. 'Well,' I replied, 'it's my wedding night to-night and you will have to sail without her.' He looked at me and explained that he was only second-in-command on the ship. So far as the military staff were concerned, the officer in charge, a military surgeon, was not on board at present. He was visiting his wife in Danzig and was not expected back until shortly before the ship was due to sail. He went on to say that they were desperately short of staff. However, he was sympathetic to me and said that I could take Tamara. He added that once his superior returned to the ship and he had explained to him that Tamara was now the wife of an Air Force officer, he would be in the clear. With great relief I said to him: 'You are a good sport, just tell me where I can find her.' He took me to her cabin and knocked on the door. 'Who is it?' I recognised Tamara's voice. 'It is your Sergeant-Major,' he said, 'I have a surprise for you.' She opened the door. 'Carl, Carl!' she cried and flew into my arms. I wanted to thank the Sergeant-Major but he had gone. I went into her cabin and we embraced for a long time.

'Carl, I am so glad to see you,' she said. 'And so am I,' I replied 'Come on, pack all your belongings as quickly as you can and let's get off this ship. We are going to get married.'

'But...', she began to say.

'No buts', I said, 'I will explain everything later' and I hurried her along.

'Am I not coming back for to-night's sailing?' she asked.

'No, you are not.'

She said that she wanted to say good-bye to her colleagues. I agreed but urged her to hurry. Shortly afterwards we were both standing in the office to say goodbye to the Sergeant-Major and then we walked down the gangway and off the ship.

Only when we were walking in the direction of the town did I tell Tamara that while I was sorry to rush her, I was worried in case the chief officer should return and I would have to explain it all again. Also there could have been problems. I asked Tamara whether she had received my message in Riga. She had, and she told me that she was in possession of all the papers we needed. 'Fine', I said, 'Let's make straight for the Registry Office. As I expected, we could not be married there and then, but I presented all the papers and since my marriage was a military one, and the authorisation for it had been signed by a Major-General, there was no problem. All I had to do was to pay the fee and find two witnesses with passports. We were asked to return at 10 am the following day.

After we left the Registry Office we had two immediate tasks: first to find the two witnesses, second, to find some accommodation. As we walked past the police station, it occurred to me that this would be the best place to find our witnesses. The officer on the desk gave us a big smile when I explained what we wanted and said that he would see what could be done. When I asked him where I could make a donation, he became very friendly. I placed a 100 mark note on the desk.

Finding accommodation was much more difficult and here even the policeman could not help. It seemed that a political conference was due to start in two days' time, which had made accommodation almost impossible to find. All hotel rooms appeared to be fully booked.

After a prolonged search, we discovered a friendly middle-aged woman who, on hearing that we were getting married next day, decided to help us. She gave us her address and told us how to reach it. 'Just knock on the door three times,' she said, 'and my daughter will let you in. Give her this note and she will make you comfortable until I come home.'

Next morning we were awake by 5 am, very excited and already planning our day. After the ceremony at the Registry Office, we would return to this house and collect our luggage. Then we hoped to catch a train to my home town and go to see Hugo. There, all being well, Tamara would be able to stay. At 7.30 am our hostess knocked on the door to say that breakfast was ready. We did not eat very much and we both admitted to being nervous. Our hostess told us that she was not on duty until 1 pm that day. She would allow her daughter to have a day off from school so that we could all have lunch on our return.

Everything went as planned. The two policemen who were to act as witnesses were waiting for us and at 10 am we entered the Registry Office. At 10.20 am we walked out of the building as man and wife. As we said goodbye to our helpful witnesses, I gave them another donation and invited them to use it to drink our health when the duty was over.

My wife and I then made our way to the railway station to enquire about available trains. There was a train in the late afternoon which would take us as far as Stettin. From there we had to change trains and, if everything went according to plan, we should pick up the post van and be with Hugo by lunchtime the next day. Arm in arm we walked back to the home of our generous hostess just in time for lunch. As we entered the living room, we found the table beautifully set with flowers in the centre. This surprised me as I had looked for flowers myself but had failed to find any. Even the dining chairs were decorated with flowers and greenery. After a delightful meal we took our leave of these kind people, thanking them for all they had done for us and promising to keep in touch.

CHAPTER FOURTEEN.
INTERLUDE AT HUGO'S FARM

Our train left on time. It was packed with soldiers but we managed to find two seats in the first class compartment. To me it seemed a very long night. Tamara slept with her head on my shoulder, only occasionally waking and looking at me briefly before closing her eyes again. As we got off the train in Stettin, we were immediately struck by the difference in temperatures. It was very cold, whereas the train had been pleasantly warm.

When we arrived in Hugo's village, we walked down the main street. It was the only street and was deserted, but as we rounded the last bend I could hear the hissing noise which I knew to be the sound made by the saw blade biting its way through the big tree trunks at Hugo's saw-mill. We could see Hugo himself talking to some people and when he spotted us, he left them and half ran to meet us.

I introduced Tamara saying, 'Well Hugo, I have brought you some help.'

'Carl, I told you that she would be welcome at any time and so would her parents. As you know, I have plenty of room. I cannot say how long this will be, the time may come when we shall all have to run away.'

'Unfortunately, Hugo, you may well be right.'

'But you must be hungry', he added, and went into the kitchen to arrange for some food. He directed us upstairs to the first door on the right. That, he added, would be our room. We went up to the room and I opened the window, which overlooked the lake and the river. 'Come here a minute, Tamara, and look at this beautiful picture. It looks so peaceful.' I pointed out to her how the water reflected all the reeds and the trees, and told her that in summertime the surface of the water was covered in water lilies. Just for a second my mind returned to Marianne.

Hugo was calling and we went downstairs for something to eat. He went out to stop his saw-mill and then joined us for the meal. I told him that we had travelled through the night and asked him if he minded if we rested for a while after the meal. We would catch up on our conversation that evening. I added that there must be a bottle of his home-made wine somewhere, and he replied that there most certainly was. We enjoyed a splendid meal and I could see that Hugo was genuinely pleased to have us there. I asked him whether it was really convenient for Tamara to stay on. He waved a hand and said that she was most welcome and that it was really the only thing he was able to do for me. I could see that Tamara was convinced that Hugo meant every word he said. When we got to our room, I commented to Tamara that this was the first private moment we had had since our marriage and we took advantage of it.

When Tamara woke me I felt much better. She said that she had woken to the wonderful smell of cooking from the kitchen. It was about 8 pm. Tamara was right. The house-keeper had cooked a lovely dinner and Hugo had changed from his working clothes ready for the evening. We talked before, during and after the meal, and at midnight we were still talking. The conversation began with what had taken place in the village since I had last heard from Hugo. Slowly and inevitably the conversation led to the current situation, and we considered what our fate might be should the war be lost. We agreed that we would not wish to fall into the hands of the Russian Army. We arranged that if the Oder/Neisse line failed to hold, Hugo and Tamara would take to the road and set out for the West, aiming to reach as near to the British troops as they could get. Hugo assured me that he would take care of Tamara. Even though he was in the Home Guard, he would keep a pair of horses and a cart ready to leave at any time. I had to admit that things were more difficult for myself as, being in the Armed Forces, I was, of course, subject to orders. To leave my post without permission amounted to desertion and the punishment for this was immediate execution by the firing squad. On a subdued note we ended our evening and went to bed. As we said goodnight to Hugo, we attempted to be a little more optimistic, saying that miracles sometimes happened and we must just hope.

When Tamara and I came down the next morning, Hugo had already left the house. His housekeeper told us that he had gone to his fields to do some harvesting. The weather was ideal for it, a beautiful autumn day.

After breakfast we went to see the Buergermeister, to register Tamara's presence at Hugo's house. It was with nostalgia that I walked along the street I had run along so often as a boy, stopping occasionally to greet a familiar face, until we reached the Buergermeister's office. Fortunately he was in and remembered me. After the introductions, he asked me how things were going at the front. I cautiously reassured him, knowing very well that some Party members were still hoping for a miracle and did not really want to know the truth. He was one such member. My view was that he could believe whatever he wished, provided that he accepted Tamara as a helper on Hugo's farm.

It was not quite lunchtime, so we walked along the river and round the lake. I told Tamara how we used to swim there in summertime almost every day and I told her how when I was fourteen, I had been attracted to a girl two years older than myself. I described the risks I had taken in that lake to get water lilies for her and how I had almost drowned in the effort. Even now, however, I could not bring myself to tell her the whole story. It must have been the last day of the schools' autumn holiday, as several children were swimming in the lake. The water was so tempting, I commented to Tamara that it was a pity that we did not have swim-suits. She smiled and said that she had one. I hoped to borrow some trunks from Hugo and we arranged to go for a swim in the afternoon. It was a lovely afternoon and we spent it at the lake, swimming and lying in the sun. For a couple of hours we were able to forget the horrors of the war. It was as if time stood still for us and the war had been just a bad dream.

That evening I told Hugo that I had two tasks to perform before I left and that they should be done next day: to visit the bank in the town and open an account for Tamara, and also to make my Will. 'Can I go with you?' asked Hugo. 'Of course, you can,' we both replied. He said that he too would like to make a Will, in favour of his daughter. At the same time he would like to take advantage of Tamara's presence in the town to advise him as to what would be suitable for him to buy, to send to his daughter. He would prepare his horse and cart for our transport. It would be more convenient than travelling by the post van.

There were two ways into town from Hugo's farm, through the forest or by the bus route. We took the way through the forest and passed the spot where Hugo's brother had had a fatal accident many years before. I am sure that the incident was in the minds of both Hugo and myself as we drove by, but neither of us mentioned it.

After completing my tasks, I arrived back at the horse and cart just as Hugo and Tamara came up laden with parcels. Tamara put her parcels down and came to greet me. I could see by her smile that she was very happy. She lifted her arm and showed me a bracelet she was wearing. It was a wedding gift to her from Hugo. She went on to say that he had tricked her by asking her to help him choose a really good present for his cousin's 21st birthday. She had advised him to buy the one she was now wearing. After he had bought it, he handed it to her saying: 'Here, Tamara, this is a little present for your wedding.' She was delighted and thought the bracelet was lovely. 'Hugo, you should not,' she exclaimed and kissed him on the cheek.

The last day of my leave came and we spent it at the lake, swimming, sun bathing and talking about the future. I was quite sure that I would have no difficulty in coming to visit Tamara whilst I was stationed in Posen, but if that should change! Well, we would have to wait and see. Sadly the day came when I had to leave my wife of one week. I said goodbye to Hugo, telling him that I was sure that Tamara would help him in any way she could and that I hoped to see them both very soon. Tamara went with me to the place where I had to wait for the post van. As we walked down the street, I asked her if she was happy with the situation she now found herself in – I meant, staying at Hugo's without me. She replied that it was certainly better than being on board the Robert Moering. 'Oh, Tamara, I love you so much. Now you try not to worry about your family. I am sure that Heinz will do his best to allow me to see you as often as possible, and I will try to be back very soon.'

As the post van started to move off, we could not control our emotions any longer. As I saw big tears rolling down her cheeks, I too could not hold back my tears.

PART IV.
THE WAR GOES ON

CHAPTER FIFTEEN.
THE BOMBING OF DRESDEN

For a time it appeared that the Russian advance was being halted in the northern sector. More and more volunteers from the three Baltic States were fighting to defend their homeland. Despite all their efforts, however, by the end of September Russian troops were advancing to Riga.

The following two weeks were spent evacuating the remaining sections of our Headquarters from the city. Heinz and myself were desperate for information about Tamara's family and about Freda. Had they managed to get away? If so, where had they been sent. Heinz spent much time on the telephone. The lines were either out of order due to war damage or else engaged. Eventually he managed to find out that our people were scheduled to leave by train within the next few days. They were, however, to be split up. Mum, Dad and Alfred would be sent with a maintenance unit to the region of Magdeburg, while Freda, with a Red Cross unit, was to go to the region of Dresden.

As soon as Heinz told me this, I thought of a way of telling Tamara about the family. I was aware that transport left our camp almost daily for the distribution centre in Frankfurt/Oder. If, just once, Heinz could arrange for me to replace the regular driver, I could then drive the extra half an hour from the distribution centre and be with Tamara. 'Go on,' he said, 'Get the papers ready, but be back by to-morrow night.' Once again I was grateful to him and before long I was on my way. Tamara was jubilant at seeing me, and even more so when I told her about the family and Freda. Hugo stopped his saw-mill and said it was an occasion to celebrate and once again we all sat round the table. This time I had brought quite a supply of food and drinks, which I had saved up.

Again we discussed the situation and came to the conclusion that unless a miracle happened, the war was lost. German troops were retreating everywhere, and both British and American Forces had almost reached the German border. Desperate efforts were being made to strengthen the Oder/Neisse line, but the 'men' consisted mainly of sixteen and seventeen year-olds; the rest were too old to fight. We were all praying that the Oder/Neisse line would hold until the British and American troops reached it. The alternative did not bear thinking about. In view of this, Tamara felt that her family had been lucky to be sent to Magdeburg, since it was nearer to the Western front. Hugo and Tamara were getting on quite well. She was helping him wherever she could. As they waved me off the next day, I felt a little happier in my mind, but the war was still going on.

Riga fell into the hands of the Russians at the beginning of October 1944, but we knew that the family and Freda had left on the last train out of the city. Two weeks later Russian troops had reached the East Prussian border.

Heinz had applied for three days' leave over Christmas. His wife had had her operation and was convalescing at home. His leave was granted and in his absence responsibility for the whole unit fell once more upon my shoulders. Heinz promised me that I would be given three days' leave when he returned. He considered that, in addition to his leave, he had a bonus in that he was required to attend a meeting in Dresden, where the main part of our Headquarters was now based. This meant, of course, that he would also be able to visit Freda. Freda sent her best wishes to us all. She was working as a hairdresser in a large military hospital in Dresden and was quite happy there. Not a single bomb had fallen on that city and she considered herself fortunate to be there.

When Heinz returned from the meeting in Dresden, he called me into his office together with two other colleagues. It had already been decided, he told us, that our Section of the Headquarters must also move to Dresden, which up to this time had not been bombed. Perhaps the Western powers would spare it for its historic value; at least this was what had been anticipated by the commanding general. The timing of our move to Dresden would be in accordance with the progress of the Russian advance. We were, of course, pleased to be moving further from the danger area, but in my case it also meant that I would be further away from Tamara. This, of course, was far from what I would have wished.

Christmas came and Heinz went off to see his wife. I looked forward to his return when I could go and see mine, and that was all that mattered to me. When Heinz returned from his leave, he was not at all happy with the situation. On the Isle of Ruegen his wife's health was giving him cause for concern, and to make matters worse, many people had left the Island to be with relatives in Germany. It was feared that the Russians would launch an attack from the Baltic Sea and take the Island for its strategic value. I tried to comfort him and suggested that, if the situation should become any worse, he might simply go and get his family off the Island. 'That is easier said than done', was his reaction. I told him that I was going to see Hugo, who would have been happy to take Tamara's family. Perhaps he would now take Heinz's family. I asked Heinz if I should mention it to Hugo. Heinz considered it a very good idea, but he was not sure whether it would be possible to get them out. I offered to go for them and if we could fix some papers, I did not see why we should not be successful. He was worried that Tamara might mention the existence of Freda in his life. I reassured him that she would not. I asked him to think it over and we said we would discuss it again after I had seen Hugo.

The following day I was on my way to Hugo. To my surprise, one of the first people I saw on my arrival was Tamara. Naturally she was delighted to see me, and we walked back to Hugo's house arm in arm. On the way she brought me up to date with all that had happened since my last visit.

When Hugo saw us coming, he stopped the saw-mill as he always did and we all went into the house. Tamara proudly showed me the Christmas tree which Hugo had brought from his own wood and which she had decorated. I opened the case and placed the presents I had carefully wrapped under the tree. I suggested that we open them in the evening but Tamara could not wait. So we agreed to open them there and then. She opened her parcel first. It was a box of chocolate liqueurs. I knew that she was particularly fond of them. They had been bought on the black market and so had the 200 cigarettes which Hugo found in his parcel. I wanted to do something special for Hugo and I handed over to him a box containing 500 marks. I explained that it was for his daughter from Tamara and myself. I opened my parcels. In the first was a pullover which Tamara had knitted for me. Hugo gave me three bottles of his best home-made wine. 'Oh', I said, 'I have one more present – I nearly forgot.' With that I took a small box from my pocket and handed it to Tamara. She opened it. It was a diamond ring. She could not believe it. 'Carl, it can't be. Wherever did you get it?' I told her how I had come by the ring. One of my Polish workers had been in desperate need of some German money and had offered the ring for sale. I thought it was rather a lot of money but then, what could I do with money? So I bought it. He was happy and I was happy that I had such a fine Christmas present for my wife. Tamara put it on and it fitted. Then we started to celebrate.

The three days passed very quickly and leaving Tamara behind once again was hard. The now familiar feeling of depression that came over me every time I left her was with me once again, and I tried to think of happier times to come.

By mid-January 1945, the Russians had taken Warsaw and we began our preparations to move the Unit by rail to Dresden. As mine was by far the busiest section, Heinz decided that we should be the last to go. The trains were ordered to arrive at intervals of one week.

On the 10th of February 1945 we began loading the last train, and as night fell we were rolling out of the goods yard. Heinz, myself and one of the remaining sergeants had a coach to ourselves and we passed the time playing cards. Apparently there had been an accident on one of the lines, and this had resulted in a long detour for our train. Thus on the 12th February we were still a long way from Dresden. We calculated that it would be at least the 14th before we arrived at our destination.

About 11 pm on the night of the 13th we had settled down for the night and I must have fallen asleep when I was awakened suddenly by the screech of the brakes as the train was attempting to make what was obviously an emergency stop. We all three sprang to our feet, put on our boots and searched for our overcoats. When Heinz opened the door, it was as light as daytime outside and we saw dozens of lights floating down from the sky. The air was vibrating with the noise of aircraft overhead. Having been through a similar experience before, I shouted a warning to the others to run and take cover. Everyone jumped out of the train and started to run in all directions as bombs whistled through the air, exploding as they hit the ground.

At first the bombs seemed to be exploding farther away from us, but as more and more waves of aircraft flew over, they came much closer. The earth began to tremble beneath my feet as I ran in an attempt to find some escape from the increasing number of explosions. Suddenly I felt that my left foot was trapped in the railway line and I fell, forcing my foot out of the boot and leaving the boot itself behind. It was only afterwards that I realised that my foot had been caught at the junction between the lines. I tried to get up and run but I could not stand. I thought that I had broken my ankle. As I lay between the lines trying to find out what had happened to my ankle, I could hear the terrifying high-pitched whistle of a falling bomb, which I knew from the sound was close by. I rolled over in an automatic attempt to cover my face. I felt the ground beneath me shaking and objects were being hurled through the air.

When I opened my eyes, I could see a great fireball in the distance. Railway wagons were standing on end, silhouetted against the sky, as were many of the railway lines, which had twisted and lifted forming a bizarre abstract pattern around the silhouetted wagons. Standing directly over me was a stag, his big antlers looking like spooky shadows against the background of devastation. I could hear the sound of voices. People were shouting. I began to shout to attract attention. I tried once more to get up, but my left leg would not take my weight and I could feel that it was badly swollen. The sound of the shouting voices seemed to increase. I managed to find a piece of timber which I used as a crutch, and made my painful way towards the place from which the voices seemed to be coming.

Eventually a couple of my own men picked me up and gradually more and more of them joined us. We found our own train and as daylight broke we were able to establish that we had all survived. Some had suffered injuries, mainly from flying debris. Quite a number of men had fallen on the lines as I had done, but I had come off worse than the others. The Red Cross orderly assured me that the ankle bone was not broken; it was very badly sprained. We had been very lucky and owed a great debt of gratitude to the train driver who, realising how close we were to the goods yards of Dresden, had made his emergency stop and, as a result, had probably saved our lives. Both the railway station and the goods yard were badly damaged, and we heard that Dresden itself was almost completely destroyed. The few bombs which had fallen near to us were in fact off target, and I would have been far better off if I had stayed close to the train. I sent a couple of men out to search for my boot. It was not long before they found it just where I had left it, still wedged between the lines. It was around midday when we started unloading, after sending two dispatch riders to Headquarters with a report of what had happened to us and at the same time to request orders as to how we should now proceed.

It was, in fact, exactly 12 noon when we heard the sound of several sirens and shortly afterwards we saw wave after wave of aircraft again bombing Dresden.

Some hours later one dispatch rider arrived back with the most dreadful news. Our Headquarters had suffered heavy casualties, including our Adjutant. The staff living accommodation was completely destroyed. He told us that the city was like a ghost town with hundreds of people lying dead in the streets. He reported that he had seen trams still on the lines filled with people who were all dead. The other dispatch rider had been killed just yards in front of him during this second attack. The written order was to stay where we were and to report the following morning to the commanding officer in charge of clearing operations in the town.

I could see Heinz growing visibly paler and I knew that it was because of Freda. She had been living in the staff quarters. The dispatch rider went on to report that most of the camp had been destroyed. One of the administration buildings and a few garages were still partly standing but the living quarters had been reduced to rubble and every able-bodied person was digging for survivors. Many dead bodies were already piled up on the parade ground. I looked at Heinz and said that he should not assume the worst but should wait until tomorrow. I hoped to be in better shape by then and could look after the company whilst he went on to the camp to see what he could find out. I told the men of the unpleasant duty which had been given to us for to-morrow, searching the rubble for survivors. They already knew that the centre of the city had been almost totally destroyed. I reminded them that it was expected of everyone that he would do his duty to the utmost in this terrible situation. The duty could be for as long as one week. Camp leave would not be allowed. Everyone must take as much rest as possible when not on duty, as the strain of our task would be tremendous.

The next morning my foot was considerably better. Most of the swelling had gone and I could manage to stand on it. At least I was able to dispense with the crutches but I still felt the need of a walking stick. With the aid of this I found that I was able to limp about. We made our way into the town and the nearer we got the plainer the damage was to us. Bulldozers were working in an effort to clear the roads. We passed a large building block and saw that one half was broken away. A four-engined bomber was embedded in the top of the remaining half in such a way that the tail section was standing almost vertically up into the grey sky. A wing which had broken off was swaying in the wind. In the street below three trams were still standing on the tram line. The trams were full of people still sitting in their seats, but all were dead. Eventually we arrived at the Command Post to which we had been directed. Our journey through the city to this spot had revealed to us some gruesome sights. We had seen people digging desperately in the rubble and pulling out bodies. These could well have been members of their own families or friends or neighbours. It was possible to spare ourselves some of the tragic scenes at this time by simply closing our eyes or turning away. That was no longer possible once we were put into groups to perform this task ourselves, pulling out bodies or parts of bodies and lifting them on to vehicles. The bodies were then transported to a clearer area and heaped up. These were indeed pictures of horror which the eye could see but which the brain refused to register.

As the grim work went on, occasionally the rescuers would be rewarded by recovering people who were still alive, and this of course increased morale. Darkness had fallen as I assembled my men and when we returned to our camp site, I supervised the distribution of whatever extra tinned food had come to hand. Everyone was given a little brandy. It was not long before they had all disappeared into their tents, obviously physically and mentally exhausted. Heinz had returned from his trip to Headquarters. He looked haggard and grim. Freda had simply disappeared along with some 15 more civilian workers from Riga and 28 members of his Unit.

Heinz told me that the Headquarters was now to be set up somewhere in the country, and that the whole operation of the Eastern Defence was no longer functioning. Such personnel as remained had been ordered to Bavaria for re-grouping. Our Unit was to remain behind in Dresden for an indefinite period, to continue the task of clearing up the city. Heinz also said that the Russians had taken advantage of the situation by increasing their offensive on the Oder/Neisse line. It was thought that in the absence of a controlled air defence, a breakthrough would soon be possible.

'What can I do about my family?' he asked. 'What can I do about Tamara?' I replied. We decided to have a drink. I went for a bottle of brandy and we had first one drink and then another. Finally we must have been so exhausted that we fell asleep.

My leg was getting better and the limp was less pronounced. Heinz had to return to the Headquarters for further instructions and the rest of us started where we had left off the previous night. Some local teams had begun to identify bodies and those that had been identified were sprinkled with lime and chlorine in an attempt to prevent any epidemics from breaking out. The most mutilated bodies were covered in paraffin and burned.

It was the grimmest duty I ever had to perform.

CHAPTER SIXTEEN. WITHDRAWAL TO MARTHA'S FAMILY HOME

Back at the camp that night I had a talk with Heinz. He told me that the Headquarters were assembling for the move, which would take place in two days' time. Our orders were to remain where we were for another week or so and Heinz would remain with us.

'Well, Heinz,' I said, 'this is our chance.' I could see that he did not understand me. I explained that it was our chance to rescue his wife. If the Headquarters were on the move, no one was likely to be in touch with us for a little while. I could go off in a lorry with faked papers, showing that my journey was to deliver equipment to the Island. The same load could be brought back, shown on the log as equipment collected from the Island. The women could be shown as office staff. Together we worked out the distance and prepared the necessary documents. It was a calculated risk but I was prepared to take it. Heinz looked at me and said: 'And you will do that?'

'Of course, I will', I replied, 'I will take your wife and your mother-in-law to Hugo, and if it is too risky there I will bring them and Tamara to wherever we are. If we have to go down, Heinz, we may as well go down together.' We shook hands, had a drink, and went to sleep. The following day Heinz took over my job and I stayed in camp to prepare all the papers. It was a relief for me to stay behind, because although I was in a state of numbness as I worked in Dresden, I was glad of the opportunity of a brief respite from it. I kept my faithful batman behind with me. He was a very reliable man and we had decided that he should accompany me on the journey. I told him what was at stake but he did not mind. We loaded a three-ton wagon with some office equipment, some tinned food and a supply of fuel. I worked out the journey and meticulously planned each section of it, so that the most alert patrols would not be able to find fault with our papers. Heinz already knew that after our duty in Dresden was over, our Unit would be moved on to Chechoslovakia, and from there into Bavaria. He told me that he would leave messages in various railway stations so that I could find my way to him.

Two days later August, my batman, and myself set out for the Isle of Ruegen. After passing through three controls, and spending three nights in the way we had expected, we arrived on the Island. We soon found Heinz's home. The door was opened by his surprised wife Irma, who invited us in. Once I had been introduced to her and her mother, I explained the purpose and the urgency of my journey. We arranged that both ladies should pack necessities only, ready to leave with me the following day. Both they and Tamara, whom I hoped to pick up on the way back, would be shown as belonging to the Unit.

The next morning we set off at dawn and as soon as we arrived on the mainland, we ran into the first control, which we passed through without even showing our papers. The sergeant-major in charge accepted what I told him and we were allowed to proceed. We made a stop for re-fuelling and checking over our papers. After assuring ourselves that the ladies in the back were all right, we set off once again. At times we were quite close to the front and could hear the heavy artillery fire.

It was dark when we arrived at Hugo's place. Tamara was very surprised to see me and so was Hugo. I introduced the ladies, and as Tamara made coffee and sandwiches, I told her that I had come for her. I knew that Hugo could not come with us as he was a member of the Home Guard. To leave would have resulted in serious consequences for both him and me. We stayed overnight and in the morning we thanked Hugo and sadly said goodbye to him. By next evening we were back in our old camp near Dresden. As I expected, it was deserted. Heinz and the whole Unit had left but, as previously arranged, his series of messages began here. The Unit had left three days ago. My message was that we should travel in the direction of Bayreuth, leaving Dresden by the south exit, towards the Sudetenland. We had to use the minor roads to Karlsbad and Eger. The roads were very mountainous and the journey to Eger took us two days. By now we had come to know each other very well. We shared our food and our sleeping quarters, except that the batman, August, continued to sleep in the cab with extra blankets. The rest of us conserved heat by huddling close together. Tamara and Irma became good friends and Tamara told me that she liked her.

We continued our journey the following morning and were soon crossing the border into Franken. In order to get near to Bayreuth we had to use the main road, which was very busy. We found ourselves following an armoured unit when suddenly we saw two British planes, which seemed to appear from nowhere in front of us. They were opening fire as they flew directly at us. They split the column up and vehicles were exploding and moving in all directions. August, our driver, was very alert and although he hit a tree in the process, he got us off that road and into a wood. I knew that the planes would be back to attack the column again, so I jumped out, opened the back of the lorry, got the ladies out, and told them to run into the wood.

Sure enough, they were back, this time from the opposite direction, but some of the men from the armoured column were ready for them and, as the planes attacked the second time, the guns from the armoured vehicles opened fire. After this second attack a number of vehicles were left on fire. One enemy aircraft was hit as well and as a big smoke trail came from it, we saw it turn, spiral downwards and explode as it hit the ground. The other aircraft had disappeared.

The column commander must have presumed that it would not return as he ordered every man back into position and directed that the road should be cleared. Some of the vehicles were burning fiercely and a passing sergeant told me of the resulting casualties. He wanted to know whether any of us had been injured and whether we needed any help. As I did not want to reveal too much to him, I just told him that we had been lucky; that we had suffered damage to the vehicle but it was nothing that we could not fix ourselves.

The three ladies had gone quite deep into the wood and I told them to stay there until the armoured unit had gone. Then August and myself inspected the damage to our vehicle. The mudguard had penetrated one of the tyres on impact and the tyre had burst. We jacked the vehicle up and took the wheel off, but then realised that we did not possess the tools we needed to effect a repair. We needed a crowbar and a couple of heavy hammers so after a short conference with the ladies, I went back into a village, about two miles away, to get some tools.

It did not take long for me to find the village blacksmith. He was most reluctant to lend me the tools I requested, saying that they were no longer his but belonged to his son who was away in the Army. It was only when I offered to deposit 200 marks with him, to be returned when I brought the tools back, that he agreed to lend them to me. The money made him a bit more amiable and he asked me what had happened in the air attack that day. He went on to tell me what he had just heard on the radio, that Cologne had fallen to British and American troops. On my way back I wondered whether we would ever find Heinz. If Cologne had been taken, it meant that either the British or the Americans had crossed the Rhine, and to me that was the one remaining obstacle on which to pin our faith.

Back in the wood again, I told the others what I had heard and added that in view of this it was possible that Heinz had already left Bayreuth. I checked our food supplies and found that we had enough for a further two days at the most. By nightfall we had completed the repair to the vehicle.

The following morning we found that after a night of heavy rain we were, in fact, well and truly stuck. Despite all our efforts, we were unable to move. I picked up the tools and took them back to the blacksmith. After assuring himself that they were undamaged, he returned my money to me. I told him that we were bogged down and asked him if he could be of any help, since he surely knew all the farmers in the area. We needed two or three heavy horses to pull us out. I offered him some money but he just pushed it back into my hand, lifted his cap from its hook, took a walking stick and whistled for his dog. We were on our way. About twenty minutes later a farm gate opened and three heavy horses were led out by a boy of about sixteen dressed in the Hitler Youth uniform. He came up to me and saluted. I commented on the smartness of his uniform and the smartness of his salute. I asked him if he had put the uniform on particularly to do this job. He replied that he had, because the task he was about to perform amounted to military service and he would be required to fill in a form. It would be necessary for me to countersign it.

It was mid-afternoon before we got our vehicle back on to the road. The ground was still drenched from the previous night's downpour. We started off by first attaching our tow rope to the horses but as they pulled, the rope broke. Fortunately our Hitler Youth young man had brought a length of chain and although we were all splattered with mud, we were winning. Our helper filled out his form and I signed it.

We resumed our journey, but I decided not to use the main roads so as to avoid any further air attacks. This, however, meant that we would be travelling a very long way round to get to Bayreuth. The road was very hilly and winding, which inevitably slowed our progress. At nightfall we stopped once again at a spot in the woods about 15 miles from our destination.

The next day we reached Bayreuth by mid-morning and made for the station, which was our pre-arranged message point. Sure enough, the station-master had a letter for Irma and one for me. Irma's hands were shaking as I handed her the letter. She walked into the station and sat down, then quickly opened it. My letter contained instructions as to where we should go from here. Heinz had received orders to move everything south into the Alps but he did not know to which part. He advised me to use the minor roads near the Chechoslovakian border and said that he would leave a further message for me at the railway station in Cham. He had left four jerry cans of petrol and some oil for us and he hoped that the fuel would be enough for me to catch them up. I went straight to the stationmaster, and found that the fuel was indeed there.

Mentally praising Heinz, I now realized that our only remaining problem was food. Even though I had plenty of money, shopkeepers were reluctant to part with their stock as everyone sensed that food shortages would become very acute. We had just enough food for one more day; after that we would be entirely dependent on what farmers might be willing to sell to us as we passed through their villages. At this point Irma came out of the station smiling. She said that reading Heinz's letter had given her new hope and she felt so much better.

We set off in the direction of Bavaria. The road we were using was delightful from a scenic point of view, but that was all that could be described as good about it. It was mountainous and in a fairly poor state of repair. Before darkness fell we turned off that road into a little village in the hope of being able to buy some food there. By now it was very difficult indeed to obtain food, but we managed to get some milk and bread. We considered this a welcome change from the tinned food we had been using. From now on, as I realized with anxiety, I would be responsible for finding enough food to feed five of us. Of course, I could have driven into any camp or entered any town hall and obtained food or coupons under normal circumstances without any problem, but in the situation I was in, I wanted to avoid this as far as possible. It could have led to trouble. I sat down in the cab of the lorry and studied our position on a map. We were not all that far from Cham and there we would have further news from Heinz. From Cham there were only two roads out. One led to Straubing and the other to Regen, the town where Martha's mother and Ellie were living. My spirits lifted a little as I thought of Martha's mother living in Regen. I had her address and knew that she lived with her sister, who together with her husband owned a food shop. I called Tamara and asked her to sit down next to me. I pointed out to her our present position on the map and then pointed to Regen. Somewhat excitedly I said: 'Look, here is Regen and you know who lives in Regen?'

'Yes, of course,' she said, 'It's Ellie.'

We then discussed whether we should call there, and the possibility of getting some food made it strongly tempting. Tamara thought it was a good idea, but decided not to mention it to the others until we had received our further news from Heinz when we reached Cham.

Earlier than usual the next morning we left the little village and soon arrived in Cham. Just one letter was waiting for me saying that Heinz had left in a hurry. It gave his final destination as Reit Im Winkel and no further news. He added his regards to us all, and his signature. Everyone was relieved but where was Reit Im Winkel? I had never heard of such a place. I got my map out again and poured over it for a time before I found it. It was a little place in the German Alps, quite near to the Austrian border and a very long way from where we were. I made a quick calculation of my petrol and oil stocks and considered that they would be just about enough to get us there. I was not quite so confident about my stocks of log books and travelling documents, since these needed to be changed so frequently. Since the roads we would be travelling on would not have quite so many control points as some of the roads we had used before, I decided that in the event of our being stopped, I might get away with a story that we were lost. I could see that food would be the main problem. No one wanted to part with any even for black market prices.

I now told the whole party what I had already discussed with Tamara, that we would travel to Regen. I explained that although it would involve a detour at the expense of precious fuel supplies, there was a very good chance that we could obtain some food there. It was therefore to be a calculated risk. After some consideration, everyone agreed. We arrived in Regen in the early afternoon.

It was not difficult to find Martha's address and it turned out to be quite a large shop for so small a town, situated in the market place. I went into the shop alone, and the lady behind the counter asked me what I would like to buy. I told her who I was. On hearing this, she came from behind the counter and led me by the hand into the kitchen, where Martha's mother was ironing. When she saw me, she came straight to me, put her arms around me and started to cry. We sat down at the kitchen table holding hands and even I found it difficult to control my emotions. Eventually I told her that I had a problem. I explained that I had four more people outside in the vehicle. One of them was my wife, who had stayed with Hugo and had recently sent the parcels to Ellie. There was my boss's wife and her mother, and a driver. I told them that we had been on the road now for two weeks or so, and that we were running out of food. Although I had plenty of money, I had no coupons and I was looking for somewhere to buy food at black market prices. Our destination was Reit Im Winkel and the journey was expected to take another three days or so. Could she possibly assist?

She asked me to wait for a few minutes whilst she went into the shop. She returned with her sister and her brother-in-law. After the introductions, her sister said to me: 'Mr. Deckers, you are all our guests. We would like you to stay here to night. We have room for all of you. My sister will make you a meal, and meantime you are all welcome to have a bath. Bring your wagon into the yard and come in and make yourselves comfortable. When Ellie comes home from school, she will be delighted to meet you.'

I tried to say that I really could not impose upon them to that extent, but she simply waved my misgivings aside. Somewhat speechless at this welcome, I returned to tell the others the good news. We drove the wagon into the yard and Martha's mother let us in by the back door. The introductions were very touching, especially to Tamara, for it seemed as though these two had known each other for a very long time. Martha's mother was already preparing lunch, which would be ready for 2 pm, when Ellie would be back from school. Whilst we were out in the yard looking over our vehicle, I noticed a young girl of about 7 – 8 years old walking through the yard and into the house. Soon afterwards I was called inside to meet her. She was, as I had guessed, Hugo's daughter Ellie. Martha's mother took Ellie by the hand and said: 'Look, Ellie, this is Uncle Carl. I have told you so much about him. He has always written to us and when you were a little baby he came to see you and put some money into your tiny hand. We have saved it for you and it has grown quite a bit since then. At Christmas he sent you another 100 marks, which we also put in the bank for you. I think you would want to say thank you to him.' 'Thank you, Uncle Carl,' she said as I lifted her up and gave her a big kiss.

As we all sat round the big table for lunch, it was a happy occasion. Ellie wanted to sit between Tamara and myself, which pleased everyone. Irma and her mother had already had a bath and they looked very comfortable. There was an air of affluence about the home. It was spacious, elegant and comfortable, and looking at the delicious meal on the table, it was easy to forget for a while that there was a war on. August gazed at the plump leg of pork, the sauerkraut and dumplings on the table with a big grin on his face. Tamara and Ellie were chatting happily together and Martha's mother made it obvious that my presence was a joy to her personally, a welcome link with happier days in the past. These then were my impressions as we began to dig in to the lovely lunch, certainly, for the five of us, the best meal we had eaten in a long time and in the most comfortable surroundings.

The rest of the afternoon was spent in conversation and I knew that our host was most eager to hear news from the front. But because things were changing so very fast now, I was not able to give him an accurate picture.

It was 5 pm when we turned on the radio set to hear the news. The newsreader was saying how many enemy aircraft had been shot down and how many Russian attacks on the Eastern Front had been successfully defeated. Also that parts of the Western Front had been straightened for tactical reasons, to establish a new defence line in the Dortmund area. We looked at each other. 'Dortmund?' he said, 'What does that mean?'

'Well,' I said, 'to me it means that the whole Ruhr district has fallen into enemy hands. What does it mean to you?'

'Yes,' he said, 'you are right.'

'Forgive me', I said, 'but I do not know your political convictions. For myself, I have none. I am a soldier and committed to carrying out orders. As I interpret the news, it means that if the Ruhr has ceased to function, the heart of our war machine has stopped ticking. Nearly everything needed for fighting is made in that district. How long can we go on without tanks, without cannons and ammunition?' Just for a moment I thought of Lena-Marie and her father's factory in the area. He turned the radio off and said: 'Perhaps it is better not to listen to our news any more. They are all lies anyhow. I hope that the killing is soon over; so many innocent young people have lost their lives for nothing.' I said that I agreed with that completely.

The time passed quickly, and by early evening Tamara and I said that we would like to have a talk with Ellie's grandma. The three of us went into another room and as we sat together, I revealed to her all I knew of the secret love story between Martha and Hugo. So far as I knew, I was the only person who knew the whole story, but as I had given a solemn promise to Hugo, I had not been able to reveal it before to-day. I told her that Ellie's parents had truly loved each other, but the circumstances they found themselves in at that time had proved too difficult for them. Hugo's future had been planned for him with a girl chosen by his parents because of the material wealth of the girl's family. Hugo had never loved that girl. Then came the tragic death of Hugo's brother, and then Martha's death had followed soon afterwards. After Martha's death, Hugo had confided in me that he was Ellie's father. Since that time I had acted as the secret contact between Ellie and him, passing all the information I could get about Ellie back to him. It was only recently, when Tamara had come on the scene, that it had been discussed between the three of us. I told her of the Will that Hugo had made in Ellie's favour.

Martha's mother was crying and Tamara tried to comfort her. She told us between her tears how she had suffered at the time through cruel village gossip to the effect that Ellie's father had been a married man and how the gossip had eventually forced her to leave the area. She said that she now felt much happier and she was grateful to us for telling her and putting her mind at rest. We promised that we would write to Hugo and he would confirm this to her.

Martha's mother and her family insisted on giving us fresh food supplies, and would not accept any of the money I offered. When we left the following morning, it was with both gratitude and sadness. As I said goodbye to Martha's mother, I thought of the burdens which some people are given to carry in this world. She had lost her husband in the First World War, then she had lost her only child, Ellie's mother, whilst still little more than a teenager, leaving her with a tiny little baby to whom she had now devoted her life. I could see the strain these events had brought on her and my hope at our parting was that we had at least given her a little comfort.

CHAPTER SEVENTEEN.
SAVED FROM EXECUTION BY THE ARRIVAL OF THE AMERICANS.

Next day the rain had stopped and as we drove along, we marvelled at the scenery around us. The morning sun on the snow-covered peaks of the majestic Alps was a sight wonderful to behold and became more breathtaking with every mile. It was indeed hard to imagine that amid such beauty a war was raging all around us. We arrived in Reit Im Winkel in the late afternoon. As I entered the office, Heinz was overjoyed to see me. I told him that I had brought his wife, his mother-in-law and Tamara. He told me how deeply relieved he was to know they were safe. He had just heard that the Russians had breached the Oder/Neisse line and were now heading for Berlin. On hearing this, I too was filled with relief, because I knew now that if I had left them with Hugo they would by this time have been in grave danger. 'Well, I did the right thing then in bringing them here,' I said and we shook hands. He then said that he would drive his car and lead us to his quarters, a farmhouse about half a mile away. We arrived at the farm soon afterwards, where the long awaited reunion took place between Heinz and his family. We left them happily together and drove to my own quarters, another farm on the other side of the town. It was a beautiful place at the foot of a high mountain. I had been given an attic room, with a view from the window of the glorious mountain scenery.

For the next week nobody did very much. Heinz was waiting for new orders which failed to arrive. The quietness of the camp was almost frightening. We occupied the men as best as we could in maintenance work, but there was little that I could do. I made the most of the opportunity by taking long walks in the mountains with Tamara. We knew that the peacefulness would be of short duration, because the radio broadcasts informed us that British and American troops were slowly advancing southwards and eastwards from the Ruhr. The most distressing news came from the Russian front. They had advanced at an alarming rate, and had already reached the suburbs of Berlin. This meant that unless Hugo had already made a run for it, he would be at the least very uncomfortable, and at the worst a prisoner of war. For even if he had been captured dressed as he would have been in civilian clothes, he would still have been classified as military by the Russians, who refused to respect appearance in any way, except for age. Any able-bodied male who was of military age was, as far as they were concerned, military personnel.

Two days later Heinz attended a meeting and when he returned he was the bearer of bad news. We had orders to make yet another change in our position. We were to move further into the Alps to a place near Zell Am See. That was not too bad as far as I was concerned, but the order also said that only essential vehicles and weapons were to be taken with us and all remaining equipment was to be rendered useless. Furthermore, all female staff must be left behind. This was a terrible shock, as it meant that I was to be parted from Tamara. After the official meeting, Heinz called me back and said: 'That's it, Carl, Tamara has to stay here.'

'What about Irma and your mother-in-law?' I asked.

'They too will have to stay here,' he replied.

'You really don't mean that!' I exclaimed. 'After all the effort we made to get them as far as this, and now you are saying that you are prepared to leave them behind!'

'It is not what I want,' he said. 'It is an order which I have received. All Unit leaders have been warned that any breach of this will be severely punished.'

'How will anybody know?' I said. 'We will hide them again. I have brought them through the length of Germany undiscovered.'

'Carl,' he said, 'It is no good talking any more like that. I am ordering you now to leave Tamara here, and from now on it is Captain Klinker to you. Do you understand? To-morrow morning you are leaving to set up new quarters for the Unit around the Gross Glockner Strasse in the Austrian Alps. We will have to hand over all personnel vehicles to the SS to-morrow and you will be allocated a motor-cycle, which will be adequate for your task.'

After I had prepared my papers for the journey, I went back to my quarters and told Tamara what had happened. We sat down on the bed and tried to figure out what we should do. My own view was: 'Why should we part now?' The end of the war could not be far away. We had come so far together, so let us continue together to the end. Tamara said that if I wanted to risk it she was happy to go with me. We arranged that I would collect the motor cycle, a 750cc with sidecar, in the morning. She would get ready and start walking along the road towards Bad Reichenhall until I picked her up, as all the other roads were blocked by avalanches. I still had some blank papers, and I could simply add a name for her. I intended to find a room for us away from the Unit and I could not see why anyone should know that she was there.

The next morning I picked her up as planned and we were on our way, travelling deeper and deeper into the Alps. We bypassed Bad Reichenhall and ran into a road block just on the old Austrian border. The SS officer in charge was of Captain's rank and wore the Ritter Cross, a decoration which elevated a man regardless of his rank. He took my papers and examined them. He looked at the bike and said:

'What is the woman doing in the sidecar?'

I stood at attention and said: 'Sir, she is the wife of our Commanding Officer.'

'He should know that no women are allowed into the Alpen Fort,' he bellowed and shouted: 'Get that woman out', to some of his men.

Tamara got out and started walking away. One of the SS men winked at me and I took this to be a sign that he had told Tamara what to do. I started up my motor cycle and drove about half a mile, rounded the next bend and stopped. I must have waited a good half hour before I saw Tamara through a gap in the trees. I pulled the light cover from the headlamp and switched the light on, moving the bike so that the light was shining in her direction. She saw me and waved and it was not long before she was back in the sidecar and we were on our way again. I asked Tamara to slide down into the sidecar as far as she could so as to be less conspicuous. Then I put the cover over her. We arrived at Zell-Am-See without further difficulty. Here I had to find accommodation for the personnel and vehicles of the Unit but my first priority was to find a dwelling for Tamara and myself as far away from the Unit site as possible. We found an idyllic hillside farm where the farmers wife gave us a very nice room, normally occupied by her son, who was away in the Armed Forces. As always, the parents were greatly concerned about their son who was on the Eastern Front. I had three days in which to organise everything before the Unit arrived.

As Tamara made herself comfortable in our new home, I took the bike to try to find some food with the coupons I had.

The following morning I set out on my motorcycle to organise accommodation for the Unit when it should arrive. As I drove by, I noticed a group of men being drilled in military fashion. I could see that it was military training by the movements of the men, all of whom were armed. There was a bridge over the stream and I drove over it and joined them. As I drew closer, I saw that it was a group of Hitler Youth commanded by a young man in Hitler Youth uniform. He appeared to be quite a bit older than the others and his appearance was much smarter too. He was wearing Hitler Youth decorations which were unfamiliar to me. As I approached him, he stopped the training session, walked towards me and saluted. I commented that what he was doing looked like a full infantry drill and I wondered whether this was not too hard on the boys, some of whom looked very young. He was very serious and told me that his group now came under the direct command of an SS battalion, and would be put into active service to defend the Fatherland to the last man.

'Well', I said, 'You will not be alone here. My Unit is due to arrive to-morrow and it could well be that we shall be required to fight side by side.' I started up my bike, we saluted each other and I drove off.

On returning to our quarters, I found Tamara helping in the kitchen. Our landlady had suggested that if we pooled our food coupons we would all benefit by it and have better meals. We thought it was a good idea and readily agreed to it.

I told the farmer how I had crossed the big stream near the sports field that morning on my motor bike, seen the group of uniformed youngsters drilling there, and gone over to find out what they were doing.

'Oh, yes', said our host, 'that is our last reserve. Their leader is a son of a high ranking SS officer who is somewhere on the Western front. The son is as fanatical as his father and he is the only one in the district of his age not yet in the regular forces. But he is a big noise in the Hitler Youth and runs about in a car. He still believes that the war will be won. His family have no friends now.'

The following morning I set off on my motor cycle to finish my job. It was possible that Heinz would arrive in the afternoon. Just as I was leaving one of the farm houses I inspected, I heard aircraft noise coming from the direction of the sports field. The noise grew louder until I could see an aeroplane approaching the field from the open valley. I saw it make a turn at the far end and it looked as though it was intending to land. I jumped on my bike and rode to the sports field.

By the time I got there, the plane had landed. It was a monoplane of the Arado type, an open cockpit two-seater, a model I had not seen for a long time. I was familiar with this type of aircraft from my early days in Halberstadt, where they were used for training navigators. By the time I reached the plane, the pilot had climbed out of the cockpit. He walked towards me and saluted. He had the rank of lance-corporal and gave the impression of being newly qualified. He told me that he was a member of a team flying hastily converted Arados on a low-flying mission around Munich to harass the advancing American troops. He had been one of three such planes to-day on just such a mission. He asked if I knew that Hitler had committed suicide. I could hardly believe my ears. He went on to tell me that Hitler had shot himself and Eva Braun in the bunker in Berlin and that Berlin had fallen into Russian hands. But that was not the worst. The worst was that the SS had taken over, commanding our men to fight the enemy with their bare hands. Everyone who refused was being executed.

At this point our Hitler Youth leader returned with two men of his group. I told him that I was making him responsible for the safety of the aircraft. He promptly replied with words to the effect that my remarks were unwelcome as he had orders from higher authority.

I told the young pilot to get into the sidecar and drove him to my quarters. I took him straight into our room and introduced him to Tamara. I told him that Tamara was here illegally, and how concerned I now was at what he had told me about the SS being in charge. Jokingly I said to him:

'Come on then, you did not just land here because you ran out of fuel?'

'No', he replied, 'I was short of fuel but I was attempting to reach Switzerland. Then I realised that I would not make it. I had to fly round the Gross Glockner and the valleys I knew, into Switzerland, and I knew that it was too far for the fuel I had.'

'If I get you the fuel,' I said, 'will you take off and fly to Switzerland?'

'Yes, of course I will', he replied, 'but don't forget, if they find out that the fuel came from you, you will be in trouble.'

'No, no', I said, 'we will both come with you. If my Unit arrives this afternoon I can get you the fuel, but it is not aviation fuel.'

'It does not matter', he replied, 'whatever you can get'.

We arranged that to-night he should fill the aircraft up with fuel, and if the young guards should ask any questions, he should say that it might be necessary to move it for better camouflage. I enquired if the machine had a centrifugal starter and whether the starting handle was there. He assured me that it had everything. We arranged that I would start the engine up for him and that Tamara would appear at the very last minute. I would help her in and then climb in myself and sit on her lap. He would then run the whole length of the sports field, make a turn and take off. Up to the moment of turning, no one would suspect that we intended to take off. It would be at this point that we would need a bit of luck. We shook hands. I told him that he could have a room near the sports field and I would take him down there and then wait for my Unit to come in. As soon as I had the fuel, I would come for him. He said goodbye to Tamara and I could see how excited she was.

By mid-afternoon the first vehicles of my Unit began to arrive, led by my sergeant. He told me that before they left, the SS had sorted out fifty men for fighting but none of the drivers. Heinz would not be arriving until to-morrow as there was some difficulty. This was the official reason, but according to the sergeant he wanted an extra day with his family. They had brought some fuel but this supply was doubly precious because the supply depot had suffered an air attack whilst the driver was actually there. Fortunately, because fuel was stored in drums in various places round the depot, it had not all gone up in flames. As he spoke, I felt a sense of relief on two accounts: that Heinz would not be arriving until to-morrow, and that they had actually brought fuel with them.

Among one of the last group of vehicles to come in was August, my batman. I asked him to follow me and we drove to a farm yard. After the usual greetings, I asked him if he was carrying cans of fuel on board his vehicle. Yes, he had four full jerry cans of it. I asked him to put three of them into my sidecar as quickly as possible and to say nothing about it to anyone, which he did. I went at once to get the pilot and we drove to the plane.

As we approached, we could see the two Hitler Youth near the aircraft. We stopped and hid the tins of fuel in some bushes. We made a plan that I would distract the youth from the aircraft whilst he filled it up. As the pilot began an inspection of the plane, I started a conversation with the boys. Then I offered them a ride on my motor cycle. I took them to the far side of the field and kept their attention away from the aircraft. They were greatly enjoying the ride. Then I suggested that they walk back to the plane, because to stand around in the same spot all the time was not good for them. They must, at all times, be physically fit and the walking would be good exercise. I left them to walk and putting the throttle full in, raced over to the plane to collect the empty fuel tins. Once I had them safely in the sidecar, I drove away together with the pilot.

After dropping him off at his quarters, I returned to my sergeant, who in the meantime had conveyed my instructions to the others as to where the vehicles should be placed and where they should station themselves. I thanked the sergeant for what he had done, explaining my absence by saying that there had been other things which needed my attention at the far end of the field. As a token of my gratitude for his assistance, I was giving him the best of the accommodation and I handed him the necessary ticket to take it over. I added that I was rather tired and excused myself.

Of course, we did not sleep much that night. We talked for a long time about our plans and whether they could succeed. They had to succeed, because if we did not get out, Heinz, as already indicated, would have to report me. Report me to whom? The SS was now in command and that, I knew, would be the end of me. If Heinz did not report me, someone else surely would because of Tamara being here. Even if that did not happen, I would most likely be killed in the fighting, as we would be pushed into a position from which there could be no escape. Then Tamara would be left alone. We must try to get out with the pilot and if it went wrong, it would involve both of us. To this we both agreed. The aircraft was good enough to get us over. If necessary, I could fly it myself. The only difficulty was the lack of space in the cockpit. The sports field was long enough for take off. We would tell the two Hitler Youth boys who were still guarding the plane that we were taxiing it to the far end of the field for better camouflage. I explained to Tamara that this taxiing across the field would warm up the engine ready for take off. Once in Switzerland, we could land an aircraft of this type in any reasonably sized field. When we had considered all the circumstances, we came to the conclusion that we had little to lose and everything to gain if the attempt was successful.

The morning came and we got up as usual. Tamara got into the sidecar and I put the cover over her. I drove down to pick up the pilot and from there we drove to the plane. We explained to the two guards that we had to move it, giving the reason we had decided on. The pilot inspected the plane and got into the cockpit. He gave me the starting handle and with little effort the engine started. I indicated to the guards that they should move to the other side. I had to get them away from the side car so that I could get Tamara out without them seeing her. I got her into the aircraft and climbed in myself. We taxied to the other end of the field. As we were making the turn, we saw a Volkswagen coming towards us directly in our path making it impossible to take off. Our Hitler Youth leader jumped out of his car clutching a pistol, which was aimed at us. He was accompanied by a policeman and two more Hitler Youth members. We stopped the engine and the policeman told us to get out. I played cool and asked on what authority they were ordering us out. The Hitler Youth leader began to shout:

'You are under arrest! Out, or I will shoot!'

We were marched to the police station, where I just had time to give Tamara a kiss and say goodbye before the pilot and I were placed in separate cells. I did not know what they were doing about Tamara.

Everything was taken away from us and the Hitler Youth leader was obviously enjoying his important role in the incident. He said that he himself would send the report to the SS Headquarters in Innsbruck today and he hoped that we would get a 'fair' trial.

I sat in my cell wondering what had gone wrong. I could only think that perhaps one of the young guards had seen something yesterday when the plane was re-fuelled and had reported it to the leader.

In the afternoon my sergeant came to the police station and after lengthy persuasion was allowed to see me. I told him that it was better not to discuss the matter; nothing could be gained by him implicating himself. I asked him whether Heinz had arrived and he said that he had not. An avalanche between here and Zell-Am-See had blocked the only road. We were completely cut off by road and also all telephones were out of order. I asked him if he knew where Tamara was and he told me that they had allowed her to return to the farm. She had to report every morning and every evening to the police station.

For two days I was held in that police cell. By mid-morning on the third day, I could hear sounds of people walking about in the main part of the station. Eventually I heard the sound of foot-steps coming nearer and nearer to my cell. As they approached, I thought to myself: 'This is it. They have come for me.' I heard the sound of keys rattling and then a key turning in the lock. The door opened and in came a group of men. I could not believe my eyes. They were American soldiers. Then I saw Tamara force her way through them. She flung her arms around me and I held her tight. We were both crying. We had made it.

Three days later the war was over.

# PART V. THE AFTERMATH

CHAPTER EIGHTEEN.
LIFE IN AN AMERICAN P.O.W. CAMP

I was lying on my back in brilliant sunshine. There was just enough room for everyone to stretch himself. I did not know what day it was, only that it was my third day here in this vast Prisoner of War camp near Ingolstadt. The camp was so big that I could not even guess how many men were in it, for there must have been tens of thousands. Surprisingly enough, there was a certain amount of freedom there in that those of us who wished to be together were allowed to choose our companions and stay with them. There were no permanent buildings, and so far, all our activities had taken place under a cloudless sky. The canvas, which we used as a ground sheet during the day, also served as part of our tents by night.

Each time a newcomer joined our group, the tent expanded to accommodate him. The groups tended to be made up of men who shared mutual interests. One group would constitute music lovers and some of them, who had musical instruments such as mouth organs, were free to play them whenever they liked. Another group would be card players whilst yet another occupied the time by making toys out of empty food tins. When I had arrived at the camp myself, and seen the way the men had formed themselves, I had looked for a group wearing the blue uniform of the former Air Force. I was soon accepted into such a group and they received me with interest, particularly as I was a recent arrival and able to tell them the news from outside. They wanted to hear everything, especially how I had got into this camp. I told them how I had been arrested and kept in the police cell until I had been rescued by the Americans. I was questioned as to whether I had ever been a member of the National Socialist Party or a member of the SS or the Hitler Youth. As far as Tamara and I were concerned, we were told that we would be given transport to the nearest Transit Camp. Tamara was, for the time being, to return to our quarters but I must remain at the police station under POW conditions until the details I had provided were checked out. Tamara thanked the captain and asked him if she could come to visit me. He said that she could as the station would be manned 24 hours a day, but she would need to obtain permission for each visit. I said goodbye to Tamara and asked her to go at once to see my sergeant and ask him for my personal effects, as well as to try to get some food for herself. I asked her to wish him and the others all the best.

The American soldiers were very good to me. They gave me the same food as they had for themselves and allowed me out of the cell on request. Unfortunately, I spoke no English and they spoke no German. Two days later Tamara and I were put on a German troop carrier, which was escorted by an American jeep to Innsbruck. Our travelling companions were nearly all women from the Zell-am-See area who were being evacuated. On arrival in Innsbruck, we were taken to a school which was guarded by American soldiers. The women occupied one part of the school and the men were placed in a separate building. We were there for two days and then the whole lot of us were put on to five German Army lorries driven by former German soldiers and escorted by American soldiers driving jeeps. Four of the lorries were filled with women and the fifth one was filled with men, all ex-soldiers. Some of the men were Austrian and some had been born in Poland or the Ukraine. We all carried an envelope to be handed over on arrival at our new camp. After a long drive, the convoy stopped in the town of Ingolstadt, where all the women were ordered out of the vehicles. I could just see Tamara and waved to her. We drove on for a short while until we reached the enormous POW camp where I now found myself.

The sunshine was the best part of life in the camp; other things left much to be desired. The camp was sub-divided, each section having an independent water supply and basic toilet facilities, all very primitive. It was so large that I had no idea how many such sections there were. There were approximately 200 people using the facilities on the section where I was. Notices showing the times when food would be handed out to each section, together with the times when our section could use the washing facilities, were displayed on a blackboard. At these times I would take my place in the long queues which formed each time the services were offered. A small food parcel was handed out once a day. The information on the blackboard applied only to one particular section of the camp. Other information applying to everybody was relayed to us through one of the camp inmates, who came round the camp every day with whatever information there was for us. Before he read the notices out, he would blow a trumpet to attract our attention.

One day as I was lying in the sun with my private thoughts, I heard the trumpet in the distance. As it drew nearer, I could hear the messenger reading out various names but he was still too far away for me to hear properly. As he came nearer, I heard him shout: 'Sergeant-Major Deckers from the Air Force, report to the office.' I could not believe it. That was me. I hurriedly put on my clothes and ran to the office as fast as I could. As I entered I could see Tamara in the room. There was a desk to the left of us with an American officer sitting behind it. He pointed out that if my statement was correct, and I was not listed as being wanted for war crimes, I would be released very quickly, provided I was able to give them an address in the American sector. He asked me if I was able to supply such an address. I told him that I could. He gave me a pen and paper and I wrote out the address of Martha's mother. The officer looked at Tamara and said 'O.K.' She answered in English, thanking him for all the help he had given and the time he had taken to see her. I was astonished to hear how much English she could speak. I stood to attention and then I went over and kissed her again. She quickly said to me: 'To-morrow lunchtime at the fence on the office side.' A little later, as I was leaving the office by the back door, I could see her walking towards the main gate. She looked round and gestured to the left. I knew that she was pointing out the spot where she would try to see me the following day.

The next day around lunchtime I made my way to the fence. I could see that Tamara was already there. She was talking to a coloured American Guard. I asked her how I could locate her if I happened to be released suddenly. She promised to give me that information when she came to see me the following day.

Four more days went by and the spell of sunny weather we were having made the situation more bearable. Each day at lunchtime I went to the fence to see Tamara. There were different guards on duty each time and some, less sympathetic to us, would not allow us to get near enough together to be able to talk without shouting. It was not easy to hear everything she wanted to say to me, but over a period of two or three days of talking under these conditions I managed to find out that her papers had been examined and she was able to move about freely. She was living, together with some other girls, in premises which had previously been used as a cafe.

The living conditions in the camp became more uncomfortable each day and particularly by night, when we were pestered by lice. Every day when the trumpeter came round, I jumped up to listen to what he was shouting and as he drew nearer I was able to make out the names he was calling. Then one day, sure enough, my own name was amongst those he called out. We all had to report to the office.

I tidied myself up as well as I could and joined the others, about thirty of us altogether, queuing outside the office. After a while an American officer came out carrying a clip-board from which he called out names in alphabetical order. As each name was read out, we went into the office. Luckily I had not long to wait. There were a number of soldiers inside handling the records of each of us. As the details were read out, we were required to state whether the information was correct. Finally we were fingerprinted and were told that we would be released at 10 am the following morning.

That night I could not sleep. I put on all the clothing I possessed and sat outside the tent with my overcoat around my shoulders, looking at the stars and thinking of Tamara. I pondered on what would be the best course of action. Being unsure of the actual time of my release, I decided that I would wait until she came on her usual lunchtime visit. To-morrow I would be free – free to begin a new life with Tamara! I knew that it was not going to be easy to start a life together with nothing, but at least we had survived.

It was time to roll my belongings into my piece of canvas and say my goodbyes. As I walked towards the main gates, in spite of my happiness, I could not help feeling somewhat guilty in obtaining my release from the camp in just over a week. Those of us who were leaving that day lined up outside the office. We were still wearing our uniforms but all medals and insignia of rank had been removed. Just after 10 am an officer came out with an interpreter and a soldier. The officer told us that all our papers had been checked and found to be in order. He went on to say that it was his duty to inform us that we had now reverted to civilian status and had no further allegiance to any Military Authority. He wished us luck before he disappeared again into the office. The remaining soldier called us in turn by name and handed to us the new papers, which gave details of our change of status. The large gate swung open and we walked out into a free world. I walked up and down the street to pass the time as I knew that Tamara was not likely to arrive for another hour. She would be surprised, I felt sure, to see me outside in the street, a free man.

CHAPTER NINETEEN.
A BOAT FOR A PAIR OF BOOTS

Tamara saw me from some distance away and we both ran until we fell into each others arms. 'I knew that you would soon be out of there', she said. 'Don't ask me how I knew, I just knew. Come, let's go to my accommodation and collect our things.' So we walked along the street together and as we walked we discussed what to do next. Our first priority was to find Mum, Dad and Alfred. We knew by now that the Russians had occupied all the area east of the River Elbe. The last we had heard of the family was that they were in Magdeburg. Since the River Elbe flows through that town, we did not know whether they would be in the Russian or the American Sector. We also knew that Dad would not voluntarily stay in the Russian Sector, so we thought it most likely that they would be in the American Sector. Unfortunately, this was a very long way from where we were now. It was quite impossible for us to hope to get there in our present circumstances. We had no food, no civilian transport, and no prospect of any for some time to come. We did not know anyone in this part of Germany except Martha's mother, who lived in Regen, and this was also a fair distance from where we were. I estimated that it would take us between 10-14 days to walk there. As we could not stay where we were in any case, it seemed the logical thing to do. Tamara surprised me by producing one of my old Air Force kitbags. There were items of clothing packed in it belonging to both of us. Apparently, my sergeant had given the kitbag to her whilst I had been detained in the police cells at Zell-am-See. The bag also contained some tinned food, which she had kept, together with bread she had saved from her daily allocation of food from the American Authorities. All was packed into the kitbag and after we had said goodbye to the girls, we were on our way. We had no map or other aid to direction, but I knew that Regen was roughly en route to Regensburg, so we made our way towards Regensburg.

We had walked only a couple of miles when it began to get dark. We decided to try the next village to see if we could get a roof over our heads for the night. We knew it would be difficult as we were not the only people moving on the roads. In fact, people were walking in all directions. Some of them were easily identifiable as ex-servicemen by the parts of uniform clothing they wore. A large number of people who had been freed from forced labour camps were also on the move. The ones walking in a westerly direction were mostly French and those heading east were mainly Polish and Ukrainian. Every so often we saw people dressed in striped clothing and we knew that they were former inmates of the concentration camps who were going home.

We knocked on several doors in the next village before one was opened by an elderly gentleman who, before I had time to speak, said: 'No, no, we have no room and we have no food to spare.' I tried to keep the conversation going and asked him if he thought that things would be better in the next village. He replied that he did not think so, that people were very frightened. They thought that if they let anyone into their homes they would take over and rob them. He went on to tell us of instances of former SS men breaking into homes during the night and taking whatever they needed. He said they only moved at night and would do anything to survive. These men were well aware that they were wanted by the American Military Authorities and as they had their blood group tattooed under their arm, they were easily identifiable. Hence the reason for moving only by night. They were known to move through the forests robbing houses on the way in an attempt to reach France and the safety of the Foreign Legion. The old man closed the door and we heard him lock it. Tamara had heard what the man said and I remarked to her that things were perhaps more difficult than we had anticipated.

The best thing we could do, I suggested, was, to look for a haystack and try to sleep. Sleeping rough was not a new experience for Tamara, and certainly not for me. The important thing was that we were together and free, and for that we were extremely thankful. It was the right time of year, just after the first hay making, and a haystack in that part of the country consisted of a crude wooden tripod frame on which the hay was hung to dry and aerate. The structure, in fact, with its hollow centre, was rather like a tent. It was delightfully warm and sheltered from the winds. Fortunately, neither of us suffered from hay fever, and we found our chosen haystack a very suitable place to sleep. The only ill effect we suffered was being bitten by insects. Again, this was not a new experience for either of us.

We woke to another beautiful morning and after eating a little of our food, we set off once again. For the first couple of hours the walking was reasonably comfortable, I carried the kitbag and Tamara carried our overcoats, but as the sun climbed higher into the blue sky, it began to feel hotter and walking became uncomfortable. We decided that when we reached the next village, we would have a rest. We sat down on a bench on the village green. It was right on the River Danube and as we sat there, my mind occupied by our journey, I realized that the river was flowing in the direction of our destination. From where we were sitting we could actually see the water's edge. The water level appeared to be rather high. I pointed out to Tamara that the river we could see was, in fact, the Danube and if we could get a boat, it would take us downstream to our destination.

'That would be lovely!' Tamara sighed and suggested that we might be able to find a boat by some means. She seemed very keen on the idea. She thought it would be very pleasant to sit in a boat in this lovely weather instead of walking in the heat. We assessed our financial situation. Tamara still had all the money I had given her in Zell-am-See. She had not spent any of it, but I told her that I did not think that it would be of much use to us. If we had things to exchange, people might be more interested in supplying what we needed. Unfortunately, however, we had very little in the way of worldly goods.

Then I saw a group of boys at the other end of the green playing a ball game, similar to football. I asked whether anyone in the village owned a boat. They told me that a number of local people owned boats, which they used for fishing. I asked if they knew of anyone who had a boat for sale. They said that they did not think that anyone would sell a boat but told me of a local farmer who had salvaged a section of a German pontoon which had got stuck on a bend of the river on his land. The boys suggested that the farmer concerned might be willing to sell that or even give it away.

I went into the farmyard and spoke to a man who was just coming out of the stable. I asked if I could fill my empty milk bottle with fresh water. He directed me to a hand-operated water pump in an outbuilding, where I could help myself. 'Excuse me', I said, 'are you the owner by any chance?' 'Yes', he said, 'I am'. I told him what I had heard in the village about the German pontoon and asked him if he would consider selling it, or perhaps, exchanging it. He looked at me and asked what I had to exchange. I told him that I had not got much. I also pointed out that since the pontoon was not his property, he might not be allowed to keep it anyway. I did have a pair of new boots if he was interested in them. He asked to see them and he also demanded an assurance that our transaction would be kept secret from village people. 'Fine', I said. I explained that I had left my wife sitting on the village green with our rucksack which contained the boots.

On returning to the green, I saw that Tamara had company. Two men were sitting with her on the bench. 'I see you are in good hands', I said, 'just give me the rucksack, I may have secured some sort of transport.' The farmer took the boots, which he scarcely looked at before throwing them into a corner of the farmyard, at the same time telling me that I could do as I liked with the pontoon. He showed me how to get into his garden, which bordered the river. There, at the water's edge was the pontoon which, he said, was pretty heavy. I asked if I could examine it. It was larger than I had expected and I had my doubts as to whether we would be able to get it back into the river. There were fairly heavy ropes attached to each end, and inside were a number of wooden boards and planks.

Hoping that the two men were still sitting with Tamara on the bench, I went back to her. The men were still there. I told them that I had just acquired a pontoon section which had belonged to the German Army and had been washed from the foreshore into the farmer's garden. I asked if the two men would be willing to help us launch it. They readily agreed to help and the eldest of the two said: 'You are surely not going to attempt to travel upstream, as that would be impossible.' He went on to say that they were heading in the direction of Austria and asked me if there was any possibility of them getting a lift with us. They were both Polish, heading for home. Both had been working in a laboratory for the German chemical industry. He added that this work had not been voluntary. I told them that they were both most welcome and we made our way to the boat.

The pontoon was very difficult to launch and if it had not been for the wooden planks inside the craft, we would never have managed the task. We used the planks to get it into the water, and eventually we coped with it. We all jumped on board. The current was very strong and at first the pontoon moved round and round in circles. I corrected this by fastening a plank on one end which I used as a rudder.

Tamara enjoyed it tremendously. The sun shone down on us out of the cloudless sky and we removed as much of our clothing as we could. Whilst the other three became involved in conversation, I volunteered to do the steering. It was not as easy to control the pontoon as it probably looked; the fact that we were travelling with the stream made the rudder action very limited. Because of this, it took us at least one mile to travel from one side of the river to the other. One of our companions had a map, which was a great advantage, and we calculated that, with luck, we could go through Regensburg and Straubing to Deggendorf. From there it was only about thirty miles or so to Regen, a distance which we could easily walk. Our Polish friends would travel with us to the same destination, and would then make their way through Czechoslovakia to Poland.

We stopped for the night at an isolated farm, hoping that the farmer would not be overrun with travellers, as would certainly have been the case on the main roads. I was just able to steer the pontoon to the bank and the younger of our two companions jumped out. The other one threw the rope to the younger man, who quickly secured it around a tree. After that exercise we were quite proud of ourselves, and considered ourselves to be reasonably competent in sailing. We secured the pontoon at both ends against the extremely strong current which, we were told, was the result of the very warm weather melting the snow in the Alps. As a result, some areas had actually suffered flooding and the water of the river was running much faster than usual. We decided that it would be a good idea for me to go to the farmhouse alone, as a group of us could have caused alarm. My knock on the door was answered by a middle-aged woman. I asked her if we could stay overnight in a barn. She invited me into the house.

She said that she would speak to her husband, who was in the stable milking the cows. As I waited for her to return, I was comparing the difference in the people I had approached in the area. Some of them, not too far away from here, had been unwilling even to speak to strangers and yet this lady had invited me into her home. When she returned, she asked how many of us there were. She said that she would boil some potatoes and give us some home-made cottage cheese and cabbage. She went on to say that we could use the tack room next to the stables. There were a table and chairs in there, and even a water pump and a wash-basin which we were welcome to use. I was overjoyed but that was not all. The lady went on to say that in the morning she would provide bread and milk. When I asked her how much all this would cost, she waved both hands and said that we were the first people to find their farm and whilst they could not do it every day, they really wanted to help. I expressed gratitude on behalf of us all and said that I was sure that my wife would be more than happy to help her.

I went back to the pontoon and they were all delighted to hear my news. We all enjoyed the simple, hot meal. It was such a change. It was not long before we were all in the barn for a good night's sleep. Tamara and I did not even notice that, once again, we had been attacked by the biting insects. It had not woken us through the night, only the visual marks, together with a slight itching, reminded us of what had taken place. We said goodbye to the good farmer and his wife, who, in addition to all they had done for us, gave us a full loaf of bread and a bottle of milk for our journey. We stood and watched as Tamara embraced the farmer's wife and promised to write when existence returned to something like normal for us. We were off once again. As we sat in the pontoon, we were all making guesses as to the distance we could eventually cover. We came to the conclusion that we were travelling at the rate of three to four miles an hour. If the river ran in a straight line, we guessed, we would cover about fifteen miles an hour, but at the numerous bends in its course the water circled round, taking the pontoon with it. We found ourselves just going round in circles, sometimes being brought to a complete halt.

As we rounded one of the many bends, we saw a bridge ahead of us. It had obviously been destroyed by the retreating German troops.

As we drew nearer to it, we could see that most of the structure was lying on the river bed. We could see as well the power of the river currents as the water splashed high into the air in a white fury on impact with the metal structure of the bridge. I saw a gap in the middle and thought that this would be the best place to take the pontoon through. As we drew nearer and nearer, I could feel it gathering momentum until there was no stopping it. I knew that we had to go forward. As we reached the bridge, the pontoon dived into the racing water and out again. Sensing the danger, we all gripped frantically at the ropes and held on. It was a very frightening experience and we were soaking wet but we were through. Alas, it was only to find ourselves confronted by another obstacle.

This time it was a pontoon bridge which had been built by the American troops to replace the original one. As we bore down upon it we could see armed soldiers on the river bank around the bridge. Shortly afterwards one of them began to walk along the banks towards us, indicating that we should pull over to his side and stop. I just about managed to do that, whereupon we were asked to step on land and show our papers. These they took into a small hut. After a while the soldiers emerged again and began to ask questions in English which only Tamara could answer. They wanted to know at which university in Poland the professor taught, and what the doctor did in Poland. Of course, these were our companions. The officer in charge told us to stay where we were for a moment. A few minutes later a big crane wagon appeared. It picked up our pontoon and deposited it on the other side of the bridge. We jumped in and continued our journey, which would otherwise have been very difficult.

Tamara then expressed pleasure and surprise at having such distinguished companions, as we had previously been completely unaware of their status. They both laughed and said it made no difference at all, they were both enjoying our company. Our stop that night was very different from the night before. There was no welcoming farmhouse or hot meal. All we could find were some haystacks. However, we did not mind as the weather was so warm. By now we were all four sporting a healthy-looking tan. We had a meal together of the milk and bread from the farmer's wife and Tamara opened a tin of meat which she had saved from Zell-am-See. After the meal we had a walk and then the two Polish travellers disappeared into one haystack and we into another. I was very happy to be alone at last with Tamara.

The next day we set out once again and found ourselves passing through conditions very similar to those of the previous day, except that the river was wider now. When we reached the place where a second bridge had fallen into the water, the gap through which we had to pass seemed to be wider and less daunting. Also we did not feel the pontoon dip as it had done previously. Therefore we approached it in a happier frame of mind and passed through it safely. As we floated through, we could see that once again a pontoon bridge had been built to take the place of the one which had been destroyed. Again we were signalled to stop when we reached it by the American soldiers. We went through the same procedure, producing our papers for examination, but this time we felt that the sergeant who performed this duty was not surprised to see us. We formed the impression that the previous Military personnel had radioed ahead. The sergeant was very friendly and offered us coffee. On hearing the word 'coffee', Tamara exclaimed: 'Coffee, real coffee?' 'Yes', he said, 'Would you like some?' Whilst the soldiers were lifting our pontoon from one side of the improvised bridge to the other, we were sitting on the grass drinking coffee and eating cookies. The cookies which were left in the packet after our refreshment break was over were handed to us together with two packets of cigarettes.

After we had started our journey once more, we all felt that the hospitality the soldiers had extended to us was all the more remarkable in view of the fact that the whole company were negroes. Towards the close of day we began to look around for a suitable place to spend the night. There was no sign of any buildings, so we settled for a most pleasant spot in an area where a group of Christmas trees was growing. The trees were 6-8 feet high, and were very densely grouped. After we had eaten our evening meal, we crept into the thickest part of the growth and settled down to sleep, using my canvas and our overcoats as an improvised bed. We clung very close together to conserve heat. So close, in fact, that if one turned during sleep, the other had to turn too. We knew that we were not far from Regensburg and the following day we decided to make a stop there, if only briefly, to try and find some food. We knew that it would have been quite hopeless to find accommodation in that town, due to the heavy bombing it had suffered. But perhaps a soup kitchen would have been set up somewhere. We decided to try.

As we continued our journey, we noticed a gradual change in the landscape; we could no longer see trees and fields. Houses appeared, and as we rounded a large bend in the river, we saw in the distance yet another destroyed bridge in the water. This one appeared to be much larger than the two previous ones we had managed to negotiate. We could see that a large part of the structure was protruding from the water. There were two possible places to pass through, one in the centre and one to the right. We conferred together as to which of the openings we should attempt. Both looked forbidding, which caused us to consider attempting neither and stopping the craft on the bank. We decided against stopping, as it would have meant a long walk into Regensburg. So we had to make a decision about the two possible openings. The presence of this massive structure in the water had created a terrifying swell, and this appeared to be somewhat less violent at the opening to the right. We had previously passed through two similar structures and had been lucky. So why should we not be lucky again?

I steered the pontoon over to the right and felt the acceleration almost carrying us through. Indeed it would have done so had not the pontoon hit a submerged part of the structure. The impact catapulted the rear end right out of the water and threw all four of us into the swirling current. I felt myself being sucked down by the power of it and carried round in circles. With all the physical strength I could muster, I tried to force myself upwards. I had been underwater and unable to breathe. I managed to get my head above water but found myself being carried by the current towards the centre of the river. Being a strong swimmer, and wearing only trousers and a shirt, I managed to struggle to the bank about half a mile down stream. I clawed my way up the bank on to the footpath and started running back towards the bridge, where a large number of people were gathering. I heard the sound of a car stopping abruptly behind me. I looked round and saw two or three soldiers in a jeep jumping out. They were shouting something but I did not understand what it was.

Believing that it was not directed at me, I carried on running. The jeep followed and overtook me. The driver jumped out and blocked my way. In the meantime the other two had caught up and taken hold of me. All I could do was to point to the bridge and say: 'My wife, my wife!'. I could not understand one word but they kept repeating: 'Documents'. Now at last I realized that they were demanding to see my papers. It was only then that I realized where my papers were. I always kept them in an inside jacket pocket, which was secured by a safety pin. The jacket was in the pontoon and the pontoon was in the river. I tried to explain this to the soldiers, but they indicated that I should take off my shirt. This was difficult as it was soaking wet, but I managed to get it off. The soldiers made a careful inspection of my armpits, and I knew what they were looking for, the giveaway tattoo carried by all SS personnel showing their individual blood group. They had obviously thought that I was an SS man on the run. One of them pointed to the large scar on my back, which was still very visible after the appalling injuries I had suffered in Berlin. All three of them examined the scar, and whilst they were doing this I remembered that I had, in fact, transferred my documents from my jacket to my trousers pocket and had secured them with the same safety pin. I shouted an international word: 'Moment', and indicated to them my back pocket. I opened it and pulled out the leather wallet, which astonishingly was not even wet. It must have been the only thing on my body that was not. The soldiers examined my papers thoroughly before handing them to the sergeant. He then apologised to me, all three jumped into the jeep and drove away. I quickly put the papers back into the wallet and ran to the bridge as fast as I could. My only thought was 'Tamara, Tamara, is she all right?' Then I saw her sitting on the concrete embankment. There was a group of people standing round her. I could see that she was extremely distressed, holding her head in her hands as she cried. 'Tamara!' I shouted. She looked up and catching sight of me ran to me, and we hugged one another again and again.

When we eventually turned our eyes from each other, we saw that all the people had disappeared except for our two travelling companions. 'Thank goodness you are safe,' I said. 'We were all worried about you,' they replied. 'You just disappeared from the back of the pontoon. There was nothing for you to hold on to and you must have been catapulted out into the turbulence. We were hanging on to the ropes and fortunately the pontoon was wedged into the structure just long enough for us to be rescued.'

We had been lucky to escape with our lives, as we heard later that a ferry boat which had tried to negotiate the centre opening had capsized. Whilst some had been rescued, twenty-seven people had drowned. Meanwhile our pontoon broke loose and we watched helplessly as it drifted downstream away from us. I told them what had happened to me after I had scrambled up the bank. How the soldiers had detained me and demanded to see my papers. It was only now that I fully appreciated the significance of the transfer of my papers from my jacket to my trousers. It had been sheer chance, and it was by that same chance that I was not once more in a POW camp.

The two Polish men looked at each other and asked each other the same question: 'Have you got your papers?' Sadly, both had to give the same answer: their papers had been in their luggage, which was at that moment floating down the Danube. We made our farewells on the bank and wished each other good luck. They gallantly kissed Tamara's hand and then set off to walk downstream. We never saw them again. 'Look, what about your papers?' I said to Tamara. 'Yes, I checked and they are there', she replied. I knew, that she kept them in her bra. We examined them and, just as I had expected, they were quite wet. Fortunately, it was a good summer's day, and we spread them out on the river bank to dry in the heat of the midday sun. They soon dried, but were of course considerably stained by the water.

CHAPTER TWENTY. THE PRICE OF A DOG

We sat on the river bank and considered our position. The few possessions we had were now gone. Apart from her underwear, Tamara was wearing a pair of trousers, a blouse, and a pair of shoes. She still had her wedding ring, a bracelet and her diamond ring. Apart from my underwear, I wore a pair of trousers, a shirt and a pair of shoes. I also had my wedding ring. In my pocket I had a handkerchief and two hundred marks, which might buy us a little bread – perhaps not even that.

'Look, Tamara, lets just forget what we have lost. Let's just think that we are still very rich.'

'Yes,' she said, 'you are right. We have got each other.'

'And more than that, Tamara. Just look at the seagull there in the air. It has nothing but its life and it seems to be happy. Come, let's go, we will make it. If our story should ever be told, we will start it from here in Regensburg, where at the end of May 1945 we started life again.'

There was no point in trying to buy anything; all the shops were closed and in any case we had no coupons. So, we decided to make our way to the Town Hall to see whether we could get either coupons or food. There was a long queue at the Town Hall, and when we eventually managed to see anyone, we were told that as we were not registered, they could not let us have either coupons or food. They went on to say that there was an acute shortage of accommodation in the town, and advised us to try the convent a few miles away, where the nuns would probably put us up for the night. The convent was on the way to Regen and so it appeared that we had nothing to lose by calling there.

It was late in the day when we arrived at the large wooden gate and

I pulled the bell cord. Shortly afterwards a small window in the gate opened and a face, which was barely visible, asked us what we wanted. We made our request and were told to wait. Shortly afterwards the gate opened and we were invited in. Two nuns greeted us. One of them said that we could stay the night but would have to sleep in separate small rooms. We would be required to attend prayers that evening and also the next morning. We would be provided with soup for the evening meal and bread and a hot drink in the morning. Then we were shown to our rooms before going into the chapel for the evening prayers, which were signalled by a bell. There was a number of other people in the chapel, refugees like ourselves – about a dozen or so. At the end of the service we were all escorted by the nuns to a dining hall, where they served us hot soup.

We then returned to our rooms. As I lay on the hard bench which served as a bed in that tiny room, I felt somewhat guilty at the comparison arising in my mind with the police cell at Zell-am-See. I marvelled at the harsh conditions the nuns accepted as their lot in life. I had no idea before coming here how they actually lived, but I felt the strongest admiration for them. In common with Tamara and me, they possessed none of this world's goods, yet they were contented and even shared the little they had.

Next morning at the sound of the bell we joined them again for morning prayers, after which came the promised breakfast of bread and a hot drink. The nuns were very early risers, and by 8 am we were on our way. As we had nothing to carry, we made good progress.

By lunchtime we had arrived at a village some ten miles or so from the convent. Realizing that we had no alternative but to knock on doors and beg for bread, and wanting to spare Tamara the humiliation of this, I left her for a while. After many refusals, I eventually reached the house of a kindly woman, who gave me half of the bread she had. Not only that, but in response to my request for a paper bag to carry it in, she provided me with a small cardboard box and a piece of string. The string was long enough to secure the carton from opening. I made two holes in the box and threaded the string through in such a way that I could hang the box around my neck. I went in search of Tamara feeling rich indeed, for we now had something once again. We had bread, the staff of life. We continued walking for several more miles and eventually reached a very pleasant spot by a small stream. We sat down by the stream and Tamara broke the bread in half. One half was to be our meal, the other was carefully replaced in the box. My training in survival techniques once more came to the fore and I automatically looked around to see what I could find to eat with our bread. There was a plentiful supply of watercress in the stream. I gathered some and washed it before I returned to Tamara, who was unaware that it was edible. I explained to her that this green plant, which she was regarding with distrust, contained the very vitamins, trace elements and iron in which we were deficient at this time. Although she did not find it palatable, she accepted what I told her and placed some in the bread for us both to eat.

Towards evening we found ourselves in another village on the edge of a forest. After walking all day, we were hot and tired. We found a farmer willing to allow us to spend the night in his barn. I asked him if he could spare us a little food. He went back into the house and reappeared with two slices of bread covered in pork dripping and salt. It was delicious. The farmer advised us to be very careful in the forest. It was known locally that SS men moved through by night and that they had formulated a system of communication by marking trees, indicating such things as the location of road controls and how to avoid them on their desperate journey to France. He went on to tell us that the activities of these SS men had necessitated the formation of vigilance groups of local people, who protected their own property by night. Otherwise, most of their possessions, normally left outside, would have been stolen. On hearing this, we realized that we had something very valuable, namely my papers. I knew that if challenged by one of these desperate men, it would be of little use to say I had none. They would not take my word for it that I had no papers. For any SS man on the run, to acquire a set of papers would be like finding gold. We could not think of a safer place to hide them than in Tamara's bra. We looked around the barn for the best spot to sleep and the many indentations in the hay told us that we were not the first guests to sleep there.

The next morning we set out again and had not gone very far when a United States Army column overtook us. The vehicles were carrying American troops, who were singing cheerfully. We waved to them and as the last vehicle passed, some kind soul must have sensed our need, for he threw two bars of chocolate into the road. What a blessing! For lunch that day we had the rest of our bread and one small bar of chocolate each.

That night we found yet another farmer willing to help us, and we were shown to a kind of room adjoining his horse stables. It contained a bed. We were told that this was where the horseman used to sleep. The bed was no longer used; he had not returned from the war. Gratefully we ate the hot potatoes and drank the glass of milk given to each of us before settling down for the night in the unexpected luxury of a bed. In the middle of the night I woke up feeling rather uncomfortable. I was being attacked by biting bugs. They were not the ones I had experienced before, this time they had attacked the area around my private parts. Tamara woke up and said that she had been bitten as well.

We left the village the following morning and had not gone very far when Tamara drew my attention to a dog which was following us. I looked round and saw that it was similar to an Alsatian. We did not worry too much about the dog at first, thinking that it would eventually leave us and return home. By this time our food supply, like ourselves, was exhausted. We found a place just off the road where we sat down to rest. I looked behind to see whether there was any sign of the dog. It was not far away from us, lying in the grass and seeming to be watching us. We watched with interest as it gradually crept towards us, finally arriving at our feet, looking at us and wagging its tail. 'We have nothing to eat', I remarked to Tamara, 'and now we have got a dog.' Tamara was certain that the dog would go home but when we got up to continue our journey, it still followed us. Even though we started to shout our discouragement, it still came after us. Three miles further along the road, we reached a Military Control Post. Tamara had some difficulty in retrieving all the papers from her bra. It was an American Post and all the staff were friendly towards us, wanting to know where we had come from and where we were heading. One of them showed interest in the dog and asked if it belonged to us. Tamara translated this to me. I told her to tell him that it was ours at the moment. The soldier asked if we wanted to sell it and again Tamara translated.

'Yes,' I said.

'How much?' he asked.

Tamara again translated, shrugging her shoulders to indicate that she had no idea of the value of the dog. Sensing this, I said to her: 'Tell him, 400 cigarettes, a loaf of bread and a box of matches.' I could see that Tamara had difficulty in controlling her amusement as she translated my terms to him, but the soldier was obviously serious in his negotiations about the dog. I noticed how fiercely he was biting into his chewing gum. He went into the big tent and came back with 400 cigarettes, a box of matches and a tin of biscuits. He offered them with his sincere apologies, and hoped we would accept them instead of the bread, since at the time he had none. He had brought a piece of rope from the tent which I slipped around the dog's neck before handing it to him. The deal was done. We patted the dog and told him to be good to his new owner. Tamara could hardly hold her laughter until we had rounded the next bend, which took us out of their sight, and then she began to laugh until the tears rolled down her cheeks.

'Carl,' she exclaimed, 'I always thought that my Dad was a good business man, but I think that you have excelled him to-day.' She then went on to say that she had been surprised that I had asked for so many cigarettes when we had no food at all. I explained to her that the cigarettes were better than money. They could be used to buy anything we needed, including accommodation. It was also a fact that we had not enjoyed the luxury of a smoke for a long time.

'Come on,' I said 'let's go into the woods to sit down and have a biscuit and a cigarette.' Tamara said that she felt guilty about the dog and I agreed that I also felt sorry for it. It was a very nice dog and we felt from the way it had attached itself to us that it was trying to find another master. It had persisted in doing so even after we had tried to reject it. However, the dog needed food, which we could not supply. Now it had found a new master who obviously wanted it and was in a position to feed it. Then too, as a result of its following us, we had benefited greatly. 'And who knows', I concluded, 'he may even take it back to America.' We opened the tin of biscuits just at the time we would have eaten lunch. We had eaten nothing since we left the farm that morning. We agreed to have three biscuits each and half a cigarette, which was all we felt we could spare, for these supplies might have to last until we reached Regen. After that we would have to see. We examined the two boxes of cigarettes we had been given. One was Camel brand and the other Chesterfield. We decided to open the Camel and were soon puffing blissfully away. The cigarettes fitted nicely into my cardboard box but not the biscuits; we had to carry them separately.

We set off once more in good spirits and walked until we reached some cross roads which I remembered vaguely from earlier days. We took the road leading in the direction of Regen and after another three miles or so we arrived at a village where we decided to try and spend the night. It did not take me very long to negotiate a deal which provided us with a room in a house, with porridge for the evening meal. The price for all this was 20 of our Camel cigarettes, and we bought some bread and milk next morning for a further 20 Camels. We felt as though we had really moved up in the world since trading the dog! Only a small portion of the proceeds had provided us with food and a real bed, and it was on that happy note that we fell asleep. But our joy was short-lived. We woke up in the night to the familiar agony. The warmth of the bed had activated the bugs embedded beneath the skin, and we scratched and scratched ourselves until we became sore. In the morning we felt pretty rotten as we realized that some of the bugs would remain in the bed and the next unsuspecting occupant would soon know of their presence. We felt we ought to do something about it but what?

The following day we set off once again, still weary from having lost so much sleep. Our progress was slow because we were both suffering from sore feet. From the top of the bridge on which we were standing we could see the village ahead. It seemed to be rather bigger than the previous ones we had passed through. As we made our way along the main street, I noticed a 'Fremdenzimmer' sign outside one of the houses, signifying that there were rooms to let there. 'Look, just the place, let's try.' I discovered the lady of the house busy with her laundry in one of the outhouses at the back. We greeted her in the traditional way, 'Gruess Gott', and told her what we wanted, adding that we had a few American cigarettes which we could offer as part payment. After some haggling she agreed that for 20 cigarettes we could have a room. For another 20 cigarettes we could have potato salad that evening and bread and goat's milk in the morning. She added that for a further 10 cigarettes we could have a hot bath. The effect on Tamara when she heard the words 'hot bath' was dramatic. 'Yes, please', she blurted out before I had formulated in my head whether to accept the terms offered. I wondered afterwards whether Tamara would have parted with every cigarette we had to obtain that hot bath. I pulled a packet of Camels out of my pocket and handed them over to the lady, explaining that the others were packed in our box and that I would give them to her later. After that she became far more friendly. She took us to see the room and also told us where we might be able to buy some fresh fish to eat with our potato salad that evening. But we would have to hurry. I eagerly replied that I was ready to go at once. She took us to the gate and pointed to a white house in the street, advising us to tell the people there that the joiner's wife had sent us. Also it would be wise to take a few cigarettes with us. Tamara wanted to come with me so we took some cigarettes from our stock and went.

The door was opened by a man, and we told him who had sent us. He said that he had a few fish left at 10 marks a pound. I asked if I could see them and since he was noticeably disabled, walking with a heavy limp, I suggested that if I accompanied him, it would save him from unnecessary walking in two directions. He did not like the idea and disappeared down some steps into the cellar. He came back with a dozen or so small fish, perch, roach and other varieties. I asked him if he had anything bigger. He said that he had a few 2 and 3 pound pike but added that they would be too expensive for me.

'How expensive?' I asked, 'I have 20 American cigarettes'.

'Oh, that's better', he said, adding that he would trade a 2 pound pike for that. 'Make it a 3 pound pike', I said, 'and you have a deal'. When he would not agree to that, I offered him 20 cigarettes and 20 marks for a 3 pound pike.

'It's a deal.' he said, and went back into the cellar bring out with him a very handsome looking pike, which he wrapped in a newspaper. For obvious reasons he asked me to keep it hidden underneath my jacket.

Tamara enjoyed every second of the deal and again she mentioned the blessing the dog had brought to us.

We had almost reached the guest house when I heard a rumble in the air which we thought was thunder. We handed our precious pike to our landlady, who promised to prepare it for us in the traditional way. She said that she had lit a fire under the boiler to heat the water for our bath, and it would be hot in another half an hour or so. She suggested that we might like to go to our room or take a stroll around until the water was ready. We thanked her and said that we would prefer to go to our room as we were rather tired. In any case, there were signs of a storm coming, for we had heard rumbles of thunder. She gave a hearty laugh. 'That was no thunder, she laughed, saying that she would let us into the secret of the sound. The man who had sold us the fish was an invalid and because of that, he had not been called up for military service. He had been given a job in an ammunition depot in the next town. As the war came to an end and the depot was being abandoned, he had seen his opportunity and had taken a quantity of hand grenades home, carrying them in his lunch box and pockets. He had two teenage sons, who spent a lot of time down by the river, where they had a boat. Apparently, they were in the habit of throwing food into the water at the same spot for several days to attract the fish. Then they would throw a grenade into the water. The resulting explosion would bring a considerable number of stunned fish to the surface, which they then collected using the boat. In this way, the village people could have a little fresh fish to supplement their diets. Everyone in the village supported the boys and kept the secret. 'That', she concluded, 'is how you came to get your pike.'

Tamara and I looked at each other and laughed as we went upstairs. Tamara was saying how much she was looking forward to having a bath. She was under the impression that as she soaked in the hot water, the bugs on her body would drown and she would be free from them. I did not want to dishearten her completely, but I knew that a much more drastic method than a hot bath would be needed to get rid of them. So I confined myself to saying: 'Well, perhaps it will quieten them down for a bit'. We did our best to brush our clothes and then had our baths.

Before long we heard our landlady calling us down for supper. On the table was our pike, nicely decorated with parsley. There was plenty of potato salad and some freshly boiled spinach. Also some gravy made from goat's milk. We asked our landlady to divide the pike into two portions so that we could take half of it with us the following day. Then we ate the remainder, which we both thoroughly enjoyed. Our hostess was very interested in us and sat at table with us during our meal. She wanted to know where we came from and where we were going. We told her that we were making for Regen. She told us that a horse-drawn carriage left the village each day carrying local people to work in an American Camp about 10 kilometres away. It followed the route we intended to take and we might be lucky enough to get a lift. We would, of course, have to go and see the driver, and she suggested that perhaps a few cigarettes would secure the lift for us. She warned us that he left at about 6 am, and if we decided to go with him it would mean getting up very early. After supper we went to see the driver, who readily agreed to take us for 10 cigarettes. After the business was settled, we went back to our room for an early night. However, as usual, we woke up in the middle of the night suffering from the familiar discomfort caused by the bugs on our bodies. The attack was no less severe than the previous ones had been. Sadly, the bathing had not helped at all.

Next morning we duly joined the group which was travelling by horse and cart. The two strong horses kept up a trot for most of the journey. In about 1½ hours we arrived at our destination, a distance which on foot would have taken us the best part of a day. Happy with our progress, we began to walk and at lunchtime we took a rest by the road side. We enjoyed the last of our pike and some of the spinach, which our landlady had so generously wrapped up for us together with some home-baked bread. Whilst we sat there eating our meal, we were joined by two ex-soldiers, very young men, who had been conscripted into the Army in the closing stages of the war. We soon found that they possessed something which to us was almost beyond price: an ointment issued by the German Army which was designed to kill the bugs which had lodged in our skin. We arranged to barter some of our precious cigarettes for a tin of this ointment and also for a razor and some soap.

After the two young men had gone on their way, we inspected our stock and found that we had just 200 cigarettes left. We made a pact that from then on we would not smoke more than one cigarette between us each day to make them last as long as possible.

That night we made our stop later than usual. As a result, we had some difficulty in finding accommodation. In the end I went to the Buergermester's house and told him a long story about my wife and how badly in need of rest she was. He told us that there was an attic room in the house but that it contained only a mattress. He had no spare bedding but we could have the use of the attic room for tonight and that was the best he could do for us. I offered him 20 cigarettes, which he declined to take, saying that no one in his family smoked. I could not believe that piece of luck. He offered us a hot drink and said we could have another in the morning. There was no electric light in the room, but we could have a couple of candles.

We were happy to have what was offered, as we were very tired and both suffering from blistered feet. Tamara went down to get the hot drink and as we still had a little bread and some biscuits left, we were quite satisfied with that. Tamara wanted to lie down and rest, but I insisted on the treatment being done first. I had no intention of having another disturbed night if it could be avoided. It was dark by this time and our two candles were burning. Of all our experiences, this particular one remains the most vivid in my memory. Even after all these years I am still amused as I recall how we shaved our pubic areas by candlelight before rubbing in the grey ointment, which smelled like paraffin. Afterwards, we lay close together under my overcoat and had our first undisturbed sleep for a long time. We did not wake up until well into the next morning.

CHAPTER TWENTY-ONE.
WE FIND MARTHA AND ELLIE

It was now well over a week since we had left the convent in Regensburg. The previous day we had got as far as Deggendorf, which I remembered having visited before on our journey from Regen to Reit-im-Winkel. In Deggendorf we had stayed the night in a refugee transit camp. This camp was a large one with every indication that the authorities here were coping quite well with large numbers of refugees. But the sexes were segregated and we slept in bunk beds in different sections. At least we both slept well and were no longer disturbed by the biting bugs. The camp had a soup kitchen and the following morning we were each given two slices of bread and marmalade and a hot drink. As we left, I estimated that the approximate distance from here to Regen was 80 kilometres. This distance could be halved if we took the route through the mountains. It would, however, be more physically demanding because the route we would have to follow climbed steadily up to one thousand feet. We decided to take the mountain road. As we walked, the scenery became increasingly beautiful but the walking became more and more taxing on our strength. The driver of an ox-cart offered us a lift for a few miles. He was going into the hills to carry back a load of timber to feed a saw-mill in the valley below. In spite of repeated whipping by the driver, the oxen did not increase their speed. He told us that oxen were more clever than people generally gave them credit for and when put to work, nothing, not even beating, could make them go faster. He went on to say that when they arrived back after the journey they would actually run to the stable, where they knew that food would be waiting for them.

When we reached the spot where he had to turn off the main road and go into the forest, we left him and walked on. There were a few houses on the roadside and we decided to try at one of them to see if I could bargain for food. The first house which came into view was an isolated cottage with a steep path leading to the front door. At my knock the door opened a crack and I saw the face of an old lady peering out. She opened the door fully and said: 'Gruess Gott, you must be a refugee. Come in.'

'Gruess Gott', I answered, 'it is very nice of you to ask me in but my wife is down on the road.'

'Bring her up', she invited.

I went back to tell Tamara. When we had climbed the steep path up to the cottage, the old lady waved us into the house saying: 'You must be hungry'. She gestured to us to sit down at the table whilst she opened a cupboard and brought out a loaf of bread and a glass jar. She told us that the bread had been provided by her daughter-in-law while the jar contained jam made from wild strawberries, which she collected every year. 'Help yourselves,' she said, 'and whilst you are having some of that I will look in the shed. I have some hens and they are laying very well just now in this warm weather.' The bread and jam was absolutely delicious. The old lady was back in no time. 'Look', she said, 'you have been lucky. I have found four eggs.' She stoked up the fire before placing a large pan on it, into which she had put some lard. When the fat was crackling, she cracked open the eggs, fried them and placed the pan on the table in front of us. As we ate, she talked incessantly, saying how pleased she was if anyone called. She lived here entirely alone and had done so for the past ten years, since her husband died. We were happy to listen as we ate the delicious food. When we had finished, the old lady made us a cup of mint tea from fresh herbs she had gathered. I tried to pay her but she would not take anything from us, saying how nice it was for her to have visitors. So we parted, wishing her good health and happiness.

We set off on our way once more. It was not long before I began to feel ill, and I realized that the rich meal of three eggs, fried in a plentiful supply of fat, had been more than my stomach could cope with after so long on a meagre diet. I became so bad that I could not go on and ended up lying by the roadside in the grip of a full-scale bilious attack. Slowly we continued our journey and by late evening we arrived in a village on the way to Regen. I was still feeling so ill that for once I left it to Tamara to find somewhere for us to spend the night. For my part, I just sat down on a wooden bench in front of a house and watched her walk across the street to a house on the other side of the village. Before long, Tamara re-emerged followed by the lady of the house. I found that the lady had not only offered to have us for the night, but would also provide me with some camomile tea which, she said, would make me feel better. At her invitation we accompanied her into the house. I sat down in the kitchen whilst our hostess showed Tamara our room. She was soon back to make me the promised camomile tea, made from fresh camomile flowers which she had collected herself and dried. She was certain that the tea would do me good and said that she would make me some porridge a little later. She added that by morning I would be recovered. When the lady's husband arrived home, we engaged in conversation and we told them that we were heading for Regen. They wanted to know who it was in Regen that we intended to call upon. When we mentioned the name, they said that they knew the people and in fact bought their groceries from that same shop. They even knew that the shopkeeper's sister and little girl were living with them.

Our host told us that the road from here into Regen was all downhill, and that if only we had bicycles we would arrive in Regen quite early the next day. We said that to have a bicycle would be marvellous as we were both suffering from sore feet as a result of all the walking we had done. I asked the husband if he knew of anyone in the village who might be willing to sell us a bike. He replied that selling for money would be a problem just now since it was generally regarded as useless in these times. I told him that we had some American cigarettes which I would gladly exchange for a bicycle, but he replied that most of the local people grew their own tobacco which they smoked in pipes. Then he remembered that there was a man in the village whose marriage had broken up and whose wife had left him. Her bicycle was still in the shed and he had seen it there not long ago. He offered to go and see the man and arrange a barter. I told him that if the bicycle was in good condition, I was prepared to give him up to 100 cigarettes for it, and whilst we were on the subject of paying, I asked how much I would have to pay him for our room that night. 'Nothing', he said, and added that they were very fortunate still to have everything they needed, including meat, living so near to the forest where there was an abundance of deer and wild boar. Also the game keeper was very good to them. He thought that it would be a good idea for me to go with him to see the man he had mentioned earlier, and I could then negotiate the deal for the bike myself. I took 100 Chesterfields from our cigarette stock and off we went, whilst Tamara helped to clear the table. The bicycle was not the most modern of machines. It was covered in dust and had flat tyres, but the man promised to put it into running order. I left the 100 cigarettes as a sign of my good faith and we left to rejoin the ladies.

The journey to Regen was great fun, Tamara took the first turn with the bike and off she went down the hill and out of sight. After rounding the bend, I could see that she had gone about half a mile before dismounting, leaving the bicycle leaning against a tree and setting out to walk. I picked it up and overtook her, waving and laughing on the way. We continued riding the bicycle in turn, and it gave us a chance to rest our feet, making it unnecessary to stop for this purpose as we had always had to do before. The result was, of course, that we were travelling further in a shorter time. As we reached the beginning of the built-up area of Regen, we stayed together on foot while I pushed the bike.

At last we reached our destination, the shop. Martha's mother, who had heard our voices, came rushing out of the kitchen to greet us and received us with open arms. She was clearly delighted and we were invited to join them all at lunch. During the meal I began to relate all that had happened to us since our last visit. As I was doing so, Ellie kept Tamara occupied in answering her many questions. I told them that we had come to them because we did not know where else to turn. But I assured them that it was our intention to travel on in due course. I hoped that it might be possible for them to assist in finding some kind of work which we could do in return for food. This, however, would only be until such time as the general situation improved, particularly with regard to transport, as we were desperately anxious to find our family. I voiced the inner feelings of both of us when I said that we clung to the hope that they had managed to cross the River Elbe and were now somewhere in the British Sector.

'Right', said our host, 'you have a rest to-day and to-morrow. We opened our shop again only last week, and although at present we have not very much to sell, we have to be there. The day after to-morrow is early closing and I will take my bicycle and see what I can find for you.'

I told him that I too had a bicycle and could perhaps accompany him. He said that he had a good friend who was a hill farmer near the Czechoslovakian border. He had previously employed a man, but he had failed to return from the war and was in fact officially missing. There was a good chance of us being able to stay there. He said that the farmer and his family, though not very well off, were good people. Failing that, he himself had relatives in farming but the problem would be one of accommodation.

We spent two very pleasant days in Regen. After leisurely mornings, Ellie would show us around in the afternoons. Our evenings were spent talking to our very gracious hosts, exchanging experiences. We felt that they enjoyed having us as much as we enjoyed being with them. They insisted that if we were lucky enough to find work locally, we should visit them as often as possible.

As arranged, on the afternoon of early closing day, which was the third day of our visit, I accompanied our host to the hill farm near Zwiesel. It was quite a tough bike ride as most of the journey was, of course, uphill. Our journey proved to be very fruitful. I was told by the kindly hill farmer, Mr Brandl, that we could indeed work for our food and that we could stay as long as we wished. There was a spare room but it had no bed, only a sofa. Though it looked a bit small for two, it would just have to do.

After two weeks on the farm, we were on friendly terms with Mr and Mrs Brandl and their teenage daughter Rosie. By this time we were accustomed to rising at 6 am. After breakfast of porridge and milk or home-made bread and treacle made from their own sugar beet, we began our day's work. We had also become familiar with the sound of the bell hung around the neck of the leading cow. With some amusement we learned that if the sound of this bell could not be heard during the night for any length of time, Mrs Brandl would never fail to rise from her bed to investigate the whereabouts of the herd, worried that they might have strayed into the neighbour's meadow. We also became accustomed to sleeping on the small sofa, which was simply not wide enough for the two of us to sleep in any other position than the rigid one we adopted after much trial and error. We were never given specified duties. Tamara simply assisted Mrs Brandl in whatever she was doing. I helped Mr Brandl, who mostly worked with two old oxen. At the period of which I am speaking, we were engaged in bringing in the hay crop from the meadows a mile or so from the farmyard.

The hay season came to an end and the next major task around the farm was to remove the trees previously marked for that purpose by the forester. Tamara and I shared the job of sawing each tree into sections, which were then transported down hill to the road by Mr Brandl and his team of oxen. The wood was then stacked and sold for firewood, the only domestic fuel available in this area at the time. As I had insufficient experience for this rather tricky operation with the oxen, Mr Brandl did that part himself. Tamara and I concentrated on the sawing of the timber. As we were working some distance away from the farm, we spent the whole day in the forest and took a packed lunch along with us. We always had a good hour for lunch and Tamara and I were curious to inspect the area on the hill beyond the trees, which was rather wild and covered by large boulders.

One day we climbed almost to the top and I spotted what appeared to be the tail section of an aeroplane silhouetted against the horizon. I pointed it out to Tamara, who urged me to go with her to investigate further. On making our way towards it, we found the remains of a Messerschmitt fighter plane strewn amongst the rocks. There was no sign of a pilot and we wondered whether he had managed to bale out. I had a good look around to see whether there was anything worth removing from the scene. Tamara sensed this and I told her that she was right, and that I thought that I had found something useful. We discussed how best we could return to the spot on the following Sunday, when I would bring whatever tools I thought necessary. We did not mention what we had found to anyone else, and retired to bed early that night with a simulated head-ache so as to have an opportunity to talk about the crashed aircraft. As usual, Tamara sensed that I had something on my mind and as soon as we got into the bed she said: 'Right, Carl, start talking, nobody is listening.'

I started by saying that I considered the situation we were in to be not bad, but not too good either. It was all very well working for food but I felt that we must make a move before the winter, when work on the farm would be minimal. I felt we would hardly be earning our bread, and would be something of a drain on the Brandls. We still had to find Mum and Dad and Alfred but we could not take to the road in our present situation without adequate clothing and a little money. I reminded her how difficult it had been to get from Ingolstadt to Regen. There was very little work around here, and we must find some which would bring in some wages. I went on to say that German money would be of no use to us; the only things of real value at this time were cigarettes, coffee and alcohol. Cigarettes are valuable, I reminded her, but many farmers grew their own tobacco, which was inferior but functional. We were smoking it ourselves. That left only coffee and alcohol. Coffee could only be obtained if one had connections with the Americans, which we had not. The only tradeable commodity left was alcohol. I knew how to make it, having closely inspected Cousin Eriks's still. (He could make an excellent schnapps, and had told me how it was done.) All this was à propos of the Messerschmitt on the mountainside.

I had spotted amongst the wreckage some very good aluminium pipes, which could be converted for use as a still. As Mr Brandl had a plentiful supply of sugar beet and potatoes, I believed that, though a long shot, the project of making schnapps from these materials was nevertheless worth a try. I knew that Mr Brandl liked a drink, yet had no supplies. I considered that he would not refuse my offer to share the liquor on a 50/50 basis. His contribution would be the materials I needed to distil it: potatoes, sugar beet and the fire wood that I would need. Our half of the proceeds of this proposed venture would go towards equipping us for the next stage of our journey. Once on the road, we would not deviate until we had found the family. The only difficulty was that we must ensure that we were not caught.

'Carl, you make it sound so easy, but I will do anything to find Mum and Dad and Alfred'. In her excited state Tamara got up and sat on the edge of our improvised bed. I could see how eager she was to find her family and felt that had it been possible, she would have made a start there and then.

The next Sunday, armed with an adjustable spanner and sawblade, we walked back to the plane. I found that the remains of the aircraft would provide me with all the materials I needed to make the still. The pipe that would be the most important part needed a threaded connector on one end, the other end did not matter so much, provided it was the required length. So we used the spanner for one end and the sawblade for the other. All the smaller pieces of equipment, such as nuts and washers, could be found here as well. Before returning to the house, we thanked Willi Messerschmitt for his generous gift.

The next day we were once more working in the forest and in the lunch break I decided to speak to Mr Brandl about my idea and test his reaction to it. I intended to mention that I had hoped to be allowed the use of the wash house in the barn for my purpose. The conversation went as follows:

'Mr Brandl, for this time of year you appear to have a lot of potatoes and sugar beet left. The animals, except for the oxen, are permanently out to grass. What are you going to do with the surplus?'

'Well', he replied, 'you never know from one year to another what will happen. Some years you are short and other years the animals go out early. If there should be an early spring, then there will be a surplus of feed, as has happened this year. It is an advantage as we don't have to feed them or muck out the stables. The cows come in for milking and that is it'.

'Yes, that makes sense, but what are you going to do with the potatoes and sugar beet?'

'We shall try to sell the potatoes,' he said, and then went on to explain that they should be thinking of making syrup from the sugar beet as soon as the current job was finished.

'Mr Brandl,' I started again, 'if I tell you how you can make much more of your surpluses, would you consider doing it?'

'I would always consider making a bit extra.'

Tamara obviously realized that we would be better left alone to discuss the proposal which, she knew, I was about to outline to him. She said that she would like to go into the woods to look for wild mushrooms.

'Mr Brandl,' I started again, 'do you know that it is possible to make schnapps by fermenting potatoes and sugar beet and then extracting the alcohol by a distilling process?'

'Yes, I know that,' he replied, 'but you can't do it here'.

'It can be done here,' I said, and proposed that we use the farm wash house as premises. I went on to explain that I had the necessary equipment and the knowledge to build the still and that if he would provide the potatoes and sugar beet, we could become partners in the project. He considered my proposal for a little while with some interest and then said that although he had known the theory of it, he had never actually known of anyone who had done it. He also expressed concern about the legal aspect and mentioned the possibility of police involvement. I assured him that his fears, although not entirely without foundation, were not perhaps as real as he believed. I had, of course, given that part of the venture considerable thought and felt that the safest way to do it was to make, say, 50 bottles of the spirit and bury it in a secret location away from the farm, known only to himself and me. The still would be dismantled and either hidden under the water of the lake or else completely destroyed before any attempt was made to sell the liquor. I told him that Tamara and I had already made an agreement about the disposal of the liquor and had decided that she would be the one actually to find the contacts. If she should be challenged, she would say that it had come into her possession as a trade-in from some unknown person. She was even prepared to say that she had slipped over the nearby Czechoslovakian border and brought it from there. We felt that it was most unlikely that her story would not be accepted, as it would be difficult to disprove.

'Look, Mr Brandl, you have been very good to us and so has Mrs Brandl, but we cannot stay here for very much longer. Winter is coming on and we would be a burden that you could well do without. Besides that, we are very anxious to find Tamara's family. We must find out if they got away from the Russians. If they did, they will be somewhere in the British Sector, as they were in Magdeburg when the war ended. And before embarking on such a journey, we must be properly equipped for it. At the present time we have virtually nothing but the clothes we are wearing. Therefore we need some means of raising the necessary money and we thought that this would be a good way to do it.'

He finally came to a decision, jumping up with the words: 'Right,

Carl, you have convinced me, have a go!' So we shook hands on it.

Tamara came back from the woods carrying a large basket of wild mushrooms. 'Look', she said, 'whilst you have been talking I have been gathering these for our supper tonight.' I gave her the thumbs up sign and she smiled at me, showing that she understood.

Tamara and I had planned to visit Martha's mother and little Ellie on our next free day, which was Sunday, but I felt that there was really no time to be lost. So, I suggested that Tamara should go alone while I remained behind to make a start on building the still. As it was not too far, she could go on the bicycle and it would be a pleasant change for her. If she went, our promise would be fulfilled and at the same time she could bring back some yeast from the shop. The yeast was vital to the distilling process. We even discussed whether we should trust Mr Hofer with our secret. Perhaps he would be able to introduce safe contacts to us.

On the following Sunday morning, Tamara went off to Regen on the bicycle and I began work on the still. My first task was to give the aluminium pipe from the aircraft a thorough cleaning, and then shape it into a spiral. I knew that before I could form the pipe into the required spiral shape it had to be filled with fine dry sand. The sand would prevent the sides of the metal collapsing where the bends were made, which would have prevented the alcoholic vapour from passing through the pipe. My next task was to connect the spiral pipe to a milk churn. This was not difficult as there were quite a few of them around the farm. In fact, when I looked round the farm, I soon found all the materials I needed for the factory to be. Since the Brandls had been in the habit of making syrup from sugar beet, all the boiling equipment was already to hand. By the evening of that Sunday I was confident that by working one hour or so each evening, it would take me no more than a week before I was ready to test the apparatus out. I would then have a trial run with water, which would clean the whole system as well as testing it. Then I would be ready for production. Whilst I was doing this, Tamara could make a start on cleaning and preparing the potatoes and the sugar beet. I calculated that in the warm spell of weather we were currently enjoying, the fermenting process would take about one week. The only difficulty I could foresee was in obtaining the yeast. So I waited excitedly for Tamara to return from

Regen.

I began to worry a little when she did not return at a reasonable time. She was away for so long that in the end we had supper without her. After supper I started to walk down the road to look for her. I must have walked for a mile or so before I saw her some distance away, pedalling hard against the rising terrain. She was happy to see me and as we walked back to the farm, she told me how much she had enjoyed the day. She then showed me two tins of corned beef, a packet of biscuits and some coffee beans which were presents to us. Then came the best news of all: she had managed to get some dried yeast. 'Hurray,' I said, 'that is what I was waiting for.'

'Wait', she said, 'that is not all'. She went on to say that Mrs Hofer knew a young girl with an American boy-friend from the nearby barracks. The girl had asked her if she could exchange coffee beans for wines and spirits, as the men liked to give parties and invite local girls for a drink and dancing. Apparently Tamara had had some serious discussions with the Hofers and they had already arranged a meeting between the girl and Tamara for the following Sunday, when they could discuss matters to their mutual benefit. This was indeed good news and inspired me to bring forward my completion date. I decided that I could have it all ready in a much shorter time and this became my prime aim. It would mean extra work in the evenings, but it would be worth while. So we set to work cleaning the potatoes and beet. We then boiled them before passing them through a large mincer to press out the liquid. We also prepared the yeast for fermentation in a large wooden tub. In addition to this, I made charcoal from birch-tree wood. This was to be used for filtering the alcohol. Mr Brandl came into the wash house occasionally and watched us at work. He did not comment, but I felt that he was somewhat doubtful whether our efforts would ever be rewarded.

Sunday came and I was ready to start production. Tamara had already left to keep her appointment with the girl, and afterwards to see Ellie. I started up my factory. A fire had been lit under the old-fashioned boiler in the wash house. Above the boiler was the milk churn, which was three-quarters full of the fermented liquid. A pipe ran from the top of the churn to the spiral tube I had so carefully fashioned. This in turn was set into a drum of cold water so as to cool down the rising alcohol vapour and transform it into a gentle flow of alcohol. It passed out from the bottom of the drum into a container of charcoal, which filtered it before it ran into a bottle as a finished product. The whole operation was delicate. Though I had proved that it could be done, the primitive methods I had been forced to use made it vital to monitor the entire process constantly if success was to be assured. The whole enterprise was not without strain or risk, but both had to be accepted as a necessary part of the price we had to pay in order to achieve our purpose.

About 11 am that morning I had the whole system working and in production and around midday, when Mr Brandl looked in, I was able to present him with the first bottle of our home-made brew. He went back to the house and returned with two glasses, but I warned him that the first couple of bottles would be very strong, somewhere in the region of 60-70% proof, almost pure alcohol. So we diluted our first fruits with water before tasting them. Mr Brandl, who had not had a strong drink for a very long time, asked for another one. I handed him the bottle saying that it was his and he could drink it at his leisure with his good lady. Before he went off with his bottle, I asked permission to be excused from farm duties the following day, as there was so much fermented juice to distil. I feared that a delay would result in a heavy loss; it could turn into vinegar. 'Look, Carl,' he replied, 'you stay at home as long as you wish and Tamara too. Just keep on making it. I have work to do in the fields just now, and I can manage quite well.' When Tamara returned at 7 pm, I had three more bottles of schnapps from the first lot.

I was very pleased with my apparatus. Tamara had brought good news as well. She had met the girl as arranged and the boy-friend as well, who turned out to be a sergeant in the American Army. Tamara told them that she was Latvian and that we were working at the farm just for food. She emphasised her anxiety about her family and how desperate she was to trace them. If they had got out of the Russian zone, they were probably in the north, which meant a long journey to find them. To finance this, we needed coffee, cigarettes, clothing and American dollars. She told them that the only thing she could get hold of was alcohol, but she was frightened of getting involved with the police. 'Is it good alcohol?' the sergeant asked. 'Yes, it is'. Tamara assured him that she could guarantee its purity. The sergeant asked how much she wanted a bottle. She told him that her husband was in need of shoes, size 10, as he had none at all. So they agreed to exchange a bottle for a pair of shoes and that the exchange should take place the following Sunday. They also arranged to meet again one week after that and make a deal for as many bottles as she could supply.

From that moment we both became very optimistic about our future, sometimes to such an extent that the excitement of it all interfered with our sleep. We lay in bed that night trying to figure out how many bottles we could make and how long it would take. We also made provisional plans for our journey and tried to estimate when we would be able to start it. Passenger transport services had still not been resumed after the end of hostilities, but goods trains were running between the large cities. By now it was mid-August and we had a sufficient stock of roots left to make about 40 bottles of schnapps. We worked out that provided the present spell of hot weather continued to speed up the fermentation process, it would take the two of us at least two weeks. We urgently needed more bottles to hold the schnapps, and if we had another fermentation container we could speed things up considerably. Mrs Brandl said that she would try and get the bottles from the man who collected the milk each day with his horse and cart. She would say that she needed them to store her home-made fruit juice. She was sure that she could persuade the man to part with some bottles in return for some of Mr Brandl's home-grown tobacco. She could also provide a container for fermentation. Accordingly, we estimated that the earliest date we could leave the farm would be the beginning of September. This would also give us four to five weeks of reasonably good weather for travelling before the onset of winter.

After supper Mr Brandl produced a map which we studied to find the best route to take us to the northern part of Germany. According to the map, the nearest railway station for the northern line was located in the town of Cham. We could see that this presented something of a problem as it was 40-50 miles away. But then, we still had the bicycle, and we saw no reason why we should not repeat the method we had used to get to our present abode, walking and riding in turn. We would go via Zwiesel and Regen, where we would call and say our farewells to the Hofers, Ellie and her grandmother. We decided that once we reached Cham, the bicycle would become something of a liability and we would try and exchange it for something useful. From Cham we would try to get to Nuernberg, then Kassel and Hanover, where we would begin our search. As we considered our plans, we all had one or two drinks, and by midnight, when we took our leave of the Brandls to go to bed, we were quite merry.

The next morning Tamara and I began working full time in our little factory. The heat from the boiling beet and potatoes, together with the warmth from the stove which heated the still, made the small room uncomfortably hot even with the door and all the windows open. At the end of the day we had four more bottles of schnapps and two containers of fermenting liquid to show for our labour. The hot weather continued as we had hoped, and because of this welcome aid to the fermenting process, I was able to start the actual distilling on Friday morning. By Saturday night I had the equivalent of 16 more bottles of schnapps. As we had not yet acquired the bottles, Mrs Brandl provided me with a milk churn to store it in. We kept it airtight with a rubber seal.

On Sunday morning Tamara set off with two bottles of the schnapps, one very carefully wrapped in a box for the American sergeant, the other for Mr Hofer. She intended to call there first and tell them that in all probability we would be leaving in two weeks' time. I saw her off and once her bicycle was out of sight, I began to work on the last lot of fermented liquid, as by now we had used up all the raw materials. I felt a bit uneasy that day as we were doing the deal with the American soldier on trust. If it should prove to be a trap, we would be in deep trouble and I would feel responsible for whatever might befall the Brandls. They had been very good to us and I was conscious of having broken the agreement which we had made about dismantling the still and removing all evidence before offering it for sale. He did not know that Tamara had taken two bottles out to-day. I knew how eager she was to find her family, and she was very confident that the American and his girl-friend would not let her down. At the end of the day I was too anxious to wait for her return and set off to meet her.

By the time we met, I had walked almost to Zwiesel. I saw from a distance that she was smiling and this was a great relief to me as it meant that nothing had gone wrong. I took the bike from her and we walked slowly home. She had a pair of shoes for me and as we walked she told me how frightened she had been when she met the girl and handed over the schnapps. The girl had asked her to wait a while for her boy-friend and two other sergeants to join, as they wanted to test the quality of the schnapps before agreeing to further deals. She said that she had panicked a little in case she had walked into a trap. Then, sure enough, a jeep came round the corner and the three sergeants got out. She went on to say how she became less frightened as they shook hands with her. She considered that it was most unlikely they would be doing that if they had come to arrest her. On the contrary, they were very friendly and she was told that they would take the bottle, drive out of town a little way, test the goods, and return to give her their verdict. Shortly afterwards the men had returned and said that the spirit was good quality. They had asked what we would charge for 20 or so bottles of the same quality. Tamara said that we were at their mercy, but we both badly needed a supply of clothing. Her husband needed shirts, trousers, socks and an overcoat. She needed what girls of her age need, as she had nothing at all. Also our German money was quite useless at this time, and a few dollars would help as well as a few cigarettes to trade in for food. He wanted to know when we could deliver the goods and Tamara told him that it could be done immediately, the only difficulty being the shortage of bottles. The three men had a conference between them. Then one of them said that if I would wait, they would go back to the camp and collect two five-litre containers. If I could return them duly filled a week the following Tuesday, they would meet me in Regen and hand over a parcel in exchange.

'What could I do?' Tamara concluded, I had to agree to that. You see Carl, even that is not all. Here are 50 dollars he gave me to buy some clothes for myself, and in my bag are 100 cigarettes. Have I not done a good job? Oh, I am so happy that we shall soon be on our way now.'

'And I am happy as well', I replied, 'but you have not told me yet what the Hofers said.'

'Yes, of course; they wished us all the best. Mr Hofer tried the schnapps and thought that it was very good. He would like to be able to order 100 bottles every week! And he gave me two tins of meat.'

By the next Sunday night we had made the equivalent of 42 bottles of schnapps. The milk collector provided only 19 empty bottles but, as it turned out, it did not matter as we had the two containers from the Americans. I wanted to give one more bottle to Mr Hofer and I told Mrs Brandl that I could see great difficulty in moving our half away from the farm in individual bottles, and that the two containers were much better for our share. I told her this because I wished to avoid telling her about the deal we had made with the Americans; in doing so we had broken the agreement we had made with them. By Monday lunchtime the wash house was put back into its original state and there was no trace of evidence of our activities. I handed over 18 bottles of schnapps to Mr Brandl and in addition a quantity left in the milk churn which Mrs Brandl had given me. The still was duly dismantled and I left the pieces with Mr Brandl to dispose of as he thought fit.

Tamara returned in the afternoon from her shopping expedition in Zwiesel, quite happy with her purchases. The next day, straight after lunch, we set off for Regen and walked all the way, using the bicycle to take the weight of the containers. A few hundred yards from the venue, Tamara took the two containers and walked whilst I found a suitable hiding place. It was not long before a jeep turned out of the side street and a sergeant got out. He took the two containers and handed over a large parcel to Tamara. It was all over in a few seconds. We took our parcel and walked to the Hofers house, telling them that we were only calling to say goodbye. They insisted that we sit down with them for coffee. As I handed our farewell gift of the bottle of schnapps to Mr Hofer, he wanted to give us some more tinned food in exchange, but we both insisted that they had already done so much for us that we wanted to give them the schnapps as a token of our gratitude and would take nothing in exchange. We said our tearful goodbyes and promised to write as soon as the mail came into operation once more.

CHAPTER TWENTY-TWO.
RE-UNITED WITH TAMARA'S FAMILY

As we walked back to the farm, we pushed the bicycle all the way and, it being a lady's model, our large parcel just fitted into the frame, wedged between the handlebars and the seat. We felt very sad to be leaving the Brandls. It was already dark when we arrived, but Mrs Brandl had left everything on the table for our supper. After we had eaten, I helped Tamara to clear away before we retired to our room. We were both very curious as to the contents of the parcel. It contained a ruck-sack, a pair of trousers, a shirt, two pairs of socks and an overcoat. All the clothing was American issue which had been used but was, nevertheless, in good condition. What was more important was that it was all of the correct size for me.

The next morning Tamara was up unusually early, and when I asked her the reason she had been unable to sleep, she said that she was far too excited and a little nervous at what we might meet on our travels. I understood how she felt and suggested that we bring our plans forward. Instead of making a start next week, as planned, we would start the journey to-morrow. 'Oh, Carl, please let's be off. We will pack to-day'.

At breakfast time I told the Brandls that we had decided to make a start on our journey the following day. I thanked them for all they had done for us and laughingly said that we hoped the whenever they had a drink, they would think about us. I told them that we had got just about everything we needed, but had forgotten the bread. I asked if they could possibly spare us a couple of slices. Mrs Brandl replied that we should not worry about that, she would make us a good breakfast and would be delighted to give us a whole loaf of her newly baked bread to take with us. She also offered us a ruck-sack which she had in a loft. I told her that although we had had one given to us only yesterday, another one would be very useful. It would make things so much easier for us if we could divide our load between us.

By late afternoon we had everything packed and were satisfied that we were as well prepared as possible for the long journey.

The next morning we said our goodbyes to the Brandl family and set out on our journey. It was not long before we reached the little town of Zwiesel, taking turns with the bicycle and each leaving it for the one on foot to pick up before setting out on the next stage. Unfortunately, after Tamara had left it for me to pick up, it was stolen before my very eyes by a young thief who then crashed it into an American jeep, damaging it beyond repair. We were forced to abandon it and continue together on foot until we reached the next town, where we decided to spend the night. I knocked on the door of a house displaying a bed-and-breakfast sign and asked if we could have a room for one American dollar. The landlady was most eager to accept, saying that she had a room. She told us in conversation that a little further up the road was a camp which was full of foreigners. Later on, after we had had a bite to eat, we walked to the camp to have a look. We found that it was full of people from the Ukraine. We enquired at the office and were told that the camp had been provided for them by the American Military Government. We told them that we were travelling through the district on our way north to look for our family. After careful examination of our papers, particularly mine, which showed that I was born in one of the Baltic States, they said that we were eligible to stay at the camp if we wished. Tamara was keen to take up this offer as there was dancing in the evening. I, however, explained to her that I had already paid for our room and wanted to go back there. My only interest in the camp was that we qualified for some food to take away with us. Before leaving we were given some very good food, which we had to sign for. On the way back to our accommodation we were both heartened to see that things were changing for the better. It appeared that both rooms and food were now easier to come by than they had been previously.

The double bed which we occupied that night was such bliss after sleeping for so long on the Brandls' small sofa, that we slept longer than usual. It was 10.30 am before we resumed our journey the following day. On the way we had to pass the camp which we had visited the previous evening. We could see from quite a distance that the camp gates were wide open. We could also see a certain amount of activity in the form of a number of men busy cleaning the pathways inside the gates, but otherwise there was no sign of life. As we reached the gates, we asked one of the men where everybody was. The man looked at me with a blank expression and in a Bavarian dialect asked me whether we were Ukrainians. I said that we were not. He then went on to say that at 6 am that morning a fleet of American lorries had arrived at the camp. Everyone had been put on to them and driven away. He went on to describe the grim scene that he had witnessed: terrible uproar in the camp and how the inmates had been put on to the transport by force. One young Ukrainian had slashed his throat with a razor and another had jumped from one of the lorries as it sped down the road. Both had died of their injuries. Apparently the cause of the uproar had been that they knew all too clearly what fate they could expect.

As we stood there in a state of shock, Tamara cried bitterly. When the conversation was over, we sat down on the grass for a while to recover, realizing how very easily we might have been included among those being forcibly repatriated. Tamara could not understand how the Americans could do such a thing. It was clear that Stalin would have every one of them shot as soon as they reached Russian soil. We were later to learn that she was right.

Within one week of leaving the Brandls' farm, we had reached Nuernberg. Our means of transport had been mainly by goods train. We had found the travelling more difficult than we had anticipated. Many of the railway lines had not yet been repaired, especially over rivers, where most of the bridges were temporary. Most of the lines were single-track, causing considerable delays. Furthermore, travelling by goods train was far from comfortable. All the enclosed wagons were sealed and the open ones were cold, draughty and very dirty. There were compensations of course, one being that we were never lonely. The numbers of people on the move amazed us. They were people like ourselves, travelling for the same reasons, many from the Baltic States. From these people we were able to glean valuable information. We learned, for instance, that the only way to get into the

British Sector by train was via Kassel, but that this was not easy as it was controlled by Military Police. Permission to cross from one sector to another was only given in special circumstances. The authorities were anxious to control the smuggling of goods from one sector to another. We discovered also that almost every town now had a Red Cross station displaying lists and records of the people who had passed through and their intended destination. Also U.N.R.R.A camps were opening up everywhere. The fact that Ukrainian people were being deported seemed to be common knowledge.

We waited around for two days to find rail transport going in the direction of Kassel, and it took us a further six days to arrive there. When the train finally rolled into Kassel goods yard around midnight, we climbed wearily down from the goods wagon on to the lines. We found ourselves surrounded by people milling around us and proceeding in all directions. We heard someone say that the train on the next line was going to Hanover and as this was as good a destination as any for us, we joined the people boarding it. As we settled down in a corner of one of the open wagons, we were grateful, as always when travelling at night, for the warmth of our overcoats. It would be around 2 am before the train began to move out, and by this time Tamara was fast asleep, as were the other five or six women who shared the wagon with us. I just kept my fingers crossed, in the hope that the information we had been given was correct and that we were in fact going in the right direction and not back to where we had come from. After about an hour the train stopped with a jerk, waking up the sleepers, who all asked the same question: 'Where are we?'

'I wish I knew,' I replied. After some time we heard the sound of feet approaching alongside the train and I asked someone whether we were in the British Sector. He replied that we were and told me that the train was heading for Goettingen. I knew that town and was able to inform the ladies that we were safely in the British Sector and give them our destination. All of them then assumed that I knew more than I did and bombarded me with all sorts of questions which I could not really answer. It was forcibly brought home to me that everyone was desperately searching for someone. I wondered if they would ever be reunited or were destined to search in vain. For here, almost four months after the war had ended, the aftermath of its misery was still with us.

After a further weary train journey we found ourselves at Celle, some thirty miles north-east of Hanover. We lost no time in finding the Red Cross station, where we were given some hot soup. Then we bent ourselves to the task of checking the records to see whether any members of Tamara's family had passed through. The first discovery we made was a heart-breaking one. While I had been snatching some sleep, Tamara had continued to search the records. When she woke me she said: 'Carl, I have some bad news for you.' I jumped up in bed and asked her what had happened. She told me that she had not been able to find anything about her parents, but she had met Juris, Eriks's cousin. He had told her that Eriks had been killed. Then she burst into tears. I asked her how it had happened, but as yet she did not know any details. Juris was coming to our room within the next half hour to tell us all about it.

We stayed in the camp for three days and could have stayed as long as we wished, but each time I saw Juris, the sadness of Eriks's death increasingly depressed me, so we decided to move on. Eriks had been killed – it was unbelievable! A man so full of life and hope and the only relative from my father's family. As the Russian troops had advanced towards Latvia, the Germans had mobilised all able-bodied men either to be sent to Germany to work or to fight in the Legion. Eriks had considered it his duty to fight for the defence of his homeland and had elected to join the Legion. As he had previous service in the Latvian Army before the war, he had been given his old rank of sergeant. Juris had had to make the same decision, but as he had been uncertain of what to do, he had been persuaded by Eriks to join the Legion too and had signed on as a corporal. Both had found themselves in the same platoon and as the unit was put into operation, they fought side by side.

Nothing had been able to stop the massive Russian advance and their Unit had been cut off in the action somewhere in the region of Ventspils fishing harbour. There had been only one way of escape and that was by sea. As they retreated along the harbour, Eriks had been wounded in the leg and had had to be carried. They had all made for the two large fishing vessels in the harbour but then had had some engine trouble and been unable to get away. They had all transferred in panic to the other vessel and managed to get out to sea. Eriks's leg had been bleeding badly, and he had been lowered, with two other wounded men, into the storage department below for what treatment they had been able to give them. When they had been about two miles out to sea, two Russian fighter planes had attacked the vessel repeatedly until it was riddled with holes and had sunk, taking most of the men down with it and giving Eriks no chance of survival. Juris had been one of the lucky ones. Being uninjured, he had managed to grab a large piece of wreckage and hang on to it. Though initially resolved to return home to Latvia, even though it was now under Russian domination, Juris had then heard of the fate of the returning Ukrainians, who had been shot as they arrived at the border. When he had heard of the Latvian camp at Celle, he had decided to go there for the time being.

As we left Juris at the camp we told him that if our efforts to find our family should prove fruitless, we would return there. The committee in Celle advised us to travel first to Uelzen, where there was a very large transit camp full of refugees of all nationalities.

We arrived at the transit camp in Uelzen at lunchtime, and were booked in. The office walls were covered with messages from people searching for their relatives. In addition to all this information, there were two large record books on a table with messages from the people who had passed through the camp. Tamara went to look through these books straight away, while I occupied myself in taking our possessions to our accommodation. When I met her again, I could see at once that she had had no success. As I concentrated on the messages around the walls, Tamara looked once again through the books. One of the office girls asked her why she had come back again and Tamara explained that if her parents had managed to get into the west, it would be somewhere here in the north of the region. The girl paused for a moment, then said that there was another record book in existence, which had been started in the very early days when the camp had first opened. She said that she would look for it and eventually pulled out a well-used desk-diary type of book. Tamara started to look through the pages. Suddenly there was a loud cry of joy and Tamara almost leaped into the air.

'Carl,' she shouted, 'I have found them, I have found them!' I went over to her and she put her arms around me. 'Come, let me look', I said. Sure enough, there was a written message from her father: 'Ferdinands Bergs is looking for his daughter Tamara.' He had added that he had gone to the Latvian camp in Hameln.

Tamara's joy was infectious and went through the whole office staff. Even the people who had searched in vain for news of their own loved ones were happy for her. She would have left at once for Hameln but I persuaded her that it was now too late in the day. For my own part, I had a little research to do, for although everyone had heard of the Piped Piper of Hameln, it was a question of how to get there. The office staff kindly supplied a map and after studying it, I concluded that we should return to Hanover via Celle. Once in Hanover, our difficulties would be over.

Three days later, in the late evening, we arrived in Hanover and made our way to the Red Cross station, where we were confident of getting hot soup and a bed for the night. As public transport was improving all the time, it was now relatively easy to find a bus to take us to Hameln.

We arrived at the office of the Hameln camp by lunchtime and after the greetings, Tamara asked for the whereabouts of her parents.

'What was their name?'

'Bergs, Ferdinands Bergs.'

'Look at the blackboard,' said the man. On the blackboard was written the information that Ferdinands Bergs and family had moved to 16 Hauptstrasse in the village of Springe. 'Springe?' I said, 'We have just come through it, half way to Hanover.' The man went on to tell us that Ferdinands had found private accommodation there and had taken his family out of the camp as he did not trust camps after the Ukrainian incident. We then pondered on the quickest way to get to Springe. I could see that Tamara would not rest until she got there. The man told us that one way was by bus. Another possibility was that just down the road someone had opened a garage recently for the repair of commercial vehicles and the owner had a set of trade plates for testing vehicles. If we could produce enough money or any suitable article to exchange, he might get us there. We thanked him and could not get away fast enough. The garage man, after hearing our proposition, shook his head and said: 'No, no! No time and no petrol.'

I waved my last ten-dollar note under his nose. At the sight of this he told us to put our luggage into a truck which he pointed out to us and jumped in. He would just tell his wife and then take us to Springe. Half an hour later we were knocking on the door of 16, Hauptstrasse, Springe, and Tamara's mother opened the door to an unforgettable reunion.

CHAPTER TWENTY-THREE.
WE BEGIN A NEW LIFE

No. 16 Hauptstrasse was a cottage owned by a local farmer who had agreed to rent the place to Dad for the time being. Part of their agreement had been that Dad would help out on the farm if required. The cottage had two bedrooms, which made sufficient room for all five of us to live there. Alfred had volunteered to sleep on the living room sofa and give up his room to us. The day after our arrival, I accompanied Dad on his visit to the farmer to explain our presence. The farmer had no objection to us being there, so long as I agreed to drive the tractor and help with the ploughing for a week or two. In return he would provide us with potatoes, bread and milk. So we began to settle down with the family and adjust to some kind of permanence again.

After the evening meal we would talk together round the table and tell of our experiences, which always ended in Tamara's mother shedding tears. They also had not had an easy time. We heard how, after the Russians had taken Berlin, they advanced so quickly that the Headquarters at Magdeburg had been abandoned in panic. The family left via Stendal for Wittenberg, only to be overtaken there by the Russian troops but Dad had never given up. He could speak both Russian and Polish, and got away by claiming to be Polish, wishing to return home to Poland. Mum had made a small Polish flag, which they fastened to the handcart which they had acquired from somewhere. They had used this to transport as many of their belongings as they could manage to get on it. They pushed this cart as far as the River Elbe. On reaching this point, the river was the only barrier between them and freedom. If only they could reach the other side! At that time the American troops were controlling the area. They hid in a wood near the river by day, and by night attempted to build a raft strong enough to take them to the other side. They managed to float the raft, but the swirling water made it impossible to control, as it spun round and round in the water. Eventually it had to be abandoned. Alfred had noticed that each evening, shortly before dark, American soldiers crossed the river in a boat half a mile away from them, and some hours later went back again. It was too dark to see them, but he could hear them singing. Dad concluded that the purpose of these nocturnal jaunts was to help the Russians drink their plentiful supplies of vodka.

The following evening Alfred ran excitedly to tell Dad that the boat was coming again. Dad, Mum and Alfred approached the landing stage. Five soldiers jumped out of the boat and Dad, with no knowledge of the English language, attempted to persuade the senior member of the group to take them across the river. He took his gold watch out of his pocket and somehow conveyed to the officer that he was willing to give it in payment for transporting him and his family across. The soldier examined the watch and, apparently being satisfied as to its value, put it in his pocket. He indicated by his fingers and thumbs the number 11 and pointed across the river. My parents returned to the wood and waited. It was close to midnight when they heard the sound of voices as the Americans approached singing, and at this they took the handcart to the boat. That was too much for the Americans, who agreed to take them and their belongings only; the cart had to remain behind. Whilst one man steered the boat, the other four rowed with oars and sang all the way across to the opposite bank. There they all got out, chained the boat to a tree, and went on their way.

The Bergs family had realised their dream. They were free. Before they had left Riga, Mum had been busy sewing all the gold and precious stones the family possessed into the seams of their underclothing, which then became their bank. They spent that night in a haystack and early the next morning their bank was opened to acquire another cart as quickly as possible. Dad felt very uneasy at their present position so close to the River Elbe, as he feared that the Americans might give more territory in that area to the Russians. So he tried to move his family and his possessions as far away from the river as possible and as quickly as they could. They walked for three days, at which point Alfred began to show symptoms of fever. They put him on the cart, covered him as well as they could, and made for Uelzen. The camp in Uelzen had only recently opened and they were lucky to find a Latvian doctor who diagnosed pneumonia. With the help of the doctor and the camp leader, they got him into Uelzen hospital. He was very ill for a time and Mum and Dad sat by his bedside day and night until he had passed the crisis. He needed a lot of care and the hospital could not keep him any longer. They could not stay at the camp in Uelzen as it was full by this time, and in any case it was only a transit camp. So the hospital authorities arranged for the family to be accommodated in a Latvian camp in Hameln, some sixty miles away. They even provided an ambulance to take them there. On arrival, they were pleasantly surprised at the facilities they found there. The rooms were comfortable and the food was good and plentiful.

Nevertheless Dad was apprehensive. His distrust of camps, even the very best ones, was now deeply rooted due to the treatment of the Ukrainians, and he resolved to find some independent domicile as soon as possible both for his peace of mind and for the safety and well-being of his family. He then lost no time in exploring the area. He went out each day on his quest and after a few days he had found and negotiated for the occupation of the cottage in which we were now sitting and listening to this story.

Tamara and I had now been with the family for four weeks and we had both benefited considerably. The pressure we had felt for so long had at last been eased. It had been such a relief not to have the worry of finding accommodation every day. I could see too that Tamara looked very much better for the break from the daily journeys. She was relaxed and happy in the knowledge that her family, as well as ourselves, had survived. We were all happy to be together and fully intended to stay together. The only real difficulty we had to face was that our time in that particular cottage was temporary. Even so, we were optimistic that together we would find our way. Dad and I helped out on the farm when required, but winter was approaching and we knew that work would diminish.

One lunchtime a jeep stopped outside the cottage and a British major and two privates got out and knocked on our door. One of the privates explained to Tamara, in a very friendly manner, that all the Buergermeisters in the district were required to report to the Military Authorities the whereabouts of any foreigners living in the area. Such information had brought him to our door. He went on to say that the policy of Military Government was that all foreigners were required to live in camps. This meant that we could no longer stay in the cottage. He told us that we would all have to move into a Latvian camp nearby. This was too much for Dad, who just exploded and vented all his wrath and deep-seated distrust on the poor major who had been so pleasant to us. We, of course, had the advantage of the bearer of this news which had so upset Dad, as we knew the reason for his outburst. He immediately concluded that an attempt was being made to round everyone up as a first stage to deportation. He was adamant that he would not go without a written guarantee from the Military Authorities that he and his family would be safe. The major very patiently and politely pointed out to Dad that the British Military Government had not forcibly evacuated any refugees and would not do so in the future. He said that he would personally guarantee that, and further explained that these camps were financed by U.N.R.R.A. under the supervision of the British Military Government. He told us that we would be provided with food, shelter, clothing and medical attention. In addition to these basic needs, certain educational facilities would be available. The visit was traumatic to say the least, and the rest of us held our breath for the greater part of it.

After a time we began to breathe more easily as it became apparent that the British major had gradually convinced Dad that this was not a trap and that he had nothing to fear. It was with great relief that we witnessed these two men shaking hands at the end of their discussion.

It was our usual practice to spend an hour or so after the evening meal playing cards or dominoes and chatting. On this particular evening, however, we dispensed with the games and our conversation was confined to the events of that day which had proved so deeply disturbing. There were a number of Latvian camps within a fifty-mile radius of us. There was the camp in Hameln, only about 20 kilometres away. We all knew of this camp because Tamara's parents had actually stayed in it for a short time and Tamara and I had seen it on our journey to Springe. In the opposite direction, just over the hill and less than 10 kilometres away, was another small Latvian camp in a large village. This particular one was quite famous in Latvian circles. This was not because of its beautiful setting at the foot of the Deister Mountains, nor because the main part of the camp had been a hotel before the war, nor yet that a number of private houses in the village were used as residents' accommodation, providing a much freer atmosphere that one would normally find in camp life. Rather it was on account of its leader, Alexander Grants. Dad had met him before and had told us his story during the first few days of our arrival.

Alexander, together with twenty or so Latvians, was working shortly before the end of the war in a German factory in the Blankenburg area. They were all aware that the American troops were nearing Blankenburg. The knowledge of this gave them a certain amount of confidence in staying where they were, as they all felt that to be in American hands would be the best thing that could happen to them in the circumstances. Everyone still remembered the fate of so many thousands of people from the Baltic States when in 1940 the Russian troops had overrun these countries. At that moment the Russian troops appeared to be a safe distance from them. The Germans were now sandwiched between the American and the Russian fronts and seemed to be concentrating their defence on the Eastern front, holding the Russians on the River Elbe. This was the state of affairs until the officer commanding the German troops, apparently realising the futility of holding out there, made a U turn, obviously in an effort to save as many of his men as possible from falling into Russian hands.

The Russians, now having little or no resistance, advanced westwards and very soon reached the Blankenburg area, taking many towns along the line. Their advance was halted only when they met the Americans ten miles or so west of Blankenburg.

Alexander and his group unexpectedly found themselves in Russian occupied territory, having just time to reach the Harz Mountains near to the factory, where they were able to hide in the dense forest and the caverns, the locations of which were well known to them. From then on Alexander took the initiative and when darkness fell he called the group together to discuss how they could escape. Alexander had worked in the area for a year and was familiar with the mountain roads. It was decided that they would try to get one of the three-ton lorries owned by the factory if they were still there. Alexander would drive it, as he had driven these lorries as part of his job at the factory. He then selected a number of men and the plan they formulated to avoid detection was to push the lorry as far as possible into the forest before starting the engine.

At midnight they set off. The lorries were still there but unfortunately one was fully loaded and the other half loaded. But the half-loaded one had no fuel and so they had no alternative but quietly to unload the first one before pushing it out of the factory premises into the side road leading into the mountains. After about half an hour they were all exhausted for they were pushing the lorry against the rising terrain of the mountains until they felt that they were far enough away to be able to start the engine. Starting up the vehicle without an ignition key might have presented an additional problem to some drivers but not to Alexander, who knew all the tricks.

Soon they were driving higher and higher along the mountain road to a place where the women and children had been instructed to wait for them. When they reached this point, they discussed their next move and decided to drive along the road to Braunlager until they reached the American troops. At this stage no one knew just where that would be, nor whether they would run into a road block. But they all agreed that they must try, whatever the cost. It was thought that it would be better to do it in broad daylight, which meant setting out from their present position the following afternoon. Everybody was to lie down flat in the back of the truck, and only Alexander, as the driver, was to be visible. Before setting off, all had agreed that whatever might happen, they would place themselves entirely in his hands.

The next afternoon Alexander was driving the truck along the chosen route, which would lead to freedom for all of them or possibly to hell. The first ten miles were uneventful. There was nothing much to see apart from the occasional burned-out vehicle at the roadside and the large numbers of German people who had left their homes to seek refuge in the mountains and were now making their way back, hoping that the possessions inside their homes were still intact. Then suddenly, as Alexander rounded a bend in the road, he saw a barrier in front of him. A large tent had been pitched beside it and two armed

Russian soldiers were standing guard, both waving him down to a halt. Alexander slowed down as though bringing the vehicle to a halt. As he did so, his mind was dwelling on his familiarity with the vehicle and what it was capable of. As the truck rolled slowly to the barrier, he put his foot down hard on the accelerator and crashed through it, breaking it into fragments which flew whistling through the air. Before the Russian guards had recovered from the shock, the truck had roared away and he had arrived in American territory and freedom. By this time the engine was boiling. The impact had smashed the radiator and the cooling fan, but the engine continued to run. Alexander spoke good English and he now explained briefly what had happened to the American guards. They waved the truck off the road and out of sight. They were certainly surprised when twenty or so people emerged, somewhat dazed, from the back of the truck. When they had all got out, they lifted Alexander shoulder high. They will probably praise him to the end of their days.

It was well past midnight when Dad had finished reminiscing, and before retiring for the night, he suggested that he and I should go to see Alexander the following day and ask him if it would be possible for him to admit us all as residents in his camp. I readily agreed to go with him, not only to ascertain whether we could live there, but to meet the man who had organised and pulled off this daring escape. Tamara and I had had to make our own attempt to escape in Zell-am-See during the last days of the war, and, though it had been different, we knew the feeling.

The walk next morning through the forest was a pleasant experience and as we made our way down the hill towards the village, we had a bird's eye view of it. Two buildings stood out. One was the church and the other the hotel. Knowing that the hotel formed part of the camp, we found it easy to locate. On arrival at the enquiry office, we asked to see the camp leader. A few minutes later we were talking to him. I judged him to be four or five years older than myself, tall and slim, with dark wavy hair. He wore rimless glasses and was talkative, friendly and direct. He readily agreed to provide accommodation for us and offered to show us round. We told him there were five of us and I explained that in my own case my father was a Latvian, but that I had been brought up by my grandparents in Germany. I had been a pilot in the German Air Force and I showed him my American demob. papers. 'Just the man,' he said, 'we are looking for a teacher of the German language for our children. The class is already in progress but the job is still vacant.' I gladly agreed to take it on, as I knew that not only would this be a worthwhile occupation for me, but that we could all benefit from the extra rewards it would bring in the way of food, cigarettes and privileges.

A couple of weeks later we had a great surprise. Juris arrived with a friend. He had received our letter and had decided to come and stay in our camp. We were delighted to have him. The first letter we received was from Martha's mother. Ellie and the Hofers had written a few lines, all saying how pleased they were to know that we had found our family.

Two weeks later a second letter came. It was from Mrs Schulz. It was a long letter in which she commented: 'Thank God, you have survived this terrible war. Unfortunately, I have no good news for you. Your grandma is dead. I suppose you did not know Mrs Richler, who was also a Jehovah's Witness and was sent to the concentration camp just like your grandma. As the Russian troops came nearer to the concentration camp in Oranienburg, all the SS guards ran away. The Russians let all the survivors out. Everyone who wanted to go home was allowed to go. The women formed themselves into groups and began their journey. There were six women in your grandma's group. At nightfall they found a barn to sleep in. In the middle of the night a group of drunken Russian soldiers burst into the barn and all the women were raped. In the morning they found your grandma dead in a pool of blood.'

I could not read any further, and silently handed the letter to Tamara before going into the bedroom. The feeling which had overcome me was not new. I had experienced it before in the bitter moments I had had to live through during the war. It was a feeling of helplessness and an awareness of the futility of it all. A mockery, in fact, of all one had been brought up to believe in. The words in Grandma's last letter to me were ringing in my ears: 'Oh, God, forgive them, for they don't know what they are doing.' The fate my grandmother had suffered created a vacuum in my own faith in God that remained with me for many years.

Shortly afterwards we called at the camp office to see if there was anything new. We found a note on the blackboard informing interested parties that there was to be a series of lectures the following week by a delegation from England on the possibilities of emigrating there. We went back to our quarters and told the rest of the family about it. Tamara and I discussed it at length in the privacy of our bedroom. We both felt that camp life here was not bad, much better in fact than our recent past, but we knew that for us it could not be permanent. We felt that we were now sufficiently recovered both physically and mentally to begin an independent life, possibly in a new country. So we eagerly awaited the arrival of the delegation to hear what they were offering.

The meeting started at 3 pm in the ballroom of the hotel and the hall soon filled up. It appeared that practically everybody in the camp was interested. The meeting began with a slide show of various parts of England where manpower was needed. It was then explained to us in what industries we would be able to find work. Five different options were given to us: coal-mining, textiles, agriculture, building and nursing. The wages, living costs, the Health Service, and other relevant information were explained to us in detail. At the same time it was pointed out that the offer was open only to certain age groups, and this seemed to be a disadvantage to the family as a whole. Tamara and I qualified, of course. Alfred was just about old enough, but Mum and Dad were too old. After the meeting was over, we said that we were very interested in emigrating to England and asked whether there was any chance of Mum and Dad being allowed into the country, as we did not wish to split the family again. We were told that if the three of us began work and were in a position to support Mum and Dad, they could apply to join us. That seemed to be satisfactory and we signed on.

Some months later we called at the camp office as usual to enquire whether there was anything new. Inside we found an unusually high concentration of people swarming round the blackboard. When we asked what it was all about, we were told that a list had been posted of the names of the people who had been accepted for emigration to England. It was quite a time before we could get near enough to the board, but when we did, we saw that the names were in three groups. Our names were listed in the first group, which was due to leave the camp in three days' time, to be taken to a transit camp near the Belgian border. Alfred's name was not on the first list. He was listed in the third section, which was due to leave the camp in four weeks' time. We rushed home and broke the news to the family. As expected, Mum started to cry; it meant that her precious family was to be divided once again. We tried to reassure her that the parting would be only a temporary one, and that as soon as ever it was possible, we would apply for them to join us.

We woke next morning with mixed emotions. There was the challenge and excitement of a new life, but also the sadness of leaving our loved ones behind. Not only our family, but the many dear friends we had made in the camp. There was our leader, there was Eriks's cousin Juris and our neighbour from the farm in Latvia. All of them were to emigrate to England too, but were all in the third group. We assembled in front of the hotel and everyone seemed to have turned out to see us off. Our friend the camp leader had provided a band and as we climbed on to the three Army lorries, which were our transport for the journey to the transit camp, the band struck up a march. The handkerchiefs came out and there were tears in everybody's eyes.

It was an early start and we travelled all day, arriving in the late evening at the transit camp near the Belgian border, where we stayed for about ten days. It was a very large camp and contained people from all parts of Germany who were to be part of the first shipload to England. It took all ten days to get through the endless paper work and medical examinations for so many people before we were taken by Army transport to Zeebrugge to join the ship.

In the early morning we stood on deck holding hands, each with our own thoughts, as the ship slipped out of the harbour and headed out to sea. We watched the land slowly disappear before turning to the front, fascinated by the way the ship sliced through the water, showing us that we were well out to sea. I remarked to Tamara that it was just like finishing reading a chapter of a book. Now we were turning over to the next page to start a new chapter and had no idea what it would contain.

'Yes, Carl, we have just finished one chapter and we are starting a new one. Let's make it a good one!'.